every last beat

INTERNATIONAL BESTSELLING AUTHOR

NICOLE S. GOODIN

BEFORE

I try not to think too hard about the fact that in order for me to live, someone else had to die.

Everyone gets to live.
    Some for longer than others.

For Violet, born with a life-threatening heart defect that has controlled her twenty-one-years, life has been anything but easy.
    When reality is a high-risk game of trial and error, Violet finds solace the only way she knows how - with a brush in her hand.

But everything can change in a heartbeat.

Surrounded by loving family and the best friend a girl could ask for, Violet must ask the universe for the biggest favour of all - the one that will keep her alive.

AFTER

This is about what my heart wants, not what it needs for once, and all that my heart wants in this moment, is him.

Life and love don't always go hand in hand
    If you're lucky you might get both.

It's been three years since the transplant that saved Violet's life... three years since the man with the blue eyes disappeared from her sight but not her dreams.

Violet is living the life she never thought she'd get - while Rylan is merely surviving his.

Fate collides past and future together in a way neither thought possible, leaving them both questioning everything they thought they knew - and all that might be.

Romantic, surreal and heart-warming, Every Last Beat will make you believe there's something bigger out there for all of us.

Every Last Beat
Published by Nicole S. Goodin
ISBN: 978-0-9951206-6-2

Cover design by Nicole Goodin
Images purchased from Shutterstock
Editing by Spell Bound

For Kate and Ruby

"Little by little, day by day."
-Author unknown

before

I try not to think too hard about the fact that in order for me to live, someone else had to die.

Chapter One

Leanne
1993 (Day of birth)

This can't be right; they can't be talking about *my* baby.

The baby I grew inside my body and gave birth to only a few short hours ago.

It just *can't* be right.

I can see the bluish-grey tinge to her skin, and I can feel the rapidness of her breathing, but it *can't* be because of her heart.

They're wrong – they have to be.

My baby, she's alive and she's beautiful...

The kind of words flying around the room right now, words like 'life threatening', 'surgery', 'heart defect', 'life or death'... they don't fit with the precious little girl in my arms.

I tug on my husband Shaun's sleeve and he turns to face me, a look of absolute horror on his face.

"I want to go home now," I tell him with wide eyes.

I know I sound like a small child, but I don't care – I'm *scared*.

He doesn't answer me; to be honest I'm not sure he hears or even sees me in this moment.

The doctor, the fifth one we've seen this morning, approaches me slowly and sits down on the edge of my bed.

"I'm so sorry, Mrs. Miller, I know this seems like an impossible situation."

I want to scream at her. *'Impossible situation...'*

This is a nightmare.

I squeeze my eyelids shut tight and try my best to wake up from this terror of a dream, but when I open them up again, she's still there, staring right at me.

That's when it hits me. This *isn't* a nightmare. This is my life.

"Our baby is *fine*," I tell her.

"I'm sorry, Mrs. Miller, but unfortunately that's not the case."

If she calls me Mrs. Miller one more time I think I might scream. Mrs. Miller was my husband's mother, and I never was a big fan of that woman.

"Call me Leanne, or Lee," I snap at her.

She smiles at me patiently, in that way people do when they feel sorry for you, and I realise that this smile will become a regular look for me. Whether my baby lives or dies, people are always going to feel sorry for me in one way or another.

This woman isn't here to give me sympathy – she's here to do her job... to *help*. She's got kind eyes, and I almost feel bad for taking out my frustration on her.

"Do you understand what's happening, Leanne? What will happen to Violet if you take her home with you now?"

Her voice is firm, but she's still being awfully nice to me considering how rude I've been.

And I understand what she's trying to get from this conversation.

She needs to know that I've been listening, that I accept the fact that my daughter will die if we do nothing.

I've heard every word they've said, but even still, none of it seems real to me.

"I need *you* to tell me what to do," I plead with her.

They all know so much more about this than Shaun or I could possibly understand, yet *we're* the ones with the power.

It feels a lot like playing God right now.

"Unfortunately, I can't do that. All I *can* do is give you all the information so the two of you can make an informed decision."

I nod my head. I know what she's saying makes sense, but I'm not sure I can do it.

"I think I need to hear it one more time," Shaun tells her.

I've never loved that man more than I do right now because I need to hear it again too.

One more time and maybe it might finally sink in... Maybe the answer I'm looking for will become clear.

I feel the bed dip as he sits down next to me.

His hand reaches across me and strokes the side of Violet's face; ever so gently as though she's made of glass – although the reality is that she's far more breakable than that.

When they put me in a wheelchair and brought us up here to the specialist unit, I never expected this to happen – I certainly didn't consider the possibility of this being something so serious.

I never thought we'd be feeling pressured like this, or that a decision would need to be made so quickly.

The doctor starts at the beginning once again, and I'm incredibly grateful that even though she's delivering blow after blow with every movement of her lips, she at least seems to be on our side.

The first few doctors we saw were horrible. We were told that intervention wasn't worthwhile and that we should just go home and enjoy the time we had with our little girl.

This doctor is more compassionate – more *hopeful*. If Violet has this operation, this woman will be the one performing it and that provides me with a small slither of comfort.

If my baby is going to be wheeled off into some cold, sterile operating theatre, then at least she'll have someone there who'll fight for her the way I would.

She introduced herself to us as Dr. Vivian Ellis, and even though I can't make sense of half the medical terms she's making reference to, I already respect her immensely.

She explains that Violet has been born with something called Hypoplastic Left Heart Syndrome.

She patiently and professionally explains what that means and what type of surgery will happen if we choose to go ahead with it.

The left side of Violet's heart hasn't developed properly, and her body isn't able to move blood around her body the way it should.

I know there's a lot more to it than that, but my overloaded mind can only handle so much information right now. It might be awfully complicated, but the basics are becoming clear – she'll require medical intervention if she's going to have any chance of survival.

The Norwood procedure is what they call the operation – the first of three surgeries that would ultimately help her heart pump blood to her little body.

Dr. Ellis pauses a moment before informing us that Violet's chest will need to be cut open, and her sternum separated while this surgery takes place.

My arms visibly shake as she goes through the survival statistics of the first surgery alone.

She explains that the only reason Violet was able to survive in the womb was due to a hormone that my body produced during the pregnancy – it kept a valve into her heart open, but now that she's been born, that valve has begun to close.

The amount of information we've had dumped onto our shoulders is overwhelming, but there's one point of clarity in my mind.

If there's anything we can do to save our daughter, Auggie's little sister – then we *have* to do it.

The moment I accept the reality of the situation and that it's happening right now, I know there isn't any other option for me to consider – I know there's no way I could take her home and watch her die.

The thing that scares me most as the team of doctors – along with Dr. Ellis, file out of the room, is that Shaun won't feel the same way I do.

He's been so quiet the entire time.

"Say something," I whisper into the silence after a few moments.

"I don't know what you want me to say."

He's staring at our little girl adoringly as she rests peacefully in my arms.

She looks so precious as she sleeps.

I know it's not a good thing that she's asleep so much and not waking to feed – it means her heart is shutting her body down, that it's not pumping enough blood to keep her functioning the way she needs to.

If we don't do something soon, she'll die.

"*Eighty percent*, did you hear her say that?" His voice is broken, and I've never known him to sound so unsure of himself.

I heard her.

I heard them all.

Every doctor we've spoken to has made it abundantly clear that there is an eighty percent chance that Violet *won't* survive this surgery.

My brain had been quick to translate that into the chance of survival.

Twenty percent.

It might not be great odds, but it's *something*, and it's a hell of a lot better than nothing.

"We have to try, right?" My voice cracks, and Shaun looks at me for what seems like the first time since we arrived up here.

"Of *course* we'll try." His words fly out in a rush and I almost fall back under the weight of them.

It's such a relief to hear him say that he wants to fight, that he too wants to give our little baby the best shot we possibly can.

"There's no doubt in my mind about that... we *will* try everything. But I'm worried about you, Lee. I'm worried about me too. There's an unfairly high chance she won't make it through this, and I'm so scared of what will happen to us if that's the case."

He's right. I'm not sure how I'll cope if we lose her, but I know that we have to try – death is inevitable otherwise.

I can't do *nothing*, and this might be the only thing I'm sure of right now, but at least I have that to hold onto.

"We'll try." I reach for his hand and squeeze it tight. "And we'll just have to worry about everything else as it comes, okay?"

If we do nothing, she dies – for certain. Twenty percent of something is better than zero percent of nothing.

It's just basic math at this point.

I focus on that – the *one* thing I can understand as Shaun pushes the button on the wall that will call the people from our nightmare back in.

Chapter Two

Violet
Present day

I flick to the next page of the photo album in front of me, like I've done at least one thousand times over before this moment.

The photos of me as a newborn baby in countless hospital beds, wires and I.V lines connected all over my body still make my stomach turn.

I have no idea how a little baby, that small and fragile, survives that.

Grown men and woman die from less... but somehow, I made it through.

When I was born, the doctors gave my parents a choice... they could take me home where I would die in their arms, or they could set up camp with me in the specialised paediatric unit where I would have my chest opened in what would be the first of many surgeries and life altering moments.

The fact that I'm still here makes it pretty clear which option they went with.

I slide my finger over the glossy pages and feel the tears well in my eyes.

It overwhelms me sometimes, just what I've been through.

I hear my mum come into the room behind me, but I don't look up.

"Do you ever wish you'd done things differently?" I ask her.

I feel her sit down next to me. She doesn't say anything, but takes the album from my hands and flicks through the pages.

I peek up at her and see her smiling down at the photos.

I don't know what she's so happy about.

There's nothing in there that's worth smiling at.

Those pictures are like torture.

Sure, I have the slightly less morbid photo albums – just like August and Charlie, my sister and brother.

But it's just not the same.

We're not the same.

Life has pretty much always been sunshine and rainbows for the two of them.

The worst injury August has ever had is a broken arm from when she fell off the jungle gym at the playground, and *my God*, you would have thought she was literally going to die.

She was eight and I was only six, yet I can still, to this very day, recall the blood-curdling scream she kept up for the entire thirty-minute drive from the park to the hospital.

Honestly, I'm glad that it's me and not Auggie that has had to go through this. Having to listen to her being her usual dramatic self about everything would have been far more painful than anything else I've endured thus far.

Charlie has always been in the wars. He's a typical boy with absolutely no fear. Ever since he could walk he was causing havoc. But surprisingly enough, he's never even broken a bone; a few cuts and bruises are all he's had to show for his years of rough and tumble.

And then there's me.

"Why would I regret a single thing?" Mum smiles as she shuts the album and picks up another one.

These pages are filled with more of the same, only I'm older and I'm past the surgeries, so most of the time my chest and my scars are covered up.

"Look at those dimples – you were always smiling. There's no regret here, Violet."

Her words are sincere – for the most part, I think she's happy I'm here. But my life isn't exactly easy most of the time, and I know she has moments where she wonders if her and Dad made the right choice by keeping me alive.

Then again, I guess sitting around looking at an album with pictures from the week or two of life I would've had otherwise, would have been far more depressing than dealing with my condition.

At least I'm alive. Most of the time I think they made the right decision, but sometimes I feel like I'm on borrowed time, like I've messed with the order of things.

I wasn't meant to live through that first surgery, but I did.

I wasn't expected to make it to five years old, but again, I did.

I never thought I'd be here at twenty-one years old... I doubt anybody did.

It almost feels like I'm not really living *my* life – my life wasn't meant to last more than a few numbered days. I don't know what to make of that sometimes.

This feeling of disconnect could be because I'm not doing the things I want to do with my life.

I don't have much in the way of independence, I don't have even an inkling of a boyfriend, and I haven't gotten through hardly any of my degree... but even if I was finished it, I can't imagine what I would possibly do with a qualification in business.

All I want to do most of the time is paint, but I also don't want to live at home with my parents for the rest of my life, however long that life might be, so at some point I'm going to have to consider getting myself a real job.

I know full well that there will never be any pressure on me to achieve anything of any real significance; the pictures in the books in front of me have ensured that nobody expects anything more from me than survival –as sad as that is.

I rest my head on mum's shoulder and watch as she flicks through page after page of the memories of my existence so far.

Chapter Three

I flick the off button on the television; I've taken to religiously watching one of those shows about people that have managed to survive in extreme conditions or outrageous situations.

The type of people, that in theory shouldn't be alive. People like *me*.

I've always thought of death as a fickle creature, it spares some who are so close to it, yet takes others that seem to be miles away.

It's a strange concept that a person can be alive and well one day, and then gone in the blink of an eye.

Here one minute, gone the next.

I know I'll die one day – we all will, and although it seems that death's chosen not to take me yet when it so easily could have, I know full well that tomorrow is a whole new day.

This instance in time is all I'm guaranteed. It's all any of us can count on if I really think about it.

Some of us will get a long forever, others a shorter one, and there's not a lot most of us can do to alter that.

There are people out there who do what they can, and I've been lucky enough to cross paths with those who *do* have the power to alter, even just a little bit... and fortunately for me they've done precisely that.

I owe my life to a long list of people, but there's one that stands out above all the rest.

The same surgeon who operated on me when I was only a few days old, and has been with me through every surgery I've had since.

My parents, both of them, have her labelled with God status, and I can't help but agree with them on this one.

The woman is nothing short of incredible.

I've heard the stories – I've seen the photos of how she saved my life on more than one occasion... and I know for a fact that if she hadn't been there when she was, I wouldn't be here today.

It's as simple and as complicated as that.

As altered as my life may be, I owe it to her.

***

Leanne
1993 (Five days old)

I look down at my tiny, beautiful miracle, defying the odds of survival with every beat of her little heart.

I think about August, at home with my sister, Rita, and how my two birth experiences couldn't have been more different.

When August was five days old we were inundated with visitors, gifts and home cooked meals.

It was an overwhelming bubble of bliss.

My biggest worry back then was if I was going to get to sleep a full night ever again, and whether or not my milk supply was keeping up with August's appetite.

I'd give just about *anything* for those to be my biggest concerns at Violet's five-day-old mark.

Shaun and I are in the same place we've been for two days – ever since our little fighter made it through her first-stage procedure.

I've barely moved from the side of her small bed. There's nowhere else I'm needed more.

Just the sight of food makes my stomach turn. I'm too stressed to eat. I know I need to, but I can't seem to bring my-self to do more than pick at something. My body needs it so I can keep expressing milk to be fed to her through the feed-ing tube that goes into her nose, but I just can't stomach it most of the time. Since I'm not really eating, I barely need to visit the bathroom either so instead I sit, and I watch, and I wait.

I glance around the room and my heart hurts for all these precious little babies.

All the parents in here are hovering the same way we are. None of us want to be here, yet we're all desperately clinging to the fact that we are.

If we're here, it means our babies are still fighting – that they're still alive.

Two doctors have just entered the room to do their rounds and instantly my nerves are kicked up a notch.

We're expecting them to remove the pacing wires from Violet's heart today. They put them in after her surgery –

they've been keeping her heart rate steady, but they can't stay in forever.

One of the doctors is Violet's surgeon, Dr. Ellis. I owe that woman more than I could ever possibly repay her. She's the reason our precious girl is here, defying those odds, alive and breathing, her heart still beating in her chest.

I don't know all the technical terms for what she did in that operating theatre a couple of days ago, but I've come to think of it as the temporary re-plumbing of Violet's heart.

It's really not something I'm able to think too hard about... if, *when* we make it outside of these hospital walls, maybe I'll worry about it all then. But today, I just need to focus on the here and now – I need to stay strong for my baby.

"Mr. and Mrs. Miller, how is Violet doing today?" Dr. Ellis asks.

Truthfully, I don't know how she is, most of what the nurses say and note down on her chart goes well and truly over my head. I don't know if it's the medical jargon, or the pressure of the situation that's doing it... I seem to be forgetting even the most basic of information; my stressed brain isn't retaining things like it normally would.

Whatever it is, I don't have much of an answer for them, so I tell them the one thing I'm sure of.

"She's alive."

Dr. Ellis gives me a small, albeit sad smile.

It really is one of those situations where it's incredibly depressing that being alive is the biggest achievement we've got to report, whilst at the same time, it's something I couldn't be more grateful for – my little girl is here and alive when others aren't.

It's all such a mix of emotions and feelings. Gratitude laced with anger, appreciation filled with despair...

"I'm glad to hear that," she replies as she scans over the chart that I've tried and failed to make sense of numerous times.

"Everything looks good here. I'd like to go ahead and remove her pacing wires."

She runs over a few of Violet's stats with Shaun and I and assures us that this is a routine procedure that is awfully common within the paediatric intensive care unit.

I trust her completely, but I'm still terrified.

While this might be a routine procedure for her, it's certainly not for us.

I can feel my anxiety levels rising as I watch her wash her hands and prepare her equipment.

She cleans the site where the wires enter Violet's small body before snipping the sutures holding them in place.

She pauses, watching the rhythm of her heart beat on the cardiac monitor next to us.

It seems so entirely wrong to just pull something out of a beating organ, but that's exactly what she does, ever so gently, pulling in time with the rhythm of Violet's heartbeat.

My stomach lurches at the sight, and I'm grateful that there's nothing in there to come up.

Shaun is squeezing my hand so tight it almost feels like my fingers might crack under the pressure, but I don't say a word. I barely breathe as the entire line is removed from her little body.

Dr. Ellis passes the wire to the other doctor whose name I've already forgotten, and I let out a deep breath of relief.

That small lapse in time, where I've allowed myself to feel content is when it happens.

The monitor that had been previously blipping away consistently and quietly is now ringing out in a piercing alarm.

There's something wrong. Something is *seriously* wrong right now.

I glance down at Violet and see she's turning blue.

I can feel my lips moving but I have no idea of the words that are coming out of them.

Times flashes in a blur but it's also somehow in slow motion.

I know that everyone is moving *so* fast around me, yet it's like they're all running like those girls on Baywatch.

Someone must have hit the emergency assist button on the wall because a whole pile of people – other doctors and nurses, have burst into the room.

I'm still speaking, maybe even yelling now as Shaun and I are dragged out of the room, along with all the other parents and families.

The last thing I hear as the doors swing closed are the words, 'I need to open her chest up', and the sound of my own ragged breath.

Chapter Four

I love it at Lucy's place.

There's no kid gloves here.

Lucy's mum, Linda, is the best. It's just the two of them over here – Lucy's dad, or her 'sperm donor' as Linda so fondly refers to him, left before Lucy was born.

It's always made me sad that he walked out on Linda; especially given that she was pregnant, but neither her nor Lucy seem particularly bothered by it, not these days anyway.

Lucy's uncle Phil lived here with them for years. He's off seeing the world now, but Luce had a pretty solid male role model for most of her life anyway. As bossy and sassy as she is, it doesn't appear she's been emotionally scarred or got too many 'daddy issues' so to speak, so maybe it was all for the best.

"What else are you girls up to today?" Linda asks as she pauses in the doorway to the living room where Luce and I are currently in the middle of a manicure session.

She's about to leave for her shift at the hospital. That's where she met my mum... and as they say, the rest is history. They've been best friends ever since.

"Oh, ya know, the usual," Lucy drawls as she focuses hard on the bright pink lacquer she's applying to my nails. "Probably get ourselves a bottle of vodka, smoke some weed... maybe get a few guys over."

I snort a laugh. That's a classic Lucy response – and one that couldn't be further from the truth. The wildest thing we're likely to get up to is burning some popcorn.

"Well make sure you smoke outside, alright? I don't want you to burn the house down, and if you're going to be running around half dressed, shut the curtains please; the old bird next door will have a heart attack if she sees."

Linda is such a good sport.

"Will do, boss," Lucy responds with a grin.

"See you later, girls."

We both yell out bye, and then it's just us.

I've always loved hanging out here. Linda has given us the same amount of freedom since we were fifteen years old, whereas my mum was always lingering somewhere in the background trying to make sure that nothing was going wrong.

I love my mum to death, but the woman has absolutely no chill.

Linda and my mum are a bit like chalk and cheese.

They've got vastly different parenting styles and ideas, but they seem to find common ground on all the important stuff, and I think in a lot of ways they help to balance each other out.

Linda helps Mum relax, and in return, Mum helps Linda to keep things in check.

As unfortunate as it is that I was in the hospital for so long as a baby, it led to a friendship that's spanned over twenty years and is still going strong today, and I can't help but think it's a sacrifice I'd be willing to make all over again.

***

Leanne
1993 (Three months old)

"Hey, Leanne, how's my favourite patient today?"

My favourite nurse, Linda, waddles in; her pregnant belly looking like it might just topple her over if given half a chance.

I smile brightly at her. My days around here are long and for the most part boring, but Linda helps brighten them significantly.

We've become close these last few months, and given that she lives only a few short blocks from me, I really hope that we'll continue to be friends after this.

I've found out pretty quickly who the real friends in my life are, and which ones are only there for the good times, when everything is going well.

Shaun has had some fantastic support from the few who *are* in it for the long haul and I'm not sure how I'll ever be able to repay them for their kindness.

This extended hospital stay hasn't been easy on any of us.

A lot of babies get to go home between the first surgery, called the Norwood procedure, and the operation that Violet will have next – the Bi-directional Glenn, but not us...

she simply hasn't been well enough. At this point it feels like we'll never make it back into the comforts of our home.

My sister Rita is living at our place for now, helping Shaun with August and taking care of the house.

She's here visiting most days too – even sitting with Violet for me so I can spend some much-needed time with my oldest daughter.

This has been tough on August – she's cried when I've had to leave her, and she's screamed when she's been taken away from the hospital without me.

Rita has become a surrogate mother to her at the moment, because at only two years old, she's far too young to understand what on earth is going on.

I really have no idea what we'd have done without my sister.

Shaun probably would have been forced to give up work to take care of Auggie, and then we would have had problems with our mortgage and paying our other bills.

There was no way Rita was going to allow that.

She really is my hero.

The nurse smiling back at me isn't far behind her in hero status – she really has gone above and beyond.

"She's going good; actually, today seems to be a good day."

I know better than to announce that it *is* a good day. I've learnt these past few months that you don't tempt fate like that.

She looks into the small bed where Violet is sleeping and smiles down at her.

"Can I get you anything before I start my shift?"

She's taken to visiting me not only during her work day, but also before she starts and after she finishes.

"I'll tell you exactly what you can do, you can take a seat." I frown at her. "I think that baby might have grown even bigger overnight."

She's always on her feet – I'm not sure I've ever seen her resting the way she should be. An 'active relaxer' is what she refers to herself as.

She rubs her very pregnant looking belly affectionately. "I know... I'm still meant to have three more weeks, but there just isn't any room left in there."

"I know that feeling... and you never know, that little girl might be getting ready to come meet you anytime now."

"I sure hope so." She smiles over at Violet again. "That precious wee poppet could do with a best friend right about now."

"You think they'll be friends?"

"I *know* they will be... we'll force them together so often they'll have no choice." She giggles.

I guess that's my question answered then – I've definitely gained a friend here, and if that's not a silver lining to this whole ordeal, then I don't know what is.

Linda bustles off for her shift with a promise to return later, and then it's just me and Violet.

It's early, so I know we won't have any visitors for hours yet.

Sometimes I take her for a walk — not outdoors or anything — a walk for Violet and I consists of nothing more than a stroll down the hallway – maybe down the lift if I'm feeling game.

I can only have her away for about ten minutes before I have to bring her back and hook her up to all the machines that are improving her stats, so we can't go far.

We've had some tough times these past few months.

We very nearly lost her.

If it weren't for the fact that Dr. Ellis happened to be doing the rounds that day, we would have.

She opened my daughter's chest – right there in the intensive care ward – and because of that, she saved her life.

If she hadn't been there... God, I shudder just thinking about the very real possibility of what would have happened.

As thankful as I am that Violet was saved, the days that followed are not something I would wish upon anyone.

No parent should have to witness their tiny baby with their chest open wide like that.

It took three days before they closed her up again.

Three days.

Three long days of a thin cover draped over my baby's front, with the words 'chest cavity open' noted on it.

I can't even begin to explain the surreal experience of watching a heart expanding and contracting inside a living, breathing human being, but it's something I'll never, ever forget.

I may not be able to recall the name of the physiatrist who visits me every few days to check I haven't lost my mind entirely, or even remember what I ate for dinner last night, but I know for a fact that I won't ever be able to rid myself of the memory of my daughter's heart visibly beating inside her body.

Chapter Five

Violet
Present day

I've painted for as long as I can remember.

Some of my earliest memories involve me with a brush in one hand, my clothes all covered in paint.

My parents told me from a young age that I was never going to be the kind of kid that would be running around outside, or swimming in anything less than the stifling heat.

They pushed me to try anything and everything that involved me sitting indoors in a warm, safe room.

I tried piano, darts, scrapbooking, guitar, stamp collecting just to name a few, but I always seemed to find my way back to making art.

I collaged, I drew, I coloured, I created...

And when I discovered painting, I found a huge piece of my soul along with it.

Even though I proved those doctors wrong – I *can* run and jump and swim – all within reason, there is still nothing I'd rather be doing than putting a brush to canvas.

Years of feelings, anxiety and medical procedures have left me with a lot of emotions and insecurities I need to express.

I don't want to be the girl who stays home and fears the world, I really don't, and with a best friend like Lucy that was never going to be possible anyway, but sometimes I need an outlet.

So, when I feel that way, that's when I paint.

The house my parents bought when we were younger has a spare bedroom. That's where I go to create.

The teenage version of August threw the mother of all fits about that one. Apparently she'd had visions of knocking down part of a wall and creating a giant walk-in wardrobe where she could display all her shoes... I always did think she watched too much of that show with those Kardashians.

Mum had halted that plan pretty quickly... she pulled the dodgy-heart card and I'd gotten my own studio.

I'd even managed to somehow talk Dad into installing a lock for me so I could work in peace, and so I knew my private things were kept private.

I knew Dad would never go in there without my permission; he respects my space and my needs. Auggie could literally not have cared less, and Charlie would probably have rather been out skateboarding with the neighbourhood kids than snooping around in my stuff.

August has moved out now, never having set a foot inside the door, and Charlie is surfing instead of skateboarding, but the real reason for the lock is still lurking around all these years later.

My mother.

The woman understands personal space about as well as a dog speaks French, so in other words, not at all.

She's always so worried.

I know it comes from a good place, but sometimes she just needs to back off and accept that I'm capable of doing things for myself.

Yes, my heart isn't what it should be – but not *everything* is about my heart.

I've painted for every reason there is. I've painted when my sister pisses me off, when Lucy drives me crazy.

I paint when I'm happy, when I'm sad and when I'm scared.

I paint when I feel love and also when I feel loss.

But I only paint for me.

I know I'm depriving Mum of something by not showing her what I'm putting on all the canvases she pays for, but I need this, and I need it to be mine alone.

Everything else in my life is public property – my health, my body, my life... it's all controlled by something or someone else.

It's on a schedule and there's nothing I can do to alter it.

It's been this way since I was little, and even though I'm okay with it for the most part, I *need* this for me.

I control my art. They're *my* feelings, *my* visions and *my* reminder of everything I've been through.

I know one day they'll be seen by others – either I'll gain the courage to share my work, or I'll die, and they'll see them then. But until either of those days come, I'm keeping the lock firmly in place on the door.

***

Leanne

1996 (Three years old)

It's so much worse this time than it was the last.

It's hard enough to watch your sleeping baby drift off into unconsciousness, but a screaming three-year-old is so, so much more distressing.

She couldn't talk or walk or do anything much the last time she was operated on, but it's all so different now.

She can not only say 'mumma', but she can hysterically cry it as she writhes in fear against the hands that are here to help her, not hurt her.

That's the thing though, in order to help her, they *do* have to hurt her. And I have to stand back and allow it to happen.

I know it's for the best, that this operation, referred to as the 'Fontan', will do so much to improve not only her quality of life – but also to extend her life too.

She's been poked and prodded, sedated and dressed for surgery and now, finally, she's being put under anaesthetic.

I hold her hand as the medication takes her into a peaceful sleep.

It's only then that I let the tears fall.

I have to stay strong for her while she's watching. I know full well that if I fall apart, she will too.

"Thank you, Leanne, we'll take it from here."

I glance back down at my baby one last time. I whisper that I love her and I'll see her soon before I leave the room.

I'm once again so grateful for Dr. Ellis – I'm not sure I could leave my precious little girl in the hands of someone I didn't trust – but I know I can trust her. She'll do everything she can to create the best outcome for my daughter.

I wander back out the hallway and into the room we'll spend the next five or so hours in. We are allowed to leave, in fact it's been encouraged – the nurses have suggested that we go out and get ourselves a decent meal or have a sleep as one of us will be glued to Violet's bedside when she comes out, but I don't think either one of us could stomach food or rest right now.

I can't imagine looking at a menu or making conversation. I'm right where I need to be. Right here, as close to my little girl as I can get.

I drop into the seat next to Shaun and neither of us says a word to the other.

We don't need to – we've been here before, and I don't doubt that we'll be here again.

***

She won't stop crying, and honestly, I don't blame her. I'd probably be crying if I'd been through what she did two days ago.

Nothing is working to settle her.

We've offered her new toys, books, and movies, but she's refused all of it.

Shaun has bought Auggie in this morning to see if she might be able to distract her sister for a few minutes, but it's been to no real avail.

There doesn't seem to be anything in the world that can soothe my little girl right now.

I'm at breaking point myself – it's awful having to watch your child in this much distress.

She's only three years old... she shouldn't be dealing with this kind of thing.

It's not fair. Her whole life has been a struggle – a battle to stay alive and she deserves to catch a break.

My body is starting to shake as my emotions threaten to overwhelm me. Tears are pooling in the corners of my eyes and I have to turn around as they begin to fall. The last thing I need is for Violet to see that I'm not coping.

Shaun's arm slides around my waist as his mouth finds my ear.

"Go and take a break," he whispers so only the two of us can hear.

I don't need to be told twice. I walk out of the room on shaky legs. I go just far enough that I can't hear my daughter's cries and collapse into the nearest chair.

I sit there for what feels like forever – my head in my hands as I try to figure out why.

Why her life is destined to be such a challenge when it could have been so simple instead.

I'm so deep in the thoughts inside my own head that I don't even notice Shaun until he's right next to me, gently shaking my shoulder.

"Lee, you need to come and see this."

His expression is one of disbelief and I'm on my feet, moving in an instant.

I can't hear any screaming or crying as I approach the door and I'm so intrigued about what's finally calmed her down that I have to stop myself from breaking into a run to cover the final few steps.

I burst through the door into the silent room.

I can understand the look on Shaun's face as I take in the scene in front of me.

Both of my beautiful girls are sitting on Violet's bed, and there's paint *everywhere* – but for the first time in over forty-eight hours, she's relaxed. She's not tugging on the tubes and lines that are poking out all over her body, she's not thrashing around restlessly, nor does she have tears streaming down her face. She's not been the least bit interested in lollies or ice blocks, but the brush in her hand – that certainly has her full attention.

"Want to try some yellow?" Auggie holds out the pot of yellow paint to her sister and my heart melts.

I stop in the doorway and lean against the frame, just watching the magic in front of me.

"August pulled out the art supplies and she just *stopped*," Shaun murmurs from next to me. He too, seems content to just watch.

"Violet really likes to paint, Mummy," Auggie announces proudly.

Violet stops painting, and I freeze, but instead of beginning to cry and scream, she holds up the painting so I can see.

She's smiling. *Really* smiling – dimples and all and I've never seen a sight more perfect.

"It's beautiful, baby," I whisper.

She goes back to her work as though she hasn't got a care in the world.

Shaun and I stand in the doorway; both of us watching each stroke of the brush heal something inside our little girl.

Chapter Six

Violet
Present day

Lucy and I have the best-friend-silent-communication thing down pat. Most of the time we only have to make eye contact briefly to know what the other thinks about something.

If eye contact isn't quite cutting it, code words or half sentences that make no sense to anyone but the two of us usually does the trick.

It's been like that for as long as I can remember.

We started doing it mainly to make sure Charlie didn't know what we were talking about, but we quickly learned that it was a really easy way to piss Auggie and her friends off – so that soon became our main focus.

It's always been my duty as little sister to try and annoy my big sister, and since Lucy doesn't have any siblings, she's taken on her own role in the game too.

We might technically be classed as adults now, but it's still not any less satisfying to make Auggie's blood boil today than it was ten years ago.

Lucy and I are blasting Aqua's 'Barbie Girl' over the sound system and reliving our younger days by dancing around the living room to our old favourite song.

I know we're far too old to be carrying on like this, but honestly, that just makes it all the more fun.

I've missed out on a lot of my childhood with my illness, my limitations and my mum's rules, so I'll be damned if I'm going to let my sister's attitude and social expectations stop me from making up for some of it now.

August is back home from school for the weekend with a group of friends in tow, including her latest boyfriend. The girl she's brought with her is an absolute bitch – there's really no other word for it. She took one look at Luce and I in our old trackies and t-shirts, and our total lack of makeup and gave us the 'bitchy girl' glare.

Auggie's new boyfriend is hot and older, but then they usually all are, and he looked at us the same way – like we were nothing more than a couple of annoying teenage sisters.

Well, 'boyfriend of the month', challenge accepted.

Lucy leaps up on the couch and does her best impression of Barbie talking to Ken at the same moment that August storms into the room and hits the pause button on the sound system, swiftly cutting off our song.

I don't even bother with an attempt to conceal my laughter and neither does Lucy. In fact, we're both almost at the point where we're laughing hysterically.

"Would you two give it a damn rest. I have company," Auggie hisses at us.

"I have company too." I smile sweetly at her.

"*She* does *not* count." She jabs a finger in my best friend's direction.

She might be being incredibly rude, but she's right. Lucy hasn't been classed as a visitor here virtually ever, but that's *not* the point.

Lucy shoots me a 'shall I mess with her?' look and I nod eagerly in response.

"We're just listening to some jams... you know *'chillin',*" Lucy drawls, and I know full well she's ripping the absolute piss out of Auggie. "You're probably not cool enough to understand, so go run along."

When we were younger, anytime August had friends over, they'd shut themselves in her room, refuse to let us join in, and state something along the lines of what Lucy has just taunted her with.

"Urrrrggghhhh!!" Auggie shrieks and stomps her foot – actually stomps it. "You two losers are *impossible*!"

She storms out of the room, leaving us in fits of laughter.

I know we're being immature, but I really don't care. It feels so good to act young and carefree again – even if it's just for one Saturday afternoon. Auggie will get over it, she always does, and tomorrow I'll go back to acting like the rational adult I really am.

Lucy sways her hips dramatically as she struts over to the sound system. She hits a few buttons and S Club 7's 'S Club Party' blasts out of the speakers.

"Oh yeah!" I yell over the music. "*This* is why we're friends."

***

Leanne
1997 (Four years old)

The girls have always been close, but never quite like this.

They're like two halves of the same piece.

They might only be four years old, but both Linda and I know that we are witnessing something special.

They play together like they've been doing it forever. I guess in reality, they have.

Ever since the day Lucy was born, they've been shoved together for play dates, but ever since Violet's last operation around a year ago, it's been less like they're being forced and more like they're being drawn together.

They rarely go a day without seeing each other and when they do, they pick up right where they left off the last time.

Even though it's a rare occasion that Violet ever stops talking, her and Lucy somehow seem to be able to communicate without any words at all. Their brains are so in sync it's almost as though one knows exactly what the other is thinking and vice versa – it's an incredibly powerful thing to witness.

Like just now, as they play Barbies and Linda and I drink coffee. Violet couldn't find the other pink high heel shoe her doll was missing. Lucy wasn't even facing Violet, and no words were spoken, yet when she came across the other pink shoe, she simply reached around behind her, holding it out. Violet took it without a word exchanged between them.

I'm starting to wonder if their brainwaves are on some secret frequency that the rest of us aren't privy to.

I can't even begin to understand their bond that's more like sisters than friends, but I'm certainly grateful.

Violet deserves to have *something* in her life that's natural and easy – even just *one* thing that doesn't involve a struggle

or a fight, and watching the two of them now, I think she
might have found it.

Chapter Seven

"What's *that*?" Amelia, one of the girls in my class points at the mark running down my front as she asks.

"It's my zip," I answer cautiously.

No one else in my class has a zip. It's just me. Not like at the hospital or the group that Mum takes me to sometimes... *everyone* there has a zip.

I glance around the other girls that are getting changed in the small room. I don't know why none of them have scars.

That's what Auggie calls them, *scars*.

"What *is* it?" she asks as she stares.

"It's from when I was little and they had to fix up my heart." No one at school has ever asked me this before and I don't really know what I'm supposed to tell her. "It's called a scar."

"Ohhh... I have a scar too," she tells me as she holds up her arm and shows me the small mark on her elbow. "I got it when I fell off my bike."

I lean in to get a better look. It's just a tiny mark; it's nothing like the big one I have, but it makes me feel a little better.

Maybe some of the other kids *do* have scars like mine too.

"Does that hurt?" She points at my chest again.

I shake my head and pull on my t-shirt so she can't keep looking at it.

"Not anymore. It did when I was little I think, but it's okay now."

"What's wrong with your heart?"

"It was broken," I tell her while I stuff my wet towel into my swim bag. "The doctor had to fix it."

"I had to get an injection once, you know. I didn't even cry," she tells me proudly.

I've had lots of injections too.

"It was a really big needle and they stuck it right here in my arm." She points to a spot up by her shoulder.

"I *hate* injections," I tell her.

"Me too." She nods really fast.

I like that we both hate injections. That means we at least have something the same.

We walk back to class together and she tells me all about how she got the scratch on her leg from the cat at her grandma's house, but I'm sort of busy thinking about why I'm the only one at school with a broken heart.

***

Leanne

"How come none of the other kids at school have a zip, Mum?"

The big metal ladle I'm washing slips from my grasp and falls into the sink with a loud clutter.

She's only five and a half. I wasn't expecting to have to talk to her about this just yet.

She knows she's different to her siblings and she's never seemed particularly bothered by it, but I can tell by the quiet curiosity in her voice that she's beginning to question things now.

I shake the bubbles off my hands and turn around to face her.

She's sitting at the bench, perched up on a stool, writing out the spelling words that she was given for homework this week.

Seeing her sitting there like that, her brain ticking over, it makes me so unbelievably grateful. There are so many children with her condition that aren't as fortunate as she is. I know she's still been dealt an incredibly rough hand, but all things considered, she's nothing short of a miracle.

As surprised as I am that I'm having to answer this question so early in her life, I'm also quite frankly a little shocked that it's happened now – this is the most 'normal' Violet has ever looked; with her clothes on anyway.

Only a few months ago she was put under anaesthesia, yet *again*, and had a pressure valve that was created during her last operation – known as a fenestration, closed. Ever since then her colour has improved hugely, and her oxygen saturation levels are the closest to normal they've ever been. It might not have been open-heart surgery, but it's made a huge difference to Violet.

"Where's this question come from, hon?"

She shrugs, not looking up from the piece of paper that she's scrawling the word 'the' onto over and over. "None of the kids in my class have a zip."

I know it's *her* heart that has the issues, and not mine, but right now my own feels like it's trying to leap out of my chest.

"Did one of the kids at school say something?"

"Amelia... she asked me what happened."

I feel ice slide through my veins, I know Amelia is only five years old, but if she said something to upset my little girl, I'll be speaking to her mother.

I take a deep breath and remind myself not to overreact. I need to stay calm and composed for Violet's sake, even though on the inside I'm anything but. "Was she not very nice to you?"

She looks up at me. "No, she was nice." She goes back to her spelling. This time the word is 'and'. "She had a little scar on her arm, but it's not as big as mine."

Her words are so pure and innocent, I begin to relax. Nobody was mean to her, not today anyway. She's just curious, and understandably so.

She's a smart girl, she was bound to notice that she doesn't look the same as her classmates in every way, or that she can't keep up in a running race, or that she can't swing on the monkey bars like all the kids her age can.

I should have prepared her better for these questions.

"What did you tell Amelia?"

"I just told her, you know... that my heart's broken."

The casual way in which she says it brings tears to my eyes.

I turn back around and busy myself with putting away a pot until I can get a grip on my emotions. Just the idea that she thinks of herself as broken, devastates me.

I do my best to treat all my children equally, but there's times when it's just not possible. Violet always needs an extra layer of clothing to keep warmer than the others, she can't stay outside in the cold like her siblings can, she tires more easily, and she can't ride her bike for as long.

It strikes me suddenly that maybe I've been doing the wrong thing by trying to treat them all the same way... because they're *not* the same. All three of them are very different children, and I'm sure they'll continue to be different for the rest of their lives.

I make allowances for Auggie's drama queen antics – I have no problem telling her that she's like no one I've ever met before, yet I feel bad making Violet feel like she's a true individual.

I guess in a lot of ways we've been striving for 'normal', but that's not fair on anyone, least of all Violet.

I should be celebrating Violet's diversity and giving her the tools to deal with those differences, not trying to make her fit a mould – she cuts her own mould, that girl. She always has, and if I can figure out how best to support her, hopefully she always will.

I'm not sure how I'm meant to explain this to her, but I have to try.

"Everyone is different, hon. No two people are the very same."

She drops her pencil and looks up at me with her big blue eyes. "But *they're* all the same. They all don't have a zip."

My heart breaks for her, it really does.

She's going to be faced with this her whole life, and I doubt it'll get any easier for her.

Children can be cruel, but I can't tell her that. She sees the good in people and expects the same in return.

That's one thing I fear – that one day circumstance will harden her, and that she'll stop seeing that goodness everywhere she goes. That just might be worse than watching her go through operation after operation, so I know I have to choose my words carefully.

"Okay, so you know how Max from your class has glasses?"

She nods.

"That makes him different. Nobody else in your class has glasses."

"But he can take them off, then he's just like everybody else."

She's sharp – she doesn't miss a thing.

"But if he takes them off, then he can't see, can he?"

She nods again. "I guess."

"And Stuart, he's got that bright red hair that nobody else has got – and you're just like half your class with your brown hair."

She smiles at that and it saddens me that she's been reduced to finding comfort in something as trivial as hair colour.

"And don't forget Bella," I point out.

Bella is a down syndrome girl at the kids' school. She's in August's year and she doesn't let a single thing bother her.

"I like Bella, she's really funny."

I smile down at my sweet, loving girl. "She *is* funny. And she's different too. Just like you, and me and *everybody* else. You might be different at school sometimes, but you're not different when we meet up with the Heart Kids."

She doesn't say anything, but I can tell she's thinking it through.

She smiles so big I can see the gorgeous dimples in her cheeks. "If Amelia came with me to the Heart Kids group, *she* would be different and we'd all be the same."

She's exactly right.

Difference is nothing more than a matter of perspective.

Chapter Eight

"But I haven't *got* any friends at school."

Lola, one of the little girls I'm spending the afternoon with tells me. Her bottom lip drops and her eyes well with tears.

I feel for her, I really do.

"How come?" I ask as I sit down next to her.

I'm too old for the Heart Kids group now, but know how vitally important it was for me when I was younger, so now I volunteer and spend time with the kids who are experiencing the types of things that I did while I was growing up – that I still sometimes am now.

It's an all too real possibility that not all these children will make it to be my age, so I know it's important that I give back what I can – this battle is a hard one, and it's certainly not made any easier by losing friends.

That's what everyone here is – they're friends; some are more like family, and while that's an incredible thing, it often doesn't translate into finding friends within the rest of the world... and that seems to be the problem Lola is having.

She's a really special girl. She's fourteen, but she seems a lot younger than the years on her birth certificate.

She's been diagnosed with ADHD – something that isn't uncommon in children with heart defects and those that have had surgeries as infants. She's a late developer, even more so than I was, and she's very small in stature.

I know she gets a hard time from her peers because although she's small, her personality is huge – and a lot of young people don't seem to know what to do with someone who is a little different.

Lola is outgoing and fun, and she's got the best attitude about her situation of anyone I've ever met. I know she'd be a great friend. She *is* a great friend.

I've met her best friend Jen, from outside of this group, more than once, but unfortunately the two girls don't go to the same school and that's been tough on Lola, especially as she's reaching her teenage years.

I've been lucky over the years. I've always had Lucy right there with me. But I can recall the isolating feeling if she were ever away sick or on holiday.

"They all make fun of me."

I know how that feels too.

Kids can be really cruel.

You hear people say you should just ignore bullies... that they're just looking for a reaction and if you don't give them one, then they'll just move on.

There's some truth to that I've seen. It worked just fine for Lucy when we were younger, but in my experience, it made no difference – they made fun of me whether I cried or not.

I wouldn't say I was relentlessly bullied as a child because of the defect I was born with. It wasn't anything to that extreme, and I often wonder if it weren't for my heart condition, if a bully would have just found something else to tease me about anyway.

I certainly wasn't the only kid that got picked on – so I can't blame my heart or my scars for it entirely, but it certainly gave them an easy target on the days I was the chosen victim.

I remember so clearly the way they'd point and laugh, usually two or three of the 'mean kids' would gang up on one person.

They made fun of Evelyn for her crooked teeth.

They taunted Mike about his stutter.

They picked on Mia for wearing glasses.

I was teased for the scars running down my chest.

I remember exactly how it felt. I still, to this very day, feel insecure about how I look – their chants and taunts sometimes still ring in my ears when I look at myself in the mirror. I know that they were just young kids themselves, but I was old enough to know better and so were they.

To be honest I can't recall when it all started, but I do remember the moment I decided to do something about it.

I tell Lola to take a seat and I tell her about the day I stood up and shared what I'd been through with the world.

***

Violet

2004 (Eleven years old)

It's speeches time at school again – or as I like to call it, the worst day of the year.

I usually do my best to be one of those lizard things that changes colour to blend in and not get noticed – but it's kinda hard to do that when you have to stand up in front of the whole class and talk.

I've written a really good speech this year, I know I have, but if I could pay someone to read it out for me instead of having to do it myself, I would.

Mum has gone on and on about how important this is going to be, so my classmates can understand me better, and I know she's probably right, but if she turns up in the back of the class with a video camera in her hand like some type of crazy dance mum, I am seriously *never* speaking to her again.

I even tried faking a sickie to get out of coming to school today, but for once, Mum saw right through my act.

Just my luck...

So here I am. Waiting for what feels like the end of the world.

Ella-Marie is talking at the moment, and I'm pretty sure she said her speech is about her pet rabbits, but I can't focus on anything she's saying because I'm up next and I'm freaking out big time.

My palms have gone all sweaty and I wipe them on my jeans to try and get rid of the feeling.

I know it's going to be my turn in a minute. Everyone is clapping for Ella-Marie as she finishes, and I force my hands to do the same.

"Violet." Mrs. Foreman glances around the room until she finds me with her eyes. "You're up, dear."

I force myself to get up out of my chair. I grab my cue cards and walk to the front of the room. My legs are shaking so much I don't know how my knees aren't smacking together and knocking me over.

I glance nervously at Mrs. Foreman when I get up there and she gives me a smile and an encouraging nod of her head.

I take a deep breath and stare directly at the back wall of the class room. If I keep my eyes off everyone, I might just make it through this without losing it.

I catch sight of movement out of the corner of my eye and when I look over, I see Lucy giving me a double thumbs up from her seat. She's got a huge smile on her face – unlike me, Lucy *loves* speech day.

She picks up her own set of cue cards and taps them with one hand whilst pointing at the ones I'm holding.

She's telling me to get on with it.

I guess I may as well, there's really no getting out of it now.

I take another breath and look back at the wall.

I tell myself that I can do this. I just have to look at the wall, then my cue cards, then back at the wall and back at my cue cards...

"I'm Violet," I tell the class. "I know that you all know that already, but what you probably don't know is what it means to be Violet – what it means to be me.

I was born with a heart condition – something called Hypo-plastic Left Heart Syndrome, which is also known as HLHS.

Having HLHS means that the left side of my heart didn't develop properly before I was born and that meant it couldn't pump the blood that I needed around my body.

When I was only a couple of days old I had to have a surgery to try and fix some of my broken parts. A special doctor, called a cardiovascular surgeon opened my chest so she could work on my heart. I had another similar operation when I was just a baby, and then again when I was about three years old.

When I was a baby my skin was a funny bluish-grey colour, I had trouble breathing and I had no strength to wake for milk or to cry. I slept a lot."

I brave a look and see that I have the attention of the *whole* class. No one is drawing on their workbook or writing a note for their friend. No one is staring out the windows or fiddling with their hair.

All eyes are on me.

I quickly look back down at my cue cards before I lose my nerve and stuff it all up.

"My surgeon's name is Dr. Ellis and without her fixing me up the way she did, I wouldn't have lived longer than a few days, maybe a week or two at most.

She connected my heart up so it would let me live. It's still wired differently to all of yours, and even after all my operations, it doesn't work as well as yours do.

I'm not the same as you, and that's why I can't run as fast, or swing on the jungle gym. It's why I come last in the cross country every year and why I don't swim in the pool unless it's a really hot day.

I have to be really careful with germs, because if I get sick it takes me a really long time to get better. My heart isn't as strong as most people's and it takes a lot more work for my body to fight off bugs.

I also have to watch out if I get a cut. I take a lot of medicine every day that helps to make my heart's job a little bit easier. There's one I have to take that makes my blood thinner, so that my heart doesn't have to work as hard, but that also makes me bleed a lot if I get hurt. I had to spend the night in the hospital when I was nine because I got a bleeding nose and they couldn't make it stop.

All up, I've spent close to a whole year in the hospital in the twelve years since I was born."

I feel like I've been up here talking all day, but in reality, I know it's probably only been a minute – maybe two.

"I have to visit specialist doctors a couple of times a year so they can check on my heart and other organs and make sure that everything is still working okay. They do tests on my body and make me run on a treadmill to see how quickly I get tired.

I've had a couple more operations since I was a kid, but they weren't open-heart surgeries – they've just been little procedures done through something called a cardiac catheter. The doctor inserts a thin tube in through your neck, groin or arm and they can use it to figure out and treat small problems. I've had this done a few times already and I'll have more as I grow up."

My hands shake even harder as I near the end of my speech.

"One day, when I'm older, my heart will probably get so worn out that it will stop working. When that happens, I'll need a heart transplant – that means that I'll have to get my old heart taken out and have a new one put in, but until then I'm just doing my best and living each day that I'm given.

So, if you see the scars on my body, or notice that I'm out of breath, now you know why... I might not be the same as all of you, but I'm *me* – I'm here and after everything I've been through, I'm just happy to be able to say that."

I slide my very last cue card back into place as I finish.

There's silence, not one person has clapped for me and I don't know why – maybe nobody really wanted to hear about things like operations and hearts being removed from bodies.

I take a deep breath and look up at my class.

There's about six or seven of them with their hands in the air.

They have questions.

I know it's not what normally happens after a speech, but when I look to my teacher for help on what to do she just smiles and nods again.

I guess I'm answering questions then.

I point to Joel first.

"Where do they get you a new heart?"

I didn't want to talk too much about this – it's not a very nice thing to think about, but he's asking, so I guess I don't have much of a choice but to answer him.

"When someone dies, sometimes they can use their heart and other body parts for donation. They have to find someone that's a match for my blood type and size."

"So, the person is *dead*?" he asks again before I have the chance to point to anyone else.

I nod my head. "Yeah... and if they've said they want to be an organ donor and their family says it's okay, then sometimes they'll get to save other people's lives when they die."

He mouths the word 'wow' and leans back in his chair.

Wow is right.

We've talked a lot about things like organ donation in my family – for obvious reasons, but I've never really stopped to think that maybe it's not a conversation all families have at the dinner table.

I chose the next of my classmates to ask me a question – but every time I point to someone, two more hands pop up somewhere else.

I answer questions about when I was in hospital, I tell them about the time I nearly died, I explain more about the things I struggle with... I tell them everything they want to know.

It's only once the teacher cuts in to let us know that it's nearly time for lunch that I realise how long I've been standing up here. I also notice that I'm not nervous anymore and my hands aren't sweaty like they were at the start.

Everyone is looking at me, but for the first time ever, I don't feel like they're making fun of me – I feel like maybe they're understanding me.

Chapter Nine

Violet
2008 (Fifteen years old)

"Luce, I think I might just head home, I've got a lot of home-work to get done..."

She rolls her eyes at me in an overly exaggerated gesture and sits her hands on her hips – it's her 'I'm not taking no for an answer' pose. It becomes obvious that she's got her mind set on this and I'm fighting a losing battle.

Lucy walks all over me most of the time – not in a controlling, overbearing kind of way, but the kind of way that pushes me *just* outside my comfort zone.

If it weren't for her, I'd probably never do anything exciting.

"I need a new bikini, and I want your help." She pouts.

There is no way in hell that Lucy *needs* a new bikini; the girl has more bikinis than any one person could ever need.

I know what this is. We're here for me.

Ever since she screwed up her nose at me wearing a rash shirt and a pair of board shorts swimming two weeks ago, I have been waiting for this moment to arrive.

I avoid swimming like the plague these days, not because I don't like to swim, but because I never have anything to wear when I go.

I'm the girl with the broken heart and the last thing I need is for people to see the evidence of that. So I cover up – or avoid it all together, much to Lucy's disgust.

"Pllleeeeaasseee," she begs as she tugs on my arm, and I realise I've stopped dead in my tracks.

She's giving me her best puppy-dog eyes.

"Fine," I grumble, "but we're here for *you*... I'm not joining in playing dress up."

***

Sometimes I *really* dislike my best friend.

She's tricked me into getting into a changing room by showing me a top that I actually love. I've tried it on and I'm going to buy it, but before I had the chance to escape the confines of the small room, she started bringing me bikinis.

There are three of them hanging on the hook in here, staring at me, and I haven't moved one muscle in an attempt to try them on.

"Show me when you've got one on," Lucy demands from outside the door.

"Not likely," I mutter under my breath.

"What?"

I take a deep breath and try to find the small amount of courage I do possess.

"I'm not putting these on; you're wasting your time."

"Just try *one* on, Violet, for crying out loud; what's the worst that can happen?"

I can feel the tears starting to form in the corners of my eyes.

I know she means well, but sometimes I wish she would just disappear.

I don't mean that really. She's my best friend and I love her to death, but sometimes it seems like she doesn't understand what it's like for me at all.

"Do you trust me, Letty?" Lucy asks quietly from outside the door when I don't reply.

I think about her question for a moment.

Outside of the members of my family, Lucy is the only person that really knows me. She's one of the only people that I've ever let in to my life one hundred percent.

I *do* trust her. As much as I hate her right now, I do trust her.

"Yes..." I reply, my voice cracking.

"Try the blue one, okay?" Her voice is still insistent, but it's more gentle now.

I know she's not going to give up, and she's right, the worst that will happen is that she'll barge her way in here, see the scars she's already seen one hundred times over, and then I'll go home without the bikini I never actually wanted in the first place.

Maybe a little piece of my self-esteem will be chipped away, but to be honest, at this point, there's not a lot left to lose.

"Fine," I sigh in defeat.

We both know she's going to win in the end – she always does.

I strip off my clothes and reach for the bikini.

I pull on the bottoms – I have no issues with wearing bikini bottoms, but it seems wrong to wear the bottoms without the top, so I don't.

I look at the top for a minute before hope springs to life inside me.

I've never seen a bikini like this before. The neckline is high, the back is string but the front is a large piece of fabric, rather than the two stupid, tiny triangles that swimwear always seem to consist of.

At a glance, I'm actually confident that it will cover most of, if not *all* of the large scar down my chest.

I hurriedly pull it over my head, I don't even bother to undo the ties, there's no time for that, this is the first moment I've ever been excited to try on anything that comes from a swimwear range.

I wiggle it into place and stare at myself in wonder in the floor-length mirror.

I actually look pretty good.

I've still not got even a hint of the boobs that Lucy has, but the blue of the fabric makes my eyes look so much bluer than normal, so that's a win.

"Have you got it on yet?" Lucy calls as she taps on the door.

I can't find the words to reply to her so I push the door open a fraction so she can come in and see for herself.

I can't believe it.

The worst of my scars are hidden.

I can only see a tiny little bit peeking out the bottom of my top, but only because I'm looking for it – I doubt anybody else would even notice.

"Holy moly, girl, where have you been hiding that booty?"

I feel myself blush but for once I don't care about the red staining my cheeks.

"Mainly in my pants." I grin at her.

She stands next to me and we both stare at my body in the mirror.

"You look really good, Vi."

"I look *normal*," I whisper.

I know most people don't want to be 'normal', but I wouldn't mind it. Normal isn't broken, and broken is all I've ever known.

"Pffft, screw *normal*... you look *hot*."

"I can't believe it's covered everything." I turn in the mirror to look side on.

"You're a genius, Lucy, I'm so sorry I ever doubted you." She raises her brows as she waits for me to repeat it back to her.

I laugh and hug her shoulder. "Thank you, Luce, you really are a genius."

She looks so pleased with herself and she should be, buying a bikini might not be a big deal to her, but it certainly is to me.

Today was a first for me and it gives me hope that it'll be the first of many.

Chapter Ten

Violet
2011 (Eighteen years old)

"You're going to that party whether you like it or not."

I stomp my foot and scowl my best scowl at my dad.

There's something very mixed up about this picture.

Most of the girls from school are begging their parents to let them go to this party, and more than half of them are getting told a resounding *no*. Yet here I am, arguing with my dad because he's insisting I go, when I'd really rather stay home.

Parties aren't my thing.

I'd much rather be in my studio, minding my own business and painting, but no... my father has got on one of his missions.

"If she doesn't want to go, sh—"

"She's going, Lee." He cuts Mum off with a glare.

Mum would love it if I stayed home. I know deep down she would like for me to go places and have fun, but I also know that she won't sleep a wink until I walk back through the front door, and that only makes me feel guilty for going at all.

Auggie goes out all the time, and even though Mum worries a bit, I've never seen her sit in the chair by the window for four hours straight while she waits for her to get home.

It's ironic really, August is far more likely to get herself into trouble than I am, but that's just one of the many downsides of having a bad heart – people worry.

"Dad, I'm *really* not bothered. To be honest I'm actually feeling a little bit off..."

"Don't you dare bullshit me, young lady." He raises his brows at me, daring me to argue with him.

We both know I feel fine, and it's pretty clear I'm not fooling him in the slightest.

"Lucy will be over in fifteen minutes, Violet Aubrey Miller, so I suggest you march your butt up those stairs, put something on and get ready to go."

I huff out a breath and stomp up the stairs. There's no arguing with him when he's made his mind up – I know that better than anyone and unlike August, I have no intention of wasting an hour of my life trying to change his decision.

I grumble all the way up to my room, I just don't see the big deal about turning eighteen if you can't even have a drink to celebrate the occasion.

I'll probably never have an alcoholic drink in my life.

The cocktail of medication I take each morning makes drinking, like everyone else at school does, an absolute no-go for me.

Thankfully Lucy isn't a big drinker, so I'm not totally alone when I do get forced to go to these kind of things, but honestly, sometimes I'd rather she just go have fun without me.

I've got a pretty good idea that the only reason she never has more than a couple of drinks is because I'm there with her. And while I love her for being so considerate, I don't want my messed up condition to impact on every aspect of her life as well.

I know she's not even legally allowed to drink yet, she's got a couple more months until she turns eighteen, but that's never stopped anyone I know from doing it anyway. And besides, she has to experience everything for the both of us, so I think it's fair that she gets a head start.

I frown as I search for something that might be somewhat acceptable to wear to a house party.

I don't own 'party' clothes. There's a few things here I never wear, stuffed somewhere down the back of my closet. Things that Lucy convinced me to buy and I've never worn, and considering she's apparently going to be here very soon, I figure that I should just go straight to those options and save us both the time and argument.

If I come out wearing jeans and a t-shirt, I'm not only going to get told off by my best friend, but probably my dad too if his speech in the living room just now was anything to go on.

There's a light knock at my door and it startles me.

No one knocks around here, not even Lucy – she's pretty much part of the furniture at this point in our friendship.

"Come in?" I ask cautiously.

I'm not sure what I was expecting to come through the door, but it certainly wasn't my dad holding a bright yellow box, wrapped up with a pretty ribbon.

"Here." He holds it out to me. "This is for you."

I eye him suspiciously. "But my birthday was two days ago."

"I was saving it." He pushes it even further towards me.

I take the box from his hands and turn to sit down on my bed with it.

I slowly undo the ribbon as he lingers awkwardly near the door.

I glance up at him and raise a brow. "You can come in you know, I'm not exactly healthy, but I haven't got anything you can catch."

"Oh, ha ha," he retorts sarcastically, but my statement has the desired effect. He comes into the room and perches himself, albeit awkwardly, on the corner of my bed.

Poor old Dad, he really doesn't know what to make of teenage girls.

I've got August to blame for that I think. She was quite the hell raiser for a while there, and I think Dad is just waiting for me to snap and join her in the teenage drama queen club. I hope he's not holding his breath, because me and my sister couldn't be more different if we tried.

"C'mon, buttercup, open the box already. I've got things to do and you've got a party to get to."

I roll my eyes at him in an overly large gesture and lift the lid off the box.

"It's a top – for you to wear tonight... I mean, if you want to," he rambles as I lift the black top out of the box.

It's a gorgeous fabric, sleeveless and high neck with a scoop hem at the back.

It's exactly what I need for this stupid party.

"Your sister showed me some pictures, but I wasn't sure I got the right kind..." He's rubbing at the back of his neck as though he's suddenly unsure of himself.

"*You* picked this for me?" I gape at him.

He shrugs and stands up, clearly embarrassed. "What, you think shopping is hard or something?"

I can't believe he did this for me. I've never known my dad to set foot inside a shopping centre, let alone a store selling nothing but clothes for girls, but he did – for *me*.

"It's *perfect*, thank you."

"So, you'll go then?" he asks, pausing by the door – he seems eager to make his escape.

"I didn't know I had a choice."

He sighs. "You always have a choice, Vi. I know I pushed you into it, but I just... I don't want you to miss out on anything... I want to make sure you experience it all."

He wants me to experience it all because we don't know how long I have.

He doesn't say the words, but I hear them.

They're there, hidden in virtually every conversation I have.

It used to make me sad, but it doesn't so much anymore. I'm just happy to be here, as alive and well as I'll probably ever be.

I jump up off my bed and wrap my arms tightly around his waist.

I used to hug my parents so often, and somewhere along the line I've stopped.

The realisation saddens me. I know I'm technically an adult now, but I'm still not too old for a hug.

"Thank you, Dad." My words are muffled against his jersey, but I'm sure he'll still hear them.

He leans down and kisses the top of my head and I decide that I'll try my hardest to have fun at this party, if not for my sake, then for my dad's.

***

I flop down on my bed and look up at my ceiling before letting out an excited squeal.

I don't care if I wake Auggie in the next room, in fact I hope I do – I can't wait to tell her about the night I've just had.

The party I never even wanted to go to has somehow turned out to be the best night of my life so far.

Chapter Eleven

Leanne

2012 (Nineteen years old)

I carry a lot of guilt with me every single day and I worry about anything and everything that a person could possibly worry about when it comes to their child.

I worry that it's my fault that she's in pain... I worry that every little thing is related to her heart condition.

I worry that I've done this to her – that my selfish choice has given her a lifetime full of hardships.

It was *my* choice to give her this life, and it's by no means going to be an easy one.

In the nineteen years since Violet was born, I feel like I've aged about ninety years myself.

I don't sleep deeply or peacefully like I used to, and I fret about all sorts of trivial, insignificant things.

I know this isn't my condition to live with, and that medically speaking, I'm completely healthy, but it's the things no one can see – the things that go on inside my brain that make me think I'm no better off.

I break out into a sweat at the smell of hand sanitiser – it transports me back in time to the paediatric intensive care unit where we spent far too much time, and the beeping of a reversing truck has me running to check a heart rate monitor that isn't there.

I stress about Violet the most out of my three children, as I'm sure any parent would, but I also spend countless hours worrying that August and Charlie aren't getting the attention and time that they need, because I'm always concerned first and foremost with their sister.

I'd be devastated to think that they held Violet responsible for not having an attentive enough mother, or for having permanently distracted parents.

I know Charlie doesn't begrudge his sister a thing. In fact, he's probably thrilled with the leniency he gets because my mind is always preoccupied with things other than his curfew or his cell phone bill.

August, on the other hand, isn't so easily pleased.

We've had some tough times with her over the years, and I know that a lot of that is down to the fact that her sister has been so unwell.

We've missed dance concerts and parent teacher interviews, school events and birthday parties because of hospital visits and emergency situations.

August might come across as a spoilt diva, but I know deep down that this is her way of coping.

She loves Violet something fierce, and even through all the tantrums she's thrown about having to sit through specialist appointments and blood tests, she's always the one who gets the most upset when Violet has to be admitted into the hospital. She's always the first one to notice if Violet's colour is off, or if her breathing sounds laboured.

Having a sibling with a heart condition has taken its toll on her – it's taken its toll on all of us if I'm being honest.

It's not just the kids I fret about, it's Shaun too.

I worry that I don't give my husband sufficient attention, or that he doesn't get enough of my time, but the reality for a lot of years has been that there just hasn't been *enough* time.

That's one of my biggest worries in life.

Time.

I'm *terrified* that we won't get enough time.

Time with Violet, time *together*, time to really just enjoy this life we've been given.

We're always waiting for more time to pass.

Always looking to the next stage, the next surgery, the next milestone…

It's really hard to live in the moment when you have no idea how long that moment is going to last, or how many more moments like it will follow.

I do my best, but even I can't do it all.

When Violet was younger, I wasn't so bad, or perhaps I was just too busy to think too hard about things outside of our bubble.

But now her life is just a 'wait and see' game – we're not actively doing anything new to better her condition and that's when my mind gets the better of me.

I worry that my beautiful little girl won't get the same things in life that her siblings will.

She really *is* beautiful. I know she thinks I'm just saying that because I'm her mum, but I'm not. She's got long dark hair that thickened up after her last childhood procedure and has stayed that way ever since. Her skin has evened and smoothed out into a stunning creamy tone. She's got deep dimples in her cheeks when she smiles, and her eyes, my goodness, *those eyes*, they really are something special.

All of my children have stunning, big blue eyes, but there's just something about Violet's that take my breath away. They shine like an aquamarine crystal and hold so much more depth than any nineteen-year-old's should.

She's wise beyond her years that girl, and considering we were never sure if her condition would ever allow her to reach even the 'normal' scale, it's incredibly impressive that she's turned out so well.

She's smart, kind, compassionate and funny.

If it weren't for her heart – I'd have very little to worry about where Violet was concerned... far less than August or Charlie. But in the same breath, I know that if it weren't for her heart she wouldn't be the same person she is today.

Her heart is as much a part of her as every other organ or limb, and if it weren't for the struggles that she's had, she might not feel empathy the way she does – or look for the good in those around her.

It might not be the life she deserves, but it's helped shape her into the amazing young woman she is today.

Her heart owes her a lot, but I can't help but think that maybe she owes it a little bit back in return.

Chapter Twelve

Oh. My. God.

This is bad; this is so, *so* bad.

There's blood *everywhere*. If it weren't for the fact that I've been waiting about five years for this day, I would have sworn someone had come in here and stabbed me as I slept.

I had a feeling this would be coming soon. My boobs came in about a month ago – it might sound like a weird way to explain it, but it's how it happened. I woke up one morning and there they were, like overnight implant surgery.

They might have been about six years late in arriving, but I guess it was better late than never.

It's yet another side effect of having a condition like HLHS – my body doesn't know if it's coming or going ninety percent of the time, so in turn I didn't develop like all the other girls my age did. I've had a flat chest and no curves to my body for far longer than I should have.

But even though I've been expecting this, I still was not quite prepared for what's happened here.

I ball up the sheets and my pyjamas as best I can, but there's not going to be much I can do to hide this bright red mess on the trip to the laundry – hopefully Charlie has left for school already because if he sees, it'll scar the poor boy for life.

I creep down the hallway, my crotch rustling from the huge, nappy-looking pad I've stuffed in my underwear.

I don't know how much blood I was expecting, but it certainly wasn't this much.

I manage to make it down without incident, and I stuff the sheets into the washing machine as fast as I can.

I tip half the box of washing powder in after them, because frankly, they'll need it, before hitting start and getting the hell out of there.

I *need* to call Lucy and find out what on earth I'm meant to expect from this hellish ordeal. I listened in sex-education, but it's a different story when it's happening to you.

August would know, but even if she still lived here, which she doesn't, I'm not sure I'd be brave enough to talk about this with her just yet.

I shut the door to my bedroom behind me and exhale an audible sigh of relief.

I feel like I'm cleaning up after a murder or something, and to be honest, I imagine the mess would be about the same.

I dial Lucy's number and chew nervously on my fingernail as I wait for her to pick up my call.

"Good morning," she answers cheerily.

"I'm bleeding," I blurt out by way of hello.

"What? Are you okay? Should I call someone?"

"No, Luce... I'm *bleeding*."

There's silence for a few beats as she reads between the lines of what I'm saying.

"Ohhhhh... you mean it's shark week?"

"Shark week is an *understatement*. It's like a mass murder went down in my pants. Is it meant to be this bad?"

"How bad are we talking? Like a tablespoon... or more?"

"We're talking like a full one-litre jug."

"Um ew." I can picture her screwing up her nose in disgust.

Her mum might be a nurse who deals with a lot worse than this, but Lucy didn't get that particular gene – she's *terrible* with blood.

"Right? I'm seriously concerned I'm going to bleed out."

"Maybe it's the blood thinners?"

I've already thought of that, but according to Google, the blood thinning medication I take every day shouldn't make a difference.

"Maybe... I don't think so though..."

"I guess it's been brewing for twenty years, just give it a chance... I'm sure it'll settle down."

"I hope so, or I'll be spending one week a month in one of these adult nappies." I groan.

I hear her muffle a laugh.

"At least it's finally here... now you can share my whinging about the price of tampons and getting thrush from wearing a pad."

"That sounds like a really pleasant way to spend time," I drawl.

"Well on the bright side, at least you've got a good rack now."

I groan at her crassness, even though she technically makes a good point.

She spends the next fifteen minutes telling me all the tricks of the trade, and I resist the urge to pull out a notebook and pen and jot it all down.

There was a time when I felt embarrassed that everyone else at school had their period and I didn't – some of the girls even got it before high school. By sixteen I think I was the only girl in my year without it, but now that it's here, I would quite happily have put it off for another ten years – it's far from enjoyable.

I've got cramping and my stomach feels bloated, my favourite sheets are probably going to be tinted a suspicious shade of pink, and I can feel a headache coming on.

If this is what maturing is all about, then I think I'd like to stay a teenager forever, because this sucks.

I suddenly feel the need to ring my sister and apologise for not understanding why she always turned into a bitch every month – because *now* I get it.

I was planning to go for a walk this morning and getting on with my study this afternoon, but now all I feel like doing is lying on the couch and watching movies – I also have a sudden and desperate craving for ice cream.

I roll my eyes at myself – I've turned into a walking, talking cliché of a girl on her period, but that's not going to stop me from doing it anyway.

"What's your status on binge-watching movies and eating junk food all day?"

"That would be a positive. I'll be over in ten. Try not to bleed out while you wait."

"Oh, ha ha."

I throw the phone down on the covers after she's hung up and sit down to take stock of my life for a minute.

I might finally be classed as a woman, but having a period almost feels like another little kick in the guts.

The whole point of a menstrual cycle is so your body can figure out the best time to conceive a baby. That's not something that's ever going to happen for me, so the very idea of having to have a period every month seems ludicrous and frankly, a little cruel.

It seems to be a reoccurring theme in my life and as per usual, it's not something I have an ounce of control over, so I do what I always do – push it from my mind and get on with my day.

Chapter Thirteen

I can't recall a time where I felt quite this weak.

Everything aches, I feel dizzy, it's hard to breathe, and of course this is the first time in ages that I'm home all alone.

Tonight's the first time Mum and Dad have gone out in forever, so there's no way I'm going to call them back, not even if it kills me.

I make that comment in passing, but the reality is, I actually *could* die.

A lot of people live by the motto that they could walk out in the street and get hit by a car any day of the week, so there's no point in worrying about this or that... but for me there's a number of things that not only *could* kill me, but that are actually *waiting* to do it.

I feel like a ticking time bomb most days, and right now the ticking is louder than it's ever been.

I know it's a warning sign for me to do *something* – to call someone, or to get myself to the hospital, but I'm so wary of being like Mum and overreacting that I hesitate as my finger hovers over the call button on my phone.

There's one person I can count on not to judge me if it all turns out to be nothing at all, and that's Lucy.

She still lives around the corner – the fact she's a poor student who has to live at home with her mum has been a blessing to me.

I don't know what I would have done with myself if she'd gone across the country to study.

I could have gone away to school if I'd wanted to, but truthfully, I didn't have the desire. I'd love my own space, outside of my parent's home, but with no degree and no money, getting my own place isn't likely to happen anytime soon.

I know I'm stalling by thinking about living arrangements rather than making a decision about what to do, and I'm feeling even worse now than I was before.

Suddenly I'm filled with a sense of urgency that probably should have me dialling an emergency operator, but instead I slide the screen of my cell phone open and hit call on the shortcut for Lucy.

Each unanswered ring is more agonising than the last as I struggle to get enough air.

"Hey, girl, I was just about to ring you, I'm meant to be studying but it suuuuuuucks." She drags out the word and I can feel her rolling her eyes through the phone. "You wanna go get a milkshake or something?"

"Luce..." My voice isn't much above a whisper now, and my breathing has become incredibly laboured.

"Oh my God, Letty." I can hear her feet slapping against the wooden floor of her house.

I don't even need to tell her that something's wrong, we know each other so well, it's like we're two halves of a whole.

I also know that I wasn't overreacting, this *is* bad. It's really, really bad. It's all come on so quickly my head is literally spinning.

I have a feeling that this might be it... that maybe I actually might have run out of chances this time.

"I'll be two minutes, where are you? Is anybody home?"

I try to get to my feet, but I can't seem to manage it; all the strength has gone from my limbs.

"Just me, in my room," I rasp as I let my body fall to my bed.

I hear her scream at someone to call an ambulance for me.

I listen as she gets into her car and slams the door closed behind her.

She's driving now, and even in this moment of panic, I find comfort in knowing she'll be here soon.

I can hear her mum talking – she must be with her.

That's a smart move – Linda is a great nurse. I might actually have a chance with her here.

I'm so dizzy and I can't seem to get enough air, but I know I have to hold on.

I can't do this to Lucy; she shouldn't have to be the one that watches me die.

"I'm coming, Violet. I'm coming, okay? Just hold on, I'll be there any second, just hold on, *please* hold on..."

"O... K..." I drag in a deep breath that feels like razor blades, but I have to do it, Lucy *needs* me to hold on.

I can hear her car pull up outside.

I don't need to tell her where the spare key is – she's known all of this family's secrets since she was five years old.

I can hear the rapid pace of her feet as she flies up the stairs, and also the slightly slower ones of her mum's behind her.

With Linda on the case, there should be an ambulance on its way already.

I think maybe I can hear the siren, but I can't be sure that it's not just my imagination playing tricks on me.

Lucy's hands are on my face. She's talking to me, but I can't find the strength to answer her.

My eyes are open. I can see her – but I'm not really *seeing* her.

'Help me' I want to scream, but nothing comes out.

***

Lucy

This is the worst day of my life.

My whole body is numb, and I can't stop the sobs that keep ripping from my throat.

I'm *so* scared.

I've never seen a person look the way Violet did when I found her.

I don't even know if she's alive right now.

I'm bracing myself for that moment in the movies where a doctor comes out of a set of swinging doors and shakes their head. One of those little, almost non-movements, but you still see it – and you damn well know what it means.

That's not going to happen. She *can't* leave me.

I need her.

She's my best friend.

I think back to when we were about eight years old. It was smack bang in between our two birthdays and we were having a joint party – it was only small, family only. We both had matching cakes – unicorns was what we were into back then, and we blew the candles out together.

I know you're not supposed to tell anyone your wish, but that year, we did.

"What did you wish for?" I whisper to Violet.

She looks around to make sure that no one else can hear us.

"I wished that I could be like everyone else."

Her wish makes me sad, mostly because now that she's shared it with me, it might never come true.

"What did you wish for?" she whispers back.

I'm not worried about telling her my wish – there's nothing that could stop it from coming true – not even whoever makes these rules.

"I wished that we'll be best friends forever."

"I'm going to go ask if they have an update." Mum stands up from next to me and heads for the nurse's station, pulling me from my little trip down memory lane.

She's worked here for about twenty-five years, and if anyone can get us answers, it's her.

I'm so grateful for my mum. If today hadn't have been her day off, I have no doubt that Violet wouldn't be here right now – if it had all been up to me, I hate to think what would have happened.

I panic. It's what I do.

Thankfully, I must have inherited that gene from dead beat dad, and not my mum.

She's so calm and in control in a crisis.

All I could do was sob uncontrollably.

Mum kept my best friend calm when I couldn't – by the time the ambulance arrived I was so inconsolable that they weren't sure which one of us they had been called to pick up.

I'm watching my mum as she talks yet again to another nurse at the station, she's trying to get any scrap of information she can.

I'm searching her body language for clues so thoroughly that I don't even notice one of the paramedics approach before he's right there next to me.

It's the cute one.

Yes, I might be in a total state of shock, but I'm not blind, and you'd have to be exactly that not to notice how gorgeous he is.

"How's she doing?" he asks me. His voice is kind and genuine, and I can tell he really wants to know that she's okay.

He holds up a blanket to me and when I don't object he carefully spreads it over my shoulders. It's only then that I realise I'm shaking like a leaf.

It's incredibly sweet of him to bring it for me.

"We haven't heard." I can hear my voice wobbling and I know it won't be long before I break down in tears again.

I glance back up at Mum but she doesn't seem to be having any luck.

"Thank you... for the blanket... for keeping her alive." That does it, the floodgates open and the tears start to fall.

"Oh, Lucy." He wraps an arm around me and rubs his hand slowly up and down my arm.

I don't remember telling him my name, but the whole experience is still so surreal I can't actually recall most of what I said and did – or probably more importantly, what I *didn't* do.

There's so much to think about all at once, and if there's one thing I take from this ordeal, it's that I'm not cut out for emergency medicine, so it's lucky that I decided to study teaching and not follow in my mum's footsteps like I once thought I would.

I didn't even think to call Violet's family. Thankfully my mum got hold of Leanne as soon as she got Violet into the ambulance and on her way to the hospital – they're on their way here right now.

More tears overflow as I think about just how incredible my mother is. She thought of everything.

She even called ahead to make sure the hospital had a surgeon and their team waiting in the ER and she managed to run through Violet's medical history.

Mum did *everything* possible to ensure that she had the best possible shot of making it through this.

I know there's a lot of people that Violet owes her life to, but after this, *when* she makes it through, she's going to have to add my mum to the list.

"She's a fighter," he tells me. "I've never seen someone fight for life as hard as she was, that's got to count for something, right?"

I nod in agreement. Violet is the toughest person I know.

The things she's been through are so incredibly unfair, yet she deals with it with a smile and a laugh.

I've never told her, but she's my hero.

I may only be a few months younger than her, but when I grow up I want to be just like her.

She's kind, compassionate, and she's got the most generous soul.

There's no one else like her.

She knows exactly what life is all about and how lucky she is to live each day of it.

We could all benefit from being a little more like Violet.

"I've got a good feeling about your friend."

I look right up at him and a memory of me screaming into the ambulance fills my mind. *I love you, Letty, don't you dare die on me!*

He didn't look at me like I was crazy as he pulled the doors shut; he looked at me like he was going to make sure that she did exactly what I told her – that she stayed alive.

I could seriously kiss him right now, for being so kind, and for keeping her safe for me... but I won't.

The elevator dings and Leanne comes flying out, Auggie right on her heels with Shaun, Charlie and Violet's Aunt Rita behind her.

They all look like they've been to hell and back.

"Leanne!" I call to her as she blindly swings her head back and forth, looking for anyone familiar.

"I'll leave you to it," he tells me quietly as he stands and takes a step away from me.

"Wait..." I call after him, while I still have the chance. "I don't even know your name."

Even though all around me there's tears, tension and panic, when he smiles it all feels a little bit brighter.

"I'm Emmett," he tells me. "I'll see you and your friend soon, okay?"

I smile as he walks away and in an instant, I feel something deep inside me that tells me she's going to be alright.

That she *is* alright.

My best friend is going to be just fine... and when she is, I really need to tell her about the cute guy named Emmett.

Chapter Fourteen

Leanne
Present day

I know it probably makes me a terrible person, let alone mother, but I've thought about receiving the news that Violet's gone.

I've tried to mentally prepare myself for hearing those words.

I haven't thought about it for years, but when she was younger and she was in and out of surgeries frequently, the thoughts consumed me.

I feel like a horrible person for admitting that – even if it's only to myself.

I know Violet needs positive vibes right now, not negative ones, but the very thing I worried would happen to Violet, has actually happened to me.

I've become hardened. I try to hope for the best, but I *always* end up expecting the worst. Where Shaun looks at a situation and sees a half full glass, I see one that's half empty. I look for dangers and problems where there are none.

Maybe hardened isn't the right word, maybe I'm paranoid... I'm not sure how best to describe it.

I know full well what I have to lose, and I also know if I don't hunt out the worst-case scenario, then nobody else will.

That's my role – it's my duty to my family.

I look for the worst and do my best to shield whoever I can from what comes of it.

There's no shielding anyone from this though.

I can't fix *this*.

And as hard as I've tried, there's no way to prepare yourself for the very real possibility that your child might leave this earth before you do.

I can't stop the worry of August and Charlie – that they might never see their sister smile again, I can't comfort Lucy from the absolute nightmare that life without her best friend would be. There's nothing I can do for Shaun as he sits there looking exactly the way I feel.

As much as it pains me... I *can't* fix this.

***

"Mr. and Mrs. Miller?"

I know that she's talking to me and I know I'm meant to respond – to acknowledge that it's me she's looking for, but I *can't*.

I'm so filled with fear that I can't even speak.

I'm being eaten alive by guilt. I should never have gone out and left her alone.

We've been here for what feels like forever and with every tick of the clock from the hall outside this room, I've blamed myself a little bit more.

If I had been home, we could have caught this earlier – we could have given her a better chance.

"Yes." I don't recognise Shaun's voice – he's gone into his robotic mode. I know it's him though, he's not moved from my side for even a moment. "That's us."

That mechanical voice is his coping mechanism. Mine is silence.

I don't look up as a woman I assume is the doctor approaches us.

I can hear her feet tapping lightly against the flooring, but I can't force my eyes to move up to meet hers.

She's come to tell us one of two things – either Violet is alive, or she's dead.

Until I know which of the two it is – I can't even begin to consider moving.

Her shoes appear in front of us and I brace myself for whatever will happen next.

"Mr. and Mrs. Miller, could we talk a moment in private?"

I don't want to talk to her in private, in fact I can't think of a single thing I'd rather do less than be shuffled off to some small, stuffy room where we'll be told the fate of our daughter.

"You can speak freely – we're all family here."

This might be one of the worst moments of my life, but I couldn't think of a better man to have at my side during it.

Shaun has his flaws, we all do, but he's a good man and he knows me so well he doesn't even need me to speak most of the time.

Like right now – if I could find a way to talk, I would have said exactly what he just has.

Rita, August and Charlie... they all deserve to hear whatever she's going to say as much as the two of us do – they're her family too.

Linda and Lucy might not be blood related, but they're family nonetheless – they always have been, and if it weren't for the two of them, Violet wouldn't have made it inside this building alive today.

There's no one here that Violet would want gone.

"Okay," the doctor acknowledges.

I wish Dr. Ellis were here. She's been with Violet through everything, if anyone could have saved my daughter's life – it was her.

I don't even know who the woman in front of me is, but I do hear what she says.

"I'm sorry, but due to Violet's heart defect, she's gone into what's commonly known as *heart failure*, upon arrival in the emergency department she went into cardiac arrest, not only once, but twice..."

Chapter Fifteen

Violet
Present day

I've heard people say after a near death experience, that their life flashed before their eyes... that they had a moment of perfect clarity and peacefulness.

I've never believed any of that until this very second.

I know I'm not technically living right now.

My heart, once again, has stopped beating the way it should.

This isn't the first time, and if I do make it through this, I doubt it will be the last, but it's different this time than it has been in the past.

I've seen the light before. I was young, but I remember it. I've caught a glimpse of 'the light' every time I've been put under.

This is new though, today is the first time the light has taken me in.

The movie montage of my life that I'm watching isn't at all what I expected to be presented with.

I expected – because I've contemplated death on multiple occasions, that I would see all of my most memorable moments, that I'd reminisce about things like my parents hugging me, or playing at the park with my brother and sister, my first kiss... or getting ice-cream with Lucy.

But that's not what this is at all.

In some cruel twist of fate, I'm being shown all the things that I should have lived out *after* this moment.

My graduation, moving out of home, painting... even having a family of my own.

There's a jolt to my heart at the sight of me holding a baby. Having a child of my own is something that I've always known wasn't going to happen for me.

Even if I ever made it to that stage of my life – if I found a donor and my body accepted their heart, even if I found a man who accepted me and wanted to build a life with me, even then, the risk of carrying a baby would be too great for me.

And even though I know this is nothing more than a cruel dream, I still can't take my eyes off the precious baby I'm holding.

My parents are grandparents – and we're all standing in a field of daisies, and my siblings are staring adoringly at their niece.

She's a girl... *my* baby is a girl.

The daisies, they're *everywhere*, and I'm not even sure why I'm so fixated on them. Everything I'm seeing in front of me isn't real, but for some reason, the daisies swaying in the wind seem significant to me.

I can hear my name being called and I focus as hard as I can on the sound.

The strong voice is familiar to me somehow, even though I'm certain I've never heard it before this moment.

It calls to more than my ears – it pulls at my soul.

"Violet."

"Violet."

"Violet."

It's calling to me still.

I try desperately to look around for the keeper of that voice, but I can't move. I'm frozen – fixated on the twisted home movie playing out in front of me.

"Violet."

I try so hard to call back to him – the man calling my name, but nothing comes out.

The light is dimming around me now and for the first time ever, I'm scared to die.

I've seen what my future should hold, and I want this life I've been shown so badly I can barely breathe. I want it *all*.

I want to hold my baby, I want more time with my family, and maybe more than any of that, I want to know who that voice belongs to; because I have a feeling it's important.

I just want to *live*.

But I know damn well I'm not going to get to.

The darkness is closing in on me now and I know how my story ends.

This is it, right here in this hospital room, cold and sterile.

A face comes into view, in the one spot of light I have left, and my heart jolts violently in my chest once again.

I try to reach for him but it's impossible. I will my mind to grasp onto anything it can, but it's not working.

"Hold on for me, Violet," he says. "*Live*."

This man... he has the most breath-taking dark blue eyes, and they're the only thing I see as the darkness takes over.

***

I suck in a deep breath and my eyes fly open in panic as I desperately gasp for air.

I don't know where I am.

I don't know where people go when they die.

All I know is I didn't expect *this*; I didn't expect to feel in pain, or to still feel so grounded.

My eyes are blurry, like I'm trying to look through a thick layer of fog and I can't make out my surroundings.

It's unnerving and I don't like it.

God, I'm in so much pain, I feel like I've been ripped in half and put back together all wrong.

"Help me." I try to scream, but my voice barely comes out as a whisper.

I don't even sound like me.

Maybe I'm *not* me anymore.

If this is what there is after life as we know it, then I long for the peace in the darkness.

I squeeze my eyes shut and beg the universe for nothingness, for a black hole of nonexistence to take me and hold me tight.

I hear a shrill alarm sound, once, twice, three times... as I chant internally for this to be over, for the next stage of death to take me swiftly.

I hear what sounds like feet running; slamming against a hard floor, I hear murmured voices that make no sense to me before everything fades into blackness once more.

"*Live*, Violet." I hear his voice in my mind once again, and as badly as I want to live for him, I know he's too late.

I let out a satisfied sigh as I let the darkness take me once more.

Chapter Sixteen

Leanne
Present day

It's been over a week since Violet was brought in to the emergency room, and I've still not forgiven myself for not being there for her when she needed me most.

Linda, Shaun, Rita and even Auggie and Charlie have spent countless hours with me, trying to convince me that it wasn't my fault – that I can't spend my life locked away in that house any more than Violet can, but I can't let it go.

I'm her mum and it's my responsibility to take care of her – no matter how old she is.

There's a light knock at the door and I smile at the young woman who has always been like a daughter to me as she enters the room.

She cares for Violet as much as I do, and I'm so grateful they've had each other all these years.

She's carrying a bunch of bright pink roses. She's brought in a new assortment every single day – it's going to look like a florist threw up in here when they finally wake Violet from her sleep.

"Any update?" she asks me quietly.

This is the first day I'll be able to give her any news actually worth hearing.

"All going well, they'll try and bring her out of it on Wednesday."

They've been keeping Violet in a medically induced coma. Her body, her heart, her brain... it all needs time to rest and heal.

It's been tough seeing her like this, but I know it's for the best.

When she wakes up again I don't want her to be disorientated or in pain like she was when she first woke. That was one of the more horrific experiences of my life, and given all I've seen, that's saying a lot.

So, if it means that I don't get to hear her speak, or see her open her eyes for a few more days, then so be it.

This isn't about me after all, this is about *her*.

I know Lucy is scared, hell, we all are... but I can't imagine what she's gone through, seeing what she had to see. She's only twenty-one herself and she's had to deal with so much this past week.

I know she wouldn't change Violet for the world, but it can't always be an easy thing – having a best friend with a condition like this.

Lucy doesn't reply, she just sits down the vase she's holding and comes over to hug me.

"I never thanked you," I say as I release her and she sits herself down in the seat next to me.

She reaches forward and gives Violet's hand a quick squeeze hello.

"Thank me for what?"

"For everything you did for her."

She shakes her head at me, the same amused smirk on her face that Violet has when she thinks I'm being ridiculous.

"You did thank me. *Twice* actually."

"Not properly."

"You *did*. And you don't need to thank me. She's my best friend; it's the least I could have done. Besides, Mum's the one who did all the hard work anyway... I think all I did was bawl my eyes out and scream at Letty to hold on."

I might not have been there, but I can picture it so clearly – the panic, the screams... the fear.

I know that Lucy did everything she could – there's more than one way to keep a person alive, and I know that her being there would have helped Violet hold onto life a little bit longer – to fight a little bit harder.

"She wouldn't have wanted to let you down, I bet that's what kept her going."

"You're giving me too much credit," she replies with a roll of her eyes.

She really is so much like my daughter – they've grown up together and they share so many quirks they're probably not even aware of.

"I spoke to that good-looking young man again today." I glance at her reaction out of the corner of my eye.

"You sound so old when you say things like that." She giggles, but she's not getting away with the change of subject so easily.

Violet might not be up for interrogating her about the new guy on the scene, but I certainly am.

"He came up to see how Violet was doing."

"That was sweet of him."

It *was* sweet of him, and I'm sure he does genuinely care, but I can't imagine he checks up on every patient that he brings into the hospital the way he has Violet.

I have a pretty good feeling that the reason for his frequent visits are mainly due to the pretty blonde sitting next to me.

"So, when's he taking you out?"

"Leanne!" she mock scolds me. "*As if* I'd even consider going out on a date with Letty lying here like this."

She's called Violet 'Letty' for as long as she's been able to talk. She's the only one who does it – it's a special thing between the two of them.

"Well I'll tell you one thing, Lucy Reynolds, the minute she wakes up and finds out about that boy, she's going to be pissed off you didn't go out with him sooner."

She laughs and nods her head. "Yeah, you're probably right."

We sit in silence for a few minutes, both of us watching the young woman in front of us with so much more life to live.

"I miss her," she whispers as she shuffles her chair closer to me and rests her head on my shoulder.

I'm grateful for it – we both need the comfort right now I think.

"Do you think she'll be okay when she wakes up?"

It's the same question I've asked myself at least one hundred times over. There's no telling what damage has been done during this ordeal – no matter how confident the doctors are.

"They think she'll be just fine." I lean my head down to rest against hers. "We've just got to listen to her doctors; it's all we can do."

"They've got her this far I guess," she whispers.

I might not be willing to believe anything until I see it with my own eyes, but she's right. Doctors might not get it right all of the time, but this one, she got it right for Violet this time.

I've held Dr. Ellis up on such a high pedestal for the longest time, I'm still having trouble adjusting to the fact that she's now in good company up there.

There are so many people who contributed to saving my daughter that day, but the doctor who saved Violet's life is the one I'm most grateful for. Dr. White literally brought her back from the dead.

The words she spoke to us over a week ago are still as fresh in mind as they were the moment she spoke them.

"It was touch and go for a couple of minutes there, but we managed to get her back."

I recognised the woman as soon as I lifted my head and laid eyes on her. I couldn't recall *where* I knew her from, but I was certain this wasn't the first time I'd seen her.

Regardless of who she was, I knew that I owed her my life. She saved my daughter, and whether or not it'll be plain sailing from here on out or not is irrelevant – for now, Violet is alive.

***

Violet

2009 (Sixteen years old)

"Violet, this is Dr. White, she's a cardiologist who is new to the hospital, would you mind if she sits in on our appointment today?"

I glance up at the newbie. She's got wildly curly hair that I bet is an absolute nightmare to brush, and pretty brown skin and eyes.

She looks harmless enough I guess.

"Sure, why not? I can play circus animal."

I'm feeling extra snarky today for some reason. My moods are often up and down, but lately they seem to be down more than they're up. That's probably the reason Mum booked me in for this appointment a bit earlier than it was required.

I see my doctor at least every six months, and I usually see a cardiologist and my cardiovascular surgeon once a year as well.

Apparently, I haven't been in this place enough times in my life, so they just keep on bringing me back.

I *hate* these appointments, I don't mind too much about being asked a bunch of questions, or when they check my lungs and heart, but the stress test – where they make me run on a treadmill to test my endurance, that one gets old pretty quickly.

Dr. Ellis passes the new doctor my notes.

"You'll be there a while reading those," I grumble.

"See what I mean, Vivian, she's so irritable lately."

Mum is on first name basis with my doctor these days. I normally am happy for her – that she feels comfortable enough with the informality, but as she's suggested, I'm *irritable* today, so it only irks me further.

"Sorry, Dr. Ellis, but my mum is right, I'm in *quite* the mood."

I've never seen Dr. Ellis laugh, but she looks pretty close to it now.

"She's a teenager, Leanne, I'd love to be able to tell you it's a side effect of her condition that I can fix with a medication adjustment, but unfortunately this one is all hormones."

I don't know what Mum is complaining about; I'm not near half as bad as what August was at my age – heck even the way she is now. I'd have to step it up at least half a dozen notches to even be in the same playing field as my big sister.

And besides, I've got a pretty good idea why I'm so moody.

The school dance is coming up and apparently the skankier the dress, the better, or so it would seem if you listened to the girls at my school.

I can't wear dresses like the ones in all the pictures I've seen.

It's not Halloween, and that's exactly how it would look if I put on a bright red dress with a neckline that plunges down to my belly button.

I'm not even sure I want to go.

None of the boys have asked me, and even though Lucy offered for us both to go without dates, I know that Jesse has asked her to go with him, and I can't take that away from her.

She deserves to have her fairy-tale night.

Besides, it's the dress, not the date, or lack thereof that has me in a mood.

Mum and Dr. Ellis are chatting together, and I narrow my eyes at their friendly conversation. For a long time, Dr. Ellis wasn't so informal with us, but I think my mum wore her down eventually.

Mum worships the ground that woman walks on. You'd think she was going to meet the queen anytime we come into contact with her.

I might be in a shitty mood, but that makes me smile. Just a little bit.

"Huh, you're an AB-positive blood type."

The new doctor seems to be talking to me as she flicks through my notes.

"Yup." I pop the 'p'. "Someone told me I was lucky once, isn't that ironic."

She smiles and holds back a laugh – no doubt amused by my attempt at being a drama queen.

I take a good look at her. She's very pretty, and she's young too, maybe only ten years or so older than me – I'd be surprised if she's over thirty. She's got one of those faces that just looks nice, and I feel bad for being so rude to her.

"Given your condition, and the fact that you're likely to need a transplant one day in the future, you *should* count yourself lucky. Not many people can say they have the universal recipient type blood."

I know she's right. There are plenty of kids like me whose chances of getting a heart are cut down by something as trivial as the type of blood they have.

"I'm the opposite of you; I'm type O-negative which means I'm the universal donor type," she tells me.

"Got a spare heart going?" I joke, even though it's really not funny.

She flicks my file shut and smiles at me again. "I *am* a listed donor, I can't speak for any of the other doctors in my profession, but after the things I've seen, I can think of nothing better than my organs going to help someone if I couldn't use them anymore."

"One man's trash is another man's treasure, right?" I mumble.

I should be thanking her, even though she's not technically done anything for me in particular, but because without people like *her*, people like *me* would never get the organs we need to carry on living.

"That's exactly right..." Dr. White agrees as her phone beeps in her pocket.

She hands my file back to Dr. Ellis who, if I remember the routine right, is about to start poking and prodding and asking me about one thousand questions that my mother is bound to butt in and answer for me anyway.

"I'm sorry, I'm needed on the ward. I might see you again sometime, Violet, but for your sake I hope it's not anytime soon."

I give her a genuine smile as she leaves the room.

I hope I won't be seeing her soon either. I really do. But I know damn well that all good things must come to an end.

I've had a pretty good run of luck lately, all things considered. The fact that my run of good luck is probably worse than most people's run of bad luck is beside the point.

Shitty mood or not, this is the only life I've got, and it's becoming more and more apparent that I just have to make the best of it.

Chapter Seventeen

Violet
Present day

There's something touching me. I can feel the warmth of it against my palm.

It feels nice. *Comforting.*

I can hear music too.

I blink drowsily and decide that this aspect of death I can deal with. This feels calm, serene and warm.

My eyes close again.

I like it here – I feel safe.

"Violet," I hear a voice sob.

They know me here. I must finally be in the right place.

"Oh, Violet, you're back," the relieved voice whispers.

I want to laugh. I can't be 'back', I've never been dead before.

"Thank God," another voice chokes out, and I become aware of the warmth in my other hand.

I smile.

"Open your eyes for me, buttercup."

Buttercup.

Buttercup...

My brain kicks into gear and reality hits. My dad has called me 'buttercup' for as long as I can remember.

And if *he's* here, then...

"Dad?" I croak.

My eyes fly open as my heart pounds and I blink, trying to adjust to the brightness of my surroundings.

"Charlie, the lights."

Charlie?

The light dims and I continue to blink rapidly as I try to make out the figures surrounding me.

Mum, Dad, Charlie and August... they're all here.

And so am I.

I'm here.

"I'm alive?" I choke out, my voice raspy.

"Only just, my girl... *only just.*" Mum sobs as her head falls onto the hospital bed I'm lying in.

Everyone is crying, even Auggie – and she never cries unless a celebrity dies, or she ruins her favourite pair of shoes.

I *really* must have been close to leaving this time.

My mind spins as they fill me in on the details.

They had to restart my heart twice after I was brought in; I was officially dead for two whole minutes – it's a miracle that my brain function is still normal.

I've been out for over a week and a half total. The drug-induced coma they put me in to allow my body to rest and heal was lifted this morning.

I also hear the thing nobody seems to be saying.

My heart is failing – it's giving up.

I know what it means... I need a transplant. And if this situation goes by the book then I won't have long at all to find a donor.

The clock is officially ticking.

We're all waiting for someone to die in order to save my life, and if that isn't the worst thought to ever cross my mind, then I don't know what is.

***

"Can I tell you something kinda... weird?"

"*Always*," August replies without a moment's hesitation.

I'm not really too sure how to start this without sounding like I've lost my mind, so I decide to just jump right in and hope that it doesn't send her running to the psych team.

"You know how they said that I was gone for a couple of minutes?"

She nods.

"I felt it, Auggie. I *was* dead."

She eyes me curiously as the silence stretches between us.

"What's it like... you know... dying?" she finally asks as she climbs into bed next to me.

Everyone else has gone to eat, Mum has been a nervous wreck ever since I woke up and I couldn't take anymore of her fussing and pacing the room so eventually I kicked her and Dad out. One or both of them have been here constantly for the past ten days, and they need a well-deserved break.

"It's different than I thought it'd be..."

"Tell me about it." She rests her head gently on my shoulder like a child waiting to hear a story.

It's often been like this with August and I – even though she's two years older than me, I've been like her big sister in a lot of ways.

The only things that August knows more about than I do, are makeup, clothes and most importantly, boys – which is why I figure that she'll be my best bet at making sense of what I've seen.

"There was a man there I don't know," I confide in her.

When I first woke up I wasn't sure if I was going to tell anyone about any of this, but it feels right to talk to my sister about it now.

I know I *need* to talk to someone – it feels as though the only thing crazier than saying it out loud might be saying nothing at all.

"Was he one of the doctors?"

I shake my head. "No... not one of the doctors... I've never seen him before. But he was calling to me, Auggie, it was like he needed *me* to stay with *him*."

She sits back up and looks right at me; she stares – eyes wide, and just when I expect something real to come out of her mouth, her face breaks out into a grin. "So, was he cute?"

This is a classic August response if I've ever heard one.

"I nearly died, and you're worried if an imaginary guy was hot or not?" I roll my eyes at her.

"Oh, he's not just an imaginary guy; he's the man of your dreams." She looks like she actually might believe what she's saying this time.

I want to believe it too.

"You think so?"

"I'd bet my last dollar."

I don't know what to say to that, so instead I just close my eyes and lay still, thinking about everything I saw.

"What else did you see?"

"A baby," I tell her quietly. "You, Charlie, Mum and Dad were there... Lucy too... and I had... I had a little girl."

I can feel the tears welling in my eyes, so I squeeze them shut even tighter.

I know I shouldn't let myself get upset about the things I won't have. I get to live, for today at least, and I shouldn't take that for granted.

"It sounds perfect," she whispers.

August might be pretty full of herself most of the time, but she's not blind to the fact that children are one of the things I want and probably can't have.

"It was."

She lowers her head back to my shoulder and pulls the blanket up to cover us even further.

A nurse is bound to come in here any minute and pitch a fit over her being in bed with me, but I don't care – for right now I just want to lay here with Auggie and feel alive.

"It was his voice... I think he's what kept me alive."

Rationally I know it was the doctor, nurses and the defibrillator that did all the real work, but I'm not sure I would have had the strength to hold on if not for his voice.

"So, he was important, huh?" she asks after a few moments.

I'm starting to feel really tired and the minute my mind starts to drift it's *his* eyes I see.

"I think he might be the *most* important."

"I really hope I get to meet him one day."

I smile. "I hope I get to meet him one day too."

I'm nearly asleep now – I'm so close to drifting off and it's all blue eyes and daisy fields running through my mind.

"Hey, Vi?" Auggie yawns.

"Yeah?" I reply sleepily.

"I'm really glad you didn't die."

Chapter Eighteen

Violet
Present day

It's not until the next morning that I come face to face with the woman who saved my life, and when I do, I'm hit with a sense of Déjà vu.

"It's nice to see you awake finally, Violet – you gave us all quite a scare." She smiles at me and it's then that I recall where I know her from.

She's the pretty young doctor that sat in on one of my appointments when I was younger. I've seen a lot of people in my time, but she stands out more than most of the others for some reason.

She certainly stands out now – she's a big part of the reason I'm alive.

Medically speaking, she might be the *only* reason.

"Do you mind if we come in for a chat?"

I gesture for them to go ahead.

It's just Mum here with me, and I really wish she'd go and get herself a coffee right about now, because I have a feeling this woman is about to make us re-live my entire ordeal, and while I might feel strong enough to hear it, I'm not sure my mother is.

"You remember Dr. White, Violet?" Mum asks me.

"I remember." I smile at her.

There's a male doctor by her side – one I don't recognise.

She gestures to him. "This is Dr. Reece, he's one of the surgeons covering for Dr. Ellis."

I say my hellos, and as grateful that I am that he's here, I just wish that Dr. Ellis were back already. I know everyone deserves a holiday and that she's only a few days away from returning, but I feel nervous about my condition and she's the best there is.

If something bad is going to happen to me again, I'd like it to be on her watch.

"What's the last thing you recall, Violet?" Dr. White questions me.

No one has actually asked me this yet – no one's asked me anything much at all when I think about it. I've pretty much been wrapped in cotton wool these past twenty-four hours.

"I remember I was at home... and I didn't feel right, so I called Lucy."

The memory feels hazy, like I'm trying to watch it through a thick layer of fog.

"I remember her and her mum coming to me... I think I could hear the siren from the ambulance... *maybe*. There's nothing that makes much sense after that."

"Good." Dr. White scribbles something down on the pad of paper she's holding. "That's good."

It doesn't feel particularly good.

"From that point on you were brought in here by two of our paramedics."

I try not to smile at the mention of the man I've quickly learnt is becoming smitten with my best friend.

"You lost consciousness on the drive, and upon arriving in the emergency room, you went into full cardiac arrest and were required to be revived by the defibrillator twice."

I know I've heard bits of this from my family and from Lucy, but hearing it all put together like this from someone who is essentially a stranger makes it a harder pill to swallow.

"You were *very* lucky – had Linda not called ahead to ensure we were there ready and waiting, this could have been a very different story. As it was, we still thought we'd lost you for a minute there."

I try to swallow the lump in my throat so I can say something, *anything* in response, but I can't seem to make it happen.

"I've never seen someone fight as hard as you did, I wanted you to know that. You weren't ready to go yet."

She's right – I didn't want Lucy to have to watch me die – so I held on as best I could, and after I saw *his* eyes and heard *his* voice, I wanted nothing more than to stay.

"We've been monitoring your heart closely, and while it's not in great shape, it's holding on – for now."

"What happens next?" Mum asks, startling me. I'd forgotten she was even in the room.

"We do all we can do – we wait, watch and hope for the best."

***

"Now I don't want to bore you with the basics – I'm sure you've already done the research, but unfortunately it's protocol."

She's right, I *have* done my research, but it was years ago – when the need for a new heart wasn't knocking on my front door in the way it is now, so I'll be grateful for the recap.

Dr. White is back to see me for the second time today, and if that doesn't convince me that I'm gravely ill, nothing will.

"Best case scenario, we find you a heart quickly, but as I'm sure you're aware, the wait can be long, I've had you placed on the list effective immediately, and while you're physically a good candidate for a transplant, you're not at end stage heart failure just yet, so there will be others who will take priority over you."

She continues to rattle off information and fact about blood types, antibodies, donor size, time spent on the waiting list and medical urgency.

I know things aren't exactly great for me, and I shouldn't feel glad that there are others worse off than I am, but for once, *I'm* not the worst-case scenario. That's not something I've been able to say too often in my life.

As she's just mentioned, I'm not in severe heart failure just yet, but I'm also not going to be getting out of here anytime soon either.

Dr. White wants me monitored for at least another week before I can go home and wait. And I've been informed that Dr. Ellis is on her side – I can't imagine with the two of them on the case that I'll have any chance of making an early escape.

I'm also aware how quickly things can change.

I went from feeling somewhat normal, to feeling dizzy and short of breath, to being in full cardiac arrest – all within less than an hour.

That's not something I want to repeat, but if it *is* on the cards for me, I'd rather be *here* when it happens. I'm not sure anyone's nerves could handle a repeat performance of last time.

"Geographical location is another consideration. Usually an organ will be transported from one hospital to another, in very rare cases, a donor and recipient may be in the same location. You're lucky that you live so close to the hospital where you'll receive your transplant – but unfortunately we have no way of knowing where the recipient will be when their organs are harvested."

I am lucky in that respect, I live only a short drive away from the best hospital in the whole country – if that weren't the case there would have been an awful lot of travel and emergency flights in my past.

It also means there's no need for me to locate my nearest transplant centre or find a surgeon to do the operation when a heart does become available – I've got all the support I need right here in this building, and I've got one of the best surgeons in the business who's not only available, but knows my entire medical history first hand.

There aren't a lot of patients in the world that would be able to say that.

"Where the donor and potential recipients are located is also taken into account with allocating where an organ may go – you're looking at about a four-hour window. So, a heart could become available tomorrow, but it might not get here in time to be viable, do you understand?"

I nod my head.

I'm doing my best to look at this from a medical perspective – the same way my doctors do, but when words like 'harvested' are being thrown around, it makes it hard.

It's near impossible to think of a donor as anything other than a person that's life has come to an end – usually a sudden, tragic and unexpected end where organ donation is concerned.

It's difficult not to feel guilty for thinking about how I could benefit from that type of tragedy.

"All going to plan, we'll observe you for the next week or so and then you'll be able to go home."

I want to go home more than anything – the last thing I want is to be stuck here while I wait for a heart, but there's a weight in the bottom of my stomach that's telling me not to get my hopes up.

"What do I do in the meantime?" I question.

"In the meantime we'll get all of the boxes ticked. You'll undergo a full evaluation to ensure that you *are* indeed a good candidate for the transplant. You'll need an examination physically and also emotionally and mentally. We'll make sure all of your blood work is up to date and I'm going to enrol you in the cardiac rehabilitation programme *now*, so when your time does come, you're already ahead of the game."

It sounds like a lot, but it's really nothing new for me. I'm clearly in good hands here so I nod and smile in acceptance.

This is just another shitty situation I have no choice but to make the best of.

Chapter Nineteen

Violet
Present day

"I'm sorry, sweetheart; I know you were hoping to go home tomorrow."

I don't know what he's apologising for. It's not his fault I got sick.

He's one of my favourite nurses but right now I can't even muster a smile for him. I'm anything but happy about my current situation.

I've managed to catch a nasty bacterial infection that's doing the rounds of the ward.

Every second person in here has a cough, runny nose and sore throat – and now, so do I.

I've had my fair share of germs over the years – it's something I've accepted goes hand in hand with hospital stays, but this particular bug is stopping me from leaving, and from what I've heard, people in much better shape than me have been fighting it off for close to a month – which means I'll probably have it for two.

It also means that if by some stroke of luck a heart were to turn up tomorrow, I'd probably have to turn it down.

I know that I'm nowhere near the top of the list at this point, and there's plenty of people in line before me, so it's not likely to even be an issue, but still, the set back is frustrating.

As is the reality of being confined to this drab, boring, little room for a long period of time.

It's not as though I've contracted some type of critical illness, but given the current situation with my heart, letting me go home is something that no one is willing to risk.

Personally I don't get it. I caught this bug *here*, I only have this nasty throat infection because I'm stuck in this hospital. I've tried to reason with everyone that comes through my door that I'm at a higher risk of getting sick by being here than I would be in the comfort of my own bedroom, but no one is having it.

So, for the foreseeable future, I'm stuck right where I am.

I've already been here over two and a half weeks – albeit, one and a half of those were spent unconscious, but still. I'm seriously concerned about my mental health if I have to stay for too much longer.

My face must be doing a fine job of showing how unimpressed I am about my extended stay because he laughs.

"It's not all bad in here," he points to himself, "some of us are actually pretty cool."

He's not a lot older than I am, and he's not wrong – he is *very* cool, but that doesn't mean I want to spend the foreseeable future in the place he works, so I try my hand at flattery.

"You know you're my favourite nurse in this whole place?"

He chuckles.

I pout at him. "We're friends, right?"

He shoots me a 'nice try' look. "You and I both know I can't spring you from this joint."

"There goes that plan," I grumble.

"Look, I know it's boring in here sometimes..."

I raise my brows at him in disbelief.

"Okay, so it's boring *all* the time... but you could read a book, make some photo albums, catch up on movies or listen to some music... come to think of it, I'm actually a little jealous."

"How about I trade you?" I deadpan.

He passes me my laptop off the chair in the corner and after making sure it's on the charger and ready to go, he heads for the door.

"Seriously, get lost in YouTube or something and you'll feel better before you know it."

I cave in and give him a small smile as he leaves.

I know I'm still going to be bored out of my mind after a few days of this, but there was one idea he suggested that I might actually be able to get interested in.

I've got hundreds and hundreds of photos saved on my laptop, and organising them into albums is something I've been meaning to do for years.

I'm clicking through the files when one of them jumps out at me.

It's from my high school dance.

***

Violet

2009 (Sixteen years old)

"This isn't the way home."

Mum doesn't speak but when I look over at her there's a small smile playing at the corners of her mouth.

"Mum?"

"Mmmm?"

"This isn't the way home," I repeat.

"We've got to go meet your sister in town."

"Urghhh," I groan.

The only thing worse than the stress test I just endured is the idea of shopping with August – now *that* is a painful idea.

"Can you run me home? Please, Mum, I'm not in the mood for being dragged around five hundred shops looking for something in 'the perfect shade of green.'" I mimic my sister's voice as I complain.

August is seriously the most high maintenance shopper to ever walk the face of the earth and her ridiculous antics are not something I have the patience for right now.

"No can do, kiddo, we're already running late. You'll just have to deal with it."

Mum seems to be taking great pleasure in my misery and I can't help but think that this is payback for acting like a brat these past few days.

I groan again and rest my head against the window all the way to the shopping centre.

Shopping and I barely get along at the best of times, and right now I'm not feeling anywhere near the top of my game.

I'm about to suggest that I wait in the car until they're done but before I know what's happening, Mum has rounded the front of the hood and is opening my door with a look on her face that screams 'just try me'.

Apparently I'm not getting out of this one.

We walk past various stores, Mum striding with purpose and me dawdling as best I can manage.

Every so often she shoots me a death stare and I move a little faster.

It's not until she slows down and stops that I realise she's tricked me. Standing up outside a dress store called 'Little Black Dress' is Lucy and her mum.

The penny drops.

We're not here for Auggie at all. We're here for *me*.

We're here to buy me a dress for the dance.

***

"That colour looks really pretty on you."

I know August would probably rather be out with her friends than stuck here doing my hair and makeup, but I don't think Mum gave her much of a choice in the matter.

Mum didn't give me a lot of choice either.

I finally managed to convince Lucy to accept the invite from Jesse, with the intention that I wouldn't go at all – but Mum wasn't having it.

She's normally the first one to encourage me to stay safely at home in front of my easel with a paint brush in my hand, but not this time.

It would seem that supervised, school-run events are my mother's happy place.

"You think?" I reply to my big sister. I've never really thought of myself as 'pretty'.

She nods her head. "Yeah, it really suits you."

"I'm nervous, Auggie."

She gently tugs on the long strands of my hair as she pulls them into the braid she's creating.

"What, because of Tim?"

My stomach drops.

Of course she already knows all about my humiliation.

I don't know what possessed me to think that anyone would want to go to the dance with me, let alone a guy like Tim.

He's gorgeous, incredible at basketball *and* he plays the guitar. He might not be captain of the football team, but he's still firmly a member of the 'cool crowd'. I, on the other hand, am not even close.

"How'd you know about that?" I whisper. "The whole school knows, don't they? Oh God... I'm not going..."

"Calm down, Vi, I'm friends with Reed, remember? He told me."

Unlike me, my sister has a lot of friends – one of which happens to be Tim's older brother.

If Tim told his brother, then it's anybody's guess who else he's had a laugh about my stupidity with. This realisation only reinforces my desire to bail on this whole thing and stay home tucked up in my pyjamas.

I look at my reflection and I'm as white as a ghost, with eyes as wide as saucers.

"It's not a big deal." August catches my eye in the mirror.

"It feels like a pretty big deal to me."

"You're sixteen, Vi, this is the time where you meet your bridesmaids, not your groom."

She does make a good point, as hypocritical as she might be.

"And besides, he only said no becau—"

I hold my hand out to silence her. "I *don't* want to hear it."

"Violet." Her tone lets me know she thinks I'm being ridiculous, but I don't care. My whole life has been this way – a series of disappointments, one after the other and tonight is bound to be no different.

"Just stop talking about it, *please*."

"Fine, but you're going. Even if I have to drag you there myself, got it?"

***

It feels as though *all* eyes are on me – like every laugh I hear is directed my way.

I know deep down it's possible I'm being irrational. No one in this entire place has probably even noticed me come in, let alone united together to taunt me, but I can't seem to entirely convince myself of this. In my head, they're all making fun of me for turning up alone... for being the girl with the broken heart... for being *different*.

My breath is coming out in short sharp pants as I turn around and around, trying desperately to find Lucy, but I can't see her anywhere. The panic is bubbling up inside me and I can feel it preparing to take total control of my body.

I should *never* have come here – I should have listened to my gut and not to my sister.

I spin around one more time, but it's no use, the crowds of people have all blurred into one and I can't make out individual faces any longer, no matter how hard I squint.

I clutch my chest and drag in a deep breath – my only thought now is to get out of here – to get far away from here so I can have my meltdown somewhere private.

I turn around, but before I can run away I collide with someone.

"Whoa, whoa, whoa, are you okay?"

I look up and the sudden haze that was covering my eyes lifts.

The universe must really hate me today, because of all the people in this room, it has to be the very one that rejected me that I've crashed into.

"Sorry," I squeak as I attempt to move around him.

It doesn't work – he's holding onto my shoulders, steadying me, and he doesn't allow me to escape.

"Violet?" He looks at me like he's not sure it's really me. "Wow, you look..."

I wait for an insult to be hurled, but it doesn't come.

"... you look *beautiful*."

I stare up at him. I don't know what to say to that – I've never had a compliment that feels so genuine and at the same time so unexpected.

He's smiling down at me. His hands are motionless on my arms and I still haven't come up with a single thing to say.

He probably owes me an explanation for turning me down in a text message, but I'm not sure I even care anymore. I just want to go home.

"Are you okay?" he repeats his earlier question.

I nod, although I'm still not sure why he's here, talking to *me*.

"Where are you going in such a hurry?"

"Home."

"But it's just starting."

I don't reply to that – I don't know what I could possibly say that won't make me sound like more of a loser than he already thinks I am.

"You're not leaving because of me, are you?" His voice sounds almost broken, not cocky or arrogant like I imagined it would in my head if we came face to face.

I don't answer again. His hands drop from my arms and he dips his head in what looks like embarrassment.

"I'm *really* sorry, Violet."

I don't want to talk about this – certainly not with him, yet I can't seem to make my feet or mouth move to do something about it. I'm stuck here frozen like a deer in headlights.

"I should have given you an explanation."

"It's okay," I mumble.

"It's not okay... I... I'm umm...."

I'm not sure where he's heading with this, but it seems he has something he wants to get off his chest, so I wait for him to find the words he's so desperately searching for.

"I'm gay."

It comes out in a rush and his expression looks wary – like he's worried I might say something horrible, like maybe *I* might be the one to hurl an insult.

"I haven't told many people that."

"*That's* why you turned me down?"

"Yeah. I'm sorry."

He didn't turn me down because I'm a freak or a loser... he turned me down because he likes boys.

"Stop apologising."

"Sorry," he mumbles then winces when he realises he's just done it again.

"Why didn't you just tell me?"

He looks around and tilts his head in the direction of an empty table and chairs. He takes my arm and leads me over to sit.

The crowds of people around me don't seem so threatening anymore as we move through them – my overactive imagination can be reasoned with now... *no one* is laughing at me.

"I know I should have, but I was embarrassed... I didn't know what people would say or think."

It's weird – I don't want someone else's dilemma to make me feel better about my own, but whether I like it or not, it does a little bit.

Tim might not have a life-threatening condition like I do, but he's fighting his own kind of battle, and it's comforting to know I'm not the only one who's worried about what other people might think of them. The reminder that I'm not the only person in school with personal stuff going on is gladly received.

"Well just for the record, I don't think being gay is anything to be ashamed of."

That gets a smile out of him.

"I really *am* sorry for turning you down. I like you, Violet, and I should have said yes. I just didn't know how to explain that we could only be friends without spilling my secret or hurting your feelings... but I think I've managed to do both of those things anyway."

I'm not going to lie to his face and tell him that I wasn't hurt, because I *was* – but I also don't want him to feel worse about what's happened than he already does, because it's not really his fault.

I wouldn't normally confess this, but he's just opened up to me in a way I wasn't expecting, so I feel like I owe him the truth.

"I thought you said no because of my condition."

He frowns at me. "What condition?"

"My heart?"

He stares at me for a few beats, his expression confused.

"I don't know what you're talking about."

"You know... I'm the weird heart kid..."

"I seriously have no idea what that means."

"You really don't know?"

He shrugs. "I literally couldn't know less. You're just Violet... you're quiet and nice and really good at art."

"Well...um... *wow*..."

He really doesn't know.

This wasn't about my heart or my health... this wasn't about *me* at all. This was about something else entirely and the reality check that not everything is about *me* is a welcome one.

I might not be getting a fairy-tale night with the guy of my dreams, but I can't say I'll be walking away empty-handed either.

The realisation that my dodgy heart isn't the only thing everyone sees when they look at me is the most valuable piece of information he could have ever given me, and even though he's not into girls, I think I might have just made the most real connection I've ever had with a guy.

Chapter Twenty

Violet
Present day

"So, there's this girl..."

I catch Lucy's gaze and roll my eyes.

There's *always* a girl when it comes to my little brother.

For a seventeen-year-old, he sure has had his fair share of girlfriends, but more to the point, girl *problems*.

The kid is just a magnet for trouble.

It really doesn't help that he's a good-looking guy. I know that's probably a weird thing to say about my own brother, but with his blue eyes and shaggy blond hair, he's got the whole 'surfer dude' look going on.

It's a look that girls his age are apparently going crazy for.

"Go on..." Lucy prompts him. I can see that she's trying her hardest not to laugh at his latest predicament.

I've been in this hospital for two months straight now, and Charlie's been in here at least half a dozen times already looking for advice or suggestions on how to fix his latest girl-related drama.

I really don't know why he comes to me for advice – I'm the sick girl, and my relationship experience is virtually non-existent.

He *could* ask August, but I think we both know that our big sister would chew him up and spit him out faster than he could say 'girl problems'.

There's no way in hell he's going to talk to Mum about his love life, and the last time Charlie asked Dad for help he sat him down and played him Jay Z's '99 problems', and while it *was* entertaining it wasn't exactly useful advice, so I guess he's picked the best of a bad bunch here with me and Luce.

He opens his mouth to explain, but before he gets the chance, Lucy speaks again.

"Let me just get this straight before we get started, is this the same girl as last week? Kimberly or whatever her name was?"

He looks at her blankly for a minute, and I seriously think he can't remember the name of the girl he was pining over only a few days ago.

He really needs a good shake sometimes.

I can almost see the light-bulb flicker to life over his head as he makes the connection.

"Ohhhh, *no*. Heck no, she's *old* news."

I roll my eyes again as Lucy and I catch each other's eye. I'm not sure how something that happened less than seven days ago can be classed as 'old news', but then again, I'm not a seventeen-year-old boy, so what would I know?

"How about you just tell us what the problem is." I raise my brows at him.

"Who said there was a problem?" He frowns.

"Really, Charlie George? If there wasn't a problem, why on earth would you be here?"

He smirks at me – his cocky-little-shit smirk. "Mum said I *had* to visit."

"Liar." I grin back at him.

Mum would never need to tell Charlie he *had* to visit me; he's here nearly every day.

The little teenage punk might like to pretend he doesn't care or that he's only here to talk about girls, but I know better, he's worried about me almost as much as I am.

We've been through a lot, my family and I, and we don't take anything for granted, least of all each other.

Okay, maybe August does a little bit, but every family has to have a diva, and she's ours.

"Just spill it, Justin Bieber, I've got places to be." Lucy glances dramatically at her watch, and even though I know she's joking, and that she's not going anywhere until one of the nurses throws her out, I'm still unbelievably jealous that she can leave this place whenever she wants to.

I don't have that luxury anymore. I'm officially a prisoner and this room is my jail cell.

"So, her name is Jess and I really like her, but I dated her sister Rose a while back and honestly, it's making things awkward for me."

"Making things awkward for *you*?" I stare at him in disbelief.

Charlie clearly has more of August's self-involved nature in him than I realised.

"Yeah, you know... I want to respect them both as women, and you know what, people are always saying that twins hate it when people can't see that they have their own identities..."

"Now they're *twins*?" I rub my temples with the balls of my fingers.

He looks at me like I've grown an extra head. "Not just now, they've always been twins, Violet. They were born like that."

I can see Lucy laughing behind her hand and I don't blame her. I've seriously got to wonder sometimes if Mum or Dad dropped him on his head when he was a baby.

I don't even know what to tell him. I'm at a complete loss for words with this one. Thankfully, that's where Luce comes in.

"Hey..." she nudges his arm, "*Casanova*, ditch the twins, you got it?"

"But it's just *one* twin," he protests.

Lucy shakes her head at him. "One plus one makes two, you big dummy. And seriously, any girl willing to date her twin sister's ex is not the kind of girl you want to be shaking your little fella at, understood?"

I can't contain my laughter anymore. The look on Charlie's face is one of pure horror.

Lucy is like a sister to him too, and the idea of her talking about what goes on in his pants is clearly grossing him out.

That's what I love about Lucy. She tells it like it is – even if you don't want to hear it.

"But..." He opens his mouth to protest again.

"But *nothing*, Charlie boy, this has got bad news written *all* over it."

He pouts, and I laugh.

"Just think, you'll be back in here next week and it'll be all 'Jess who?'" I reach out and ruffle his hair as I tease him – much to his disgust.

He's grumbling something incomprehensible to himself as Mum walks into the room, carrying the stack of books I asked her to get me from the library.

I don't have a love life of my own, so I settle for the next best thing – trying to stop my brother from destroying his, and reading romance novels.

She sets down the books and comes over to kiss me on the top of my head.

She follows suit with Charlie next, and finally Lucy.

Mum has always treated Lucy as part of our family – she's certainly been around long enough.

She glances between the three of us and then looks pointedly back at Charlie. "You're not making your sister regret begging so hard for a baby brother now, are you?"

"Regret *me*?" he replies cheekily, shooting her his best butter-wouldn't-melt grin. "Never."

I shake my head in amusement.

He might be a pain in the butt, little womaniser, but I love him more than he'll ever know. Mum isn't kidding when she says I begged her for another sibling – other than the heart I now need, I've never wanted anything as much in my whole life.

***

Leanne
1997 (Four years old)

I know there's nothing I need to fear about this... nothing more than the idea of giving birth anyway.

My midwife has assured me that my unborn baby's heart is perfectly healthy this time. Everything is working exactly as it should be – the ridiculous amount of ultrasounds I've had should have put my mind at ease, but I can't seem to stop myself from still fretting about it.

I never planned on having another baby after Violet, if I'm being entirely honest.

That experience wasn't something I wanted to risk repeating.

I love Violet, and I wouldn't change her for the world. At just four and a half years old, she's already taught me so much about life and love, about taking things for granted and valuing what's important... but her life is so much harder than what it should be – and I'd never wish that upon another child. Certainly not the one waiting to make its way into the world right now.

But ironically enough, it was Violet herself that changed my mind about having another baby.

Ever since she could speak, she's been begging me for a baby. 'Baby' was literally the first word she ever spoke, and she carries an old baby doll around with her everywhere she goes.

It's a brother she wants – and while I can't guarantee that part of the deal, we did eventually give in and try for the baby she so desperately desired.

That brings me to this point, eight and a half months later, on my way to the delivery ward of the hospital – the same ward both August and Violet were born in, because despite my insistence that I have this baby in a ward with specialised heart facilities, there's no medical or logical reason for us to go anywhere else. That, and I'm actually quite positive that it isn't even allowed.

I groan with another contraction. I don't care what other women say – this doesn't seem to get any easier the more times you do it.

"Nearly there, Lee Lee," Shaun promises me.

I know we're not far away, but it seems like an impossible distance.

This labour is progressing so much faster than the other two did, and I'm becoming more and more concerned by the minute that I'm going to give birth in the front seat of this car.

"This is the *last* time, I swear to God, Shaun." I ground out the words through the pain.

"Three sounds good to me, Lee, trust me."

I can see the lit-up sign for the hospital looming ahead and I breathe a sigh of relief, this baby still has to get out one way or another, but now I'm more confident that I'll make it inside the building at least.

Everything passes in a blur of contractions and pain and before I know it I hear Rebecca, my midwife telling me it's time. "Just one more push, Leanne, just one more."

I push with everything I have, and I know the second it's all over.

I collapse back onto the bed, totally and utterly spent.

"You did it, sweetheart." Shaun is totally overcome with emotion, I can hear the tears in his voice. "It's a boy, Lee, we have a son."

I open my tired eyelids and for the first time lay sight on the precious little baby that is my son.

He's absolutely perfect. Violet will be thrilled.

"Hey, little guy." I sniff, trying to reign in my tears. "I'm so happy you're here."

And I really am. I don't feel the sense of fear I expected to.

I thought I'd be encompassed with worry for his heart – that he might have the same condition his sister does, but instead I just feel at peace, knowing that my family is finally complete.

***

Leanne
Present day

I glance into Violet's studio in surprise.

This door is never open and when Violet's in here, she's always alone.

That's why I'm so shocked to see Charlie in here, rummaging around in the huge collection of paint and brushes that Violet has accumulated over the years.

He's got a big pad of paper tucked under his arm and he's tossing a seemingly random collection of things into a box.

I've been in this room only a handful of times, and always, *always* supervised by Violet.

She's a very private person, especially where her art is concerned, and as hard as that has been for me to accept, I know I have to.

Painting is her outlet... it's her therapy, and it's the only type that's ever worked for her.

I've taken her to see countless professionals, some of them costing us hundreds and hundreds of dollars per hour, but none of them have been able to give Violet the same sense of peace that she seems to find when she creates a work of art.

I've seen her pictures before. She paints me something every year for my birthday, but I've seen none of her *real* stuff. Nothing that she's painted to represent the way she feels.

I already know that they'll be phenomenal; she's an incredibly talented artist – I know that without even needing to see anything she's created in the privacy of this room for the past six or more years – I can just feel it.

"What are you doing in here?"

Charlie jumps in the air at the sound of my voice behind him.

I don't know what he's up to, but it's obvious he's not meant to be in here any more than I am.

"Christ, Mum, you scared me."

I'm so tempted to go into the room after him, but given that Violet wasn't expecting to wind up with an extended hospital stay, I doubt that she left her work in a state she'd consider acceptable for me to view, so I stay strong – and wait at the door where I know I should.

"I don't think your sister would be too happy about you being in here."

Truthfully, I'm more interested to know *how* he got in here.

Violet *never* leaves the door unlocked, and as far as I was aware, she only has the one key.

Charlie tosses a couple more things in the box and tucks it under his other arm.

"I know," he replies sheepishly. "She's gonna be pissed, but I'm hoping she'll forgive me if it means to she gets to paint."

"You're taking all that in to her?"

I'm not sure what I was expecting his excuse for being in here to be, but it certainly wasn't this.

"Yeah..." He shuffles out the door and I step out of his way.

I hold my arms out to take the box from him and he gratefully hands it over before locking the door behind himself.

"I know she's missing it. She gets all moody when she can't paint."

I can almost feel my heart swelling with pride in my chest.

I might not have been a perfect parent, but I must have done something right along the way if my seventeen-year-old son is this considerate.

A typical Saturday in the life of Charlie consists of surfing or skating, hanging out with his mates, chasing girls and trying to get his underage mitts on half a dozen beers.

He's a sweet kid – but usually he's a classic teenage boy.

But not today.

Today he's here, doing something unbelievably thoughtful for his sister.

"You're a sweet boy."

"Mum..." He blushes and dips his head as he takes the box back from me. "It's not a big deal."

He heads off down the hallway, but there's one more thing I need to ask him.

"Charlie..." I call out. "Where did you get the key?"

He laughs at my shameless attempt at getting my hands on that little treasure.

"If I told you that, I'd have to kill you." He chuckles.

Chapter Twenty-One

Violet
Present day

I smile as I watch Lucy type out a message to the guy she's been seeing.

She's so smitten with him; it's almost hard to watch.

He's head over heels for her too, I can tell. She probably had him hook, line and sinker from the moment she first smiled at him.

He wouldn't be the first guy to fall for Lucy at a glance – she's truly beautiful with her long blonde hair and bright green eyes, but there's so much more to her than that and it's obvious that he sees her for the beauty she carries on the inside as much as she does the outside.

I was there when they met. In fact, in a roundabout way; I was the one that brought them together.

Emmett was one of the emergency crew that brought me in here in the ambulance – and he's been chasing Lucy nearly every moment since.

They're so happy together. I already know that he's 'it' for her – she's found her forever. She's never been like this before, and I've never seen a man look at her the way he does.

I want what they have – I've always wanted to meet someone and find love, and after seeing the vision in my head, I want it now more than ever.

I don't expect to actually get it – a hospital room isn't exactly a great place to meet the man of your dreams, but I want it, *so* badly.

I've had just the one moment so far where I felt like maybe I might be destined for love after all.

His name was Scott Wood.

He was my first kiss, and even though I knew I wasn't going to marry him, it still gave me hope that a happily ever after was possible for me.

Out of a whole room full of girls, he wanted me.

Me. Violet Miller.

It probably wasn't a big deal for him, but it made me optimistic that one day, someone out there might want me like that again.

***

Violet
2011 (Eighteen years old)

"Letty, Mark's cousin is *totally* checking you out." Lucy attempts to whisper the words to me inconspicuously, but she's a little tipsy and it comes out loud enough for not only Mark's cousin to hear, but everyone else in the room as well.

I know that my face is bright red. I can feel it burning – my only hope is that the layer of products Lucy applied to my skin are doing a reasonable job of hiding my obvious embarrassment.

This is exactly why I didn't want to come to this party – I don't like crowds and I definitely don't care for being the centre of attention like I am right now.

I make a mental note to give my dad a hard time when I get home – it's his fault I'm at this stupid thing in the first place.

Mark, who has been hanging around my best friend like a dog does a juicy bone, laughs loudly – he's also a bit drunk.

"I keep telling you, babe, his name is *Scott*."

"Fine." Luce giggles as she drapes her arms around Mark's neck. "*Scott* is checking her out."

"Shhhh," I hiss at her. "You're *so* loud, and he is *not* checking me out so just shhhh."

Mark joins in with shushing her.

He and Lucy have been on again, off again for a couple of months now, and while I really like the guy, I don't think it'll last being 'on again' for much longer.

Luce isn't ready to be tied down yet, and she's certainly not got any shortage of admirers waiting in the wings.

"He was asking about you earlier actually." Mark's looking at me, waiting for me to take the bait and he won't have to wait long, I can't help myself.

None of the guys from our school are interested in me – I'm fairly certain they all know my history by now and honestly, I think I scare them.

Scott doesn't know me, or my history and he's really, *really* cute.

I only spoke to him briefly when we arrived, but he seems nice enough too.

"What did he say?"

Mark opens his mouth to tell me, but he's cut off before he can get a word in.

"I just asked who the pretty girl with the dark hair was."

The voice comes from behind me, and if I wasn't bright red already, I would be now.

"I toooolllld yooooou." Lucy giggles.

I've never cursed my best friend the way I'm doing in my mind right now.

She's got a lot to answer for, but I'm going to wait until tomorrow morning, when she's really feeling those tequila shots she just knocked back and deal with her then.

I turn around slowly, wishing the whole time that the ground would just swallow me whole.

I come face to face with the guy who just called me pretty and the first thing that strikes me is how kind his eyes are.

Not only is he saying something that I've never heard from a guy my age, but he's looking at me as though he likes what he sees, and I'm not sure what I'm supposed to do with that.

Where Lucy has a long list of male suitors, I have a very, very short one.

So short in fact, you can't even see it.

While most girls in my year are discussing how and when they lost their virginity, I've never even had a real kiss.

Sure, I've kissed boys, but I'm under no illusion that a peck on the lips during a game of spin the bottle counts as a *real* kiss.

I've never felt passion, or heat... lust has never even been on my radar.

I've long wished to feel a tingling up my spine from a boy touching my skin… but it hasn't happened, and I'd pretty comfortably bet everything I own on knowing the reason why.

It's the same reason for everything that hinders my life – my stupid heart.

"As your totally sober friend said, I'm Scott," he jokes as he smiles at me.

I glance over my shoulder and see that Lucy is being led away by Mark, who is shooting me a not so subtle thumbs up.

"I'm really sorry about her. I should *not* have told her it was a good idea to do shots."

He laughs and kicks at something with the toe of his shoe.

"I'm Violet," I add before I lose my nerve any more than I already have.

"I know," he replies sheepishly. "I wasn't joking when I said I'd asked about you."

Butterflies are fluttering around like crazy in my stomach as he speaks.

"Do you want to get a drink?" he asks. He looks as nervous as I am and I'm grateful for it.

I shake my head. "Nah, I'm good… I don't really drink."

He looks relieved. "I'm driving, so me either."

There's a lot of loud banging and we both look into the kitchen where Lucy appears to be playing a pot like a drum.

He shakes his head and laughs at her. "You want to come and sit outside with me?"

"Nah I'd rather stay in here and listen to that."

He eyes me curiously like he's not really sure if I'm joking or serious.

"Sarcasm," I explain with a smile. "Please... let's go."

***

We're sitting *so* close, and I know it's only a matter of time before he kisses me.

My side is pressed up against his and my shoulders are covered by his jacket.

It got chilly out here on the front porch about an hour ago but neither of us wanted to go inside.

If I could stay out here and talk to him for the rest of the night, and not have to go back in there at all, I would choose to do exactly that.

Parties might not be my thing... but *this*, sitting and talking with a guy who is actually interested in me is like a dream come true.

He's holding my hand – and those tingles I've longed for – they're racing up and down my spine nonstop.

As August would say, he's 'giving me all the feels'.

He's from out of town, and while it makes me sad to think that I'll probably never see him again, on the other hand I'm glad.

I wouldn't want to ruin tonight by bringing my heart into the picture.

Tonight, I'm just a girl, who's about to be kissed by a boy.

Neither of us has spoken a word for at least a few minutes and I can feel the tension building between us.

I can hear his breathing and I can feel his strong pulse where his wrist is resting against mine. He's so *alive* – and he wants *me*.

I tilt my head up in his direction and look at his face.

He's handsome, so handsome I almost can't believe he's spent the past two hours out here with me.

His free hand lifts to find my face and before I know it, his lips are on mine.

They're soft and warm and they're kissing *me*.

I kiss him back and even though I have no idea what I'm doing, I don't think this could be any more perfect.

My breathing is laboured in a way that has nothing to do with my heart condition as he pulls away and smiles at me.

Someone inside lets out a loud 'yeeee-haaaa' and I can't help but agree.

This fragment in time, where I can still feel his lips on mine, and my head rests on his shoulder is the most 'ye-ha' moment of my life so far.

Chapter Twenty-Two

Violet
Present day

I glance out my small window and into the hallway of the ward beyond.

I've taken to watching people to fill my time – there's not a lot else for me to do in here.

I try to figure out who the strangers strolling past are, why they're here, who they love, what they do… I make up stories in my mind about them. I'm probably dead wrong about it all, but it doesn't matter, in my mind, that's who they are.

That's the thing about people… about *all* of us. Who's to say who we really are?

The me that I believe I am, the me that I *think* the world sees, might not be me at all… it's hard to look at yourself as something outside of your own mind, but that's what I try to imagine as I lie here, the rain pelting against my window.

I'm the sick girl.

The girl with the bad heart.

That's what most people see when they look at me.

I know it's not what Lucy sees… or Auggie, or Charlie.

I know they think about my heart, but they can all see me for the person that I am outside of my condition, the person that I am to *them*.

I know that my mum mainly feels concern when she looks at me. She's apprehensive about everything and anything that a person could possibly worry about.

For years she's worried that the cough I picked up is going to turn into a chest infection, which means my body would have to work extra hard to fight it. She's worried what that strain might mean for my heart.

She worries that it'll fail.

Every little thing that happens to me results in my mum worrying about me ending up in heart failure.

I can see it in her eyes. I can feel her brain making those leaps.

I could stub my toe and she would still worry about my heart giving out.

That's been the case for as long as I can remember, and it still rings true to this day – and I guess in a way she was right to lose sleep the way she did, because here I am... in heart failure, so of course she's worrying more than she ever has.

The only person capable of reigning my mother in these days is Aunt Rita. Even Dad doesn't have that power anymore.

It's fortunate really, that where Mum's superpower has been worry, Dad's has been patience. That man seriously has the patience of a saint.

People look at our family, and they see the woman who does it all, she takes care of her sick daughter, she's a mum, a wife, and the house is somehow always clean and tidy.

What they probably don't see is that Dad is the glue holding it all together – he's literally been holding *her* together since the day I was born.

I would hate to think of how many meltdowns Mum would have had by now if it weren't for Dad and his rational thinking. It's worked for years and years, but now, when I'm confined to a bed in a way I haven't been for a long time, it seems to have lost its effectiveness.

No amount of soothing words or well-meaning suggestions on Dad's behalf have reached her since I arrived here.

Aunt Rita has a different approach. She's abrupt to the point of being rude and that seems to work for now. Just earlier she told Mum that she stunk, that she needed to, and I quote, 'bugger off home for a shower'.

That's what I love about Rita. No one messes with her. We just all simply do what we're told when she's involved. There really is no other way.

"What are you thinking about there, kiddo?" she interrupts my day dream.

I sigh and shrug. "Just contemplating life, I guess."

"Pffft." She slaps the magazine she's been reading down onto the small table in the corner. "That's for the old and the dying, and you, my dear girl, are neither of those things."

"Aren't I, though?" I gesture to the collection of drips and lines attached to my body.

It's not an unreasonable assessment, and it's certainly not the first time I've thought about this. If they don't find me a match soon, I could die.

It's just that simple and that complicated all at once.

She just shakes her head, totally unfazed by the possibility of my death. "It's not in your stars. You trust me on this; you'll be just fine for a long time yet."

I've never been sure where she gets this 'in your stars' business from, but she's been saying it for as long as I can remember.

She's actually rarely wrong – not that any of us like to admit it.

She's the only spiritual person in our family, well, her and Charlie. It seems he's been drinking whatever Aunt Rita has. He's turned into a bit of a hippy these days.

"What else do my stars say?" I ask her as I turn onto my side so I'm facing her.

I don't normally entertain her with this carry on, but in this moment, I want nothing more than for her to be right – I want to be okay.

"If you're asking if I see a Mr. Tall, Dark and Handsome, then you bet I do."

My heart starts beating erratically and the monitor to my left beeps like crazy. She knows nothing about the vision I had, but yet she's looking at me as though she's very well informed.

Rita glances at the screen briefly and grins wickedly. "Well, if just the mention of the man gets you going like that, I can't imagine what'll happen when you finally get him in the sack."

I manage to somehow choke on thin air at her statement, which does not help the rate of my heart in the slightest.

Melanie, one of the nurses appears in the doorway. "Is everything okay in here?"

She glances at the machine, and then at me – I'm coughing and spluttering as I try to wave her away to indicate that I'm okay.

"She's *fine*, all is well, lovely, I just don't think Violet here realised that people my age knew what sex was."

Oh God, I can feel my face heating now as I reach for my water and take a sip.

You can always count on Rita to keep things interesting, that's for sure.

Nurse Melanie laughs and pushes the button to silence the beeping on my monitor. "No more sex talk." She points her finger at my Aunt. "Violet needs to rest, not go into cardiac arrest."

"I make no promises," Rita replies without a care in the world.

I know Melanie is doing her best to hold herself together, but I can still manage to see her shoulders shaking with laughter as she leaves the room.

"Where's this mystery man then, huh?" I ask after my heart rate settles back into its normal rhythm.

Her eyes sparkle with a youth that doesn't match the lines on her face. "I can't tell you everything now, can I? That would ruin all the fun."

She winks at me, picks up her magazine and starts flicking through it as though she never said anything at all.

Chapter Twenty-Three

Violet
Present day

I've developed a dry, hacking cough these past few days. That, combined with my general fatigue, dizziness, rapid breathing and bluish skin tone, solidifies the fact that I'm not going anywhere anytime soon – if ever.

No one's said it out loud to me yet, but I know my heart is failing more severely now.

I've already been here for longer than any of us anticipated, and now it's becoming obvious that I won't be leaving until I get a heart.

If I get a heart, that is.

For now, I need something called a ventricular assist device, known commonly as a VAD, it's a device that basically takes the blood from my body and oxygenates it before pumping it back in again.

Essentially, it's doing the job my heart has decided is too hard – this machine should give my heart the rest it needs to hold on a bit longer.

I just need to keep holding on.

It's the same story, different day for me right now. There are more tests, more maybes... more trial and error.

This is possibly the highest staked game we're yet to play.

This choice could be the deciding factor as to whether I live or die.

The external, short-term device that Dr. White is talking to us about is the option I want to go with.

She's explained, in great depth, that this is a temporary solution – all this device will do is buy me some time.

A month if I'm lucky – but probably even less.

I don't know if that's going to be enough time – no one does, but I do know that I don't want to go through yet another open-heart surgery to have a long-term VAD put in, just to find that I could have got a new heart next week.

My mum and dad are not in agreement with my logic on the subject.

They want the long-term solution.

"It could buy you years, Violet," Mum pleads with me. "You might not have to worry about a transplant for a long time – it just seems less risky."

I understand what she's saying, I really do, but I have a shot at a *real* second chance here.

I'm a perfect candidate for a transplant, I'm still young, I'm sort of fit, I don't smoke, I've already been doing the cardiac rehabilitation program, I've got the support... and more than that, I've just got a *feeling* that this might finally be my time.

"Often a period of time spent on a short-term VAD can actually improve a patient's suitability for transplant, Mrs. Miller. I know it's a scary thing to consider, and the allocated period of time it offers may be hard to come to grips with, given that it's so short, but I really do believe that this is the best course of action for Violet right now. We can do what we need to through the cardiac catheter, and a few small incisions in her abdomen, rather than having to put her through another high risk, lengthy surgical procedure. The less stress on her heart and body, the better at this point."

I want to high-five Dr. White – she's saying all the things my parents need to hear.

"What happens if her time on that machine runs out?" Mum asks. Her voice is shaking. I hate hearing her like this. It cuts me deep to see the pain and suffering my condition causes her.

"If the short-term VAD is no longer able to sustain Violet's heart function, and a donor heart hasn't become available, then we'll have no choice but to continue with the long-term VAD."

That sounds like a terrible outcome to me. It's obviously better than dying, but it's still far from ideal.

The backup option seems to bring some peace to my parents however, so if that's what they wanted to hear, then I'm glad they did.

I know damn well there's a lot more that Dr. White *isn't* saying – my heart could fail again while I wait for a transplant, I might deteriorate to the point where I'm not strong enough for surgery... circumstances could change, and I suddenly might not be suitable for the long-term VAD anymore.

They're all very real possibilities, but I ignore them – every single one.

"It's your choice, buttercup." Dad reaches for my hand.

I know it's my choice – I'm an adult now and my mind has been made up for the better part of the last half hour.

This question and answers session has been for their benefit, not mine.

"I'd like to go ahead with the short-term VAD," I tell Dr. White.

She nods at me with a small smile – I know she thinks I've made the right decision.

"You understand that having this procedure means that you'll be restricted to a bed, and you won't be able to be discharged until either you receive a transplant, or you are fitted with the long-term VAD?"

I understand all of it.

I think that's why Mum and Dad were so set on the second option – that procedure would have meant I got to go home.

"I understand."

"Great." She closes the file she's holding in her hands. "I'll let Dr. Ellis know you've made a decision and she'll go ahead and make the arrangements."

I can almost literally feel the tension radiating from my mother as I watch Dr. White leave the room.

Dad mumbles something about coffee and before I even look up, he's gone... leaving me all alone with a sceptical set of eyes.

"Are you sure, Violet?"

"I'm sure."

"But why don't you take the long-term opt—"

"Mum, I've made my choice," I interrupt her.

I'm too tired for this argument. I know it's hard for her – having to come to terms with the fact that I make my own decisions now, but that's the reality. I'm twenty-one years old and my health is no longer her burden to carry, it's *mine*.

"I just *don't* understand."

Of course she doesn't. She couldn't possibly.

I know she's watched me endure this condition every step of the way – but she hasn't had to live it first-hand.

It's *my* life, not hers.

She's always done everything she can to keep me alive and to make the best of my situation, and I'm grateful for that, I *really* am, but this is about more than just surviving now. This is about *living* – it's about having a *real* life.

I don't want to carry around a battery pack strapped to my body for the next however many years.

I don't want to have to endure an open-heart surgery now and then again one day when the VAD stops helping.

I just don't want to do it.

I don't pull this card often, but I feel like it's justified now.

"I think I've been through enough," I croak – even my voice seems to have given up on me now. "Don't you?"

I want to take the easier option for once. I want to be hopeful.

A huge part of me feels like being fitted with a long-term solution means I'm closing myself off for the real long-term solution here – a heart.

I need to give my body and the universe a shot to make things right for me.

I have to take a chance on someone else's heart.

Her stare softens and I see her resolve wavering.

"This is what my heart *needs*... I can feel it."

She sighs.

"You've been on my side my whole life, Mum; I just need you to stick by me for this too, okay?"

She nods her head and I watch as tears well in her eyes.

"Okay."

"You promise?"

She leans over and kisses the top of my head.

"I've gotten you out of here your whole life, I'm not about to stop now."

***

Leanne

1993 (Six months old)

We're *finally* going home.

It's been so long, I was beginning to wonder if this moment was ever actually going to arrive.

Most people spend one or two nights, possibly a couple more if they need the extra support after they give birth, but we've been here a little over six months in total now and this is the very first time Violet will leave these hospital walls.

She's never even been inside the beautiful nursery I decorated for her – the space containing everything I selected carefully by hand.

Something like co-ordinating colour schemes seems so unbelievably trivial now. It's almost laughable that I visited four different baby stores just to find a blanket in the perfect shade of mint.

If only I knew nine months ago what I know now.

I wouldn't have spent my time making sure that I had the all-natural, expensive-as-hell baby lotion; I wouldn't have insisted that Shaun re-paint the ceiling in the nursery and I definitely wouldn't have bothered stressing about the fact that *all* of the baby clothes we owned weren't pre-washed, dried and folded neatly in the drawers.

If I knew then what I know now, I would have spent the time I wasted doing all of that, playing with August, or going for walks outdoors... I would have enjoyed all the simple things we all take for granted until something like this happens.

It's not so easy to take a stroll down the road anymore or shoot into town. Heck, all that was made significantly more complicated by just having a baby, let alone by having *another* baby – especially one that comes with heart complications and a feeding tube, but this is my new normal.

This is *our* new normal.

It's been about three months since Violet's last open-heart surgery – the bi-directional Glenn, and she's only just well enough to leave. That procedure has prepared her body for the final stage operation she'll have when she's three years old.

We're out of here for now – and I know all too well that our time to return will come all too soon. But for today, we're finally free.

The worry of the next surgery is for another day.

We walk down the long hallway, Shaun carrying Violet, all tucked up safe and asleep in her car seat.

Thinking back on the past ninety days is like trying to read writing on the side of a speeding train.

It's a blur.

I see some parts so clearly, yet can't recall others at all.

I notice things I didn't see at the time – no one ever told me, but I can see now that Violet was really unwell for a while there... that maybe she wasn't doing too well at all.

I wonder if maybe there were times where perhaps death was knocking, but we just weren't coming to the door to let it in.

Maybe it is like they say – maybe ignorance is bliss after all.

Regardless of what happened then, I do my best to focus instead on what's happening now. I feel like singing, dancing and making a real scene as we make our way out of here. I'm tempted to yell 'you were wrong' at the top of my lungs.

Don't get me wrong, we've received some fantastic support these past months, but I'll never forget those doctors that told us we were wasting our time – that our little girl wouldn't make it.

It may not have been an easy journey getting to this point, but we *are* here, and that's what's most important. I know we're not through it all yet, but I also know we undoubtedly made the right decision in trying.

Violet has been given six months we were told she wouldn't get, and even though I'm dying to get out of here and move onto the next stage of our lives, I couldn't be more grateful that those months have existed.

Life lately hasn't consisted of much more than the four walls of the small room we've been confined to, but I still wouldn't give it up for anything.

We walk out of the front doors, and into the fresh morning light.

Shaun straps Violet's car seat into the back of the car and I slide in next to her.

"We made it, baby," I whisper to her as Shaun starts the engine. "I promised you I'd get you out of here."

*****

"Shaun!" I hiss into the darkness of our bedroom.

"Mmmmmm," he groans in his half-asleep state.

"She's done it again."

"You're kidding," he moans.

I wish I was.

This is the third time this week alone.

Violet is starting to make a habit of pulling out her feeding tube, and each time she does it we have to make a trip into the hospital to have it put back in.

She only seems to do it in the dead of night – times when I can't call Linda and have her put it back in, of course.

I know it's necessary to have the damn thing, but I'd be lying if I didn't say I was sick to death of it.

There's only so many times you can drive a baby into the hospital in a half-asleep state before something cracks.

I'm at the point now where I'm going to insist that I be taught how to do it myself – if the on-duty doctor won't do it then I'll have Linda show me how... it can't be that bloody hard.

"I'll take her in, you stay here with Auggie."

"If you're sure?" He yawns.

"Go back to sleep," I whisper as I pull the door shut.

I know he won't need to be told twice.

We're both as exhausted as each other right now.

Ever since we brought Violet home, August seems to have forgotten what sleeping right through the night is all about.

She's up every few hours, crying or wandering around the halls.

The only thing tougher than getting up to a baby half the night is getting up to a nearly three-year-old for the other half of it.

I've had only one full night's sleep since we got home. I set Violet's tube to automatically feed her every three hours and Rita took August for the night to try and give us a break.

While the hours of uninterrupted sleep were total bliss, the overwhelming feeling of panic and terror when I woke to silence is something I could do without – I haven't been brave enough to try it again.

It's a scary thing being a parent.

It's a truly *terrifying* job to be a parent of a child with needs that differ from others – needs that make everything so much more high-risk than it should be.

Every day feels a little bit like a gamble. Like I'm betting all the money I have on the favourite in the field, but instead of crossing my fingers for a big win, I'm just hoping like hell that I'll get my money back – that I'll get the chance to make another bet tomorrow.

It's a challenging lifestyle to adjust to and one I'm not sure I'll ever consider normal – but I have to try.

This is my life now – *our* lives, and that's all there is to it.

We just have to get on with it – take it day by day and hope that our bets keep paying off.

Chapter Twenty-Four

"Alright, what'll it be first... 'Mean Girls', 'Legally Blonde' or 'Bring It On'?"

I shake my head in amusement at the offered selection. "Really?" I raise my brows at Lucy. "*Those* are the choices I get?"

She gasps in mock outrage. "These are *classics*."

I stifle a giggle. Lucy is such a sucker for these kinds of movies.

"Fine, 'Mean Girls'... unless you're going to quote the whole thing word for word, in which case, the other one with the cheerleaders."

She claps her hands together excitedly and rushes over to the TV. She's just as happy about this as I am.

Movie nights are our thing, and while it might be an awfully tame pastime for a couple of girls in their twenties, there's no other way I'd rather spend my time – we've been doing this for as long as I can remember.

I've missed hanging out with Lucy lately and while it's not the same in here, I just don't know if I'm going to get another chance to do this with her outside of this room – there's no guarantee I'm going to get to go home.

So I begged my nurses to let this slide. Hospital policy says that no visitors are allowed in the ward after eight at night, but thankfully, they agreed to turn a blind eye to our girly movie marathon.

I guess a crappy heart does have some perks after all.

I think they all feel sorry for me, and while I normally hate sympathy, in this case, I'll take it. One of the nurses even brought us in some popcorn earlier so I don't think anyone's got too much of a problem bending the rules just this once.

I'm just glad that they agreed without Lucy having to get involved. She might look sweet, pretty and innocent, but I know full well she's not someone you'd want to mess with. Her mum jokes that she's always been part wild cat – when the need arises, she's not afraid to roar.

She's always been like that... Lucy has had my back for forever.

***

Lucy
2006 (Thirteen years old)

"Seriously, Mum, she's just a *bitch*."

"Language!" Mum scowls at me.

I roll my eyes. Sometimes my mum really needs to chill – it's not like I said the 'f' word or anything.

"But she *is*."

"That might be the case, but there are things that we think, and things that we say out loud, and you, my dear girl, *really* need to learn the difference between the two."

Mum's always said I have no filter.

She's correct too. I can't understand why you'd think something but not be willing to say it out loud. I've always believed that if you shouldn't say it out loud, then you probably shouldn't think it either.

"And besides," Mum carries on, "what Julia is or isn't doesn't change the fact that *you* are the one being called into the principal's office."

"I only had to go there because I told her she was being a bi—"

"Lucy Reynolds, don't you dare," she cuts me off. "I don't know what has gotten into you."

I know exactly what's gotten into me. Julia and her little gang of airheads is what has got me all riled up.

I don't know who they think they are, and I don't care how many trips I have to take to the principal's office, there's no way I'm going to take this crap lying down.

"Mr. Filby was very concerned about your behaviour, you know."

"*Mr. Filby.*" I sneer the name, even though it's not him I'm really angry with. "*He* doesn't even know what happened."

"Well then *you* tell me what happened, because this isn't like you."

She's disappointed in me; I can see it in her eyes and I'd be lying if I said it didn't hurt, but I know she's going to be just as angry as I am when she finds out what those girls said.

"They called her Frankenstein," I growl.

I hear her gasp. "What?"

"Julia and her friends, I heard them calling Violet 'Frankenstein'… they were making fun of her scars."

"They said that?" she whispers. Her face has paled in shock.

I nod, and I see her expression shift from stunned to furious in the blink of an eye.

"Oh. No. Way. This is *not* happening. Na uh, no *damn* way… not on my watch."

She's got the phone in her hand already and I haven't got a clue who she's planning on calling, but I don't care.

Mum is on the warpath now.

If I look close enough I can probably see the smoke coming out her ears and the steam pouring from her nose.

She's royally pissed off.

"Bet I can call her a bitch now, huh, Mum?"

She points to me with a 'don't mess with me' finger at the same moment that whoever she's calling answers the phone.

"Yes, hi, Mr. Filby, this is Linda Reynolds…"

Her voice fades out as she leaves the room and shuts the door behind her.

Mr. Filby might have been a complete ass to me today by not giving me the opportunity to explain myself, but I actually feel a little bit sorry for him right now.

My mother is a firm believer in justice and fair play and she won't stop until she gets it.

It's one of the qualities that makes her such a great nurse – her sense of equality, and right and wrong means that she'll fight for as long as it takes for her patients to get what they need.

She'll go to great lengths for someone she doesn't even know, and I swear she'll literally go to the ends of the earth for the people she loves.

That unequivocally includes Violet.

She's my sister in all the ways that count, and she's been treated as a member of our family since the day she first turned up.

I know that Mum will fight as hard for Violet as she would if it were me that had been treated like this.

I'll fight hard too. No one speaks like that about my best friend and gets away with it.

Julia was lucky I didn't do more than call her names.

The look on Violet's face when they giggled and laughed and made fun of her is a look I'll never, ever forget.

The hurt I saw in her eyes will stay with me for the rest of my life.

Girls like Julia, they're the reason Violet feels like she needs to hide herself and who she is.

Girls like that, the type who can't see past a few marks on a person's skin, they're exactly the reason that Violet won't wear a bikini or a top that shows even a little bit of the scar on her chest.

They're the kind of girls that look for trouble where there is none. But they found trouble this time, that's for sure.

They might not have known that Letty and I were still in the changing room, but that's no excuse.

In fact, it might be worse. They didn't even have the nerve to say those things to her face – instead they talked about her behind her back.

Then there's the fact that they were totally wrong. Violet is no freak – she's more beautiful than all those girls put together.

If I had to take a guess, I'd say that Julia was jealous of Violet. Julia is planning to go and study art next year, and don't get me wrong, she *is* a good painter. She rates herself as one of the best in our school, but *no one* is as good as Violet – not even close. To be honest, I think she's even better than Mrs. Barkley, our art teacher.

Jealously can be an evil creature and when that group of girls had sneered those hurtful names and then told me to get lost, the jealously had been plain to see.

It breaks my heart. I know that Violet would befriend literally *anyone* that was genuinely kind to her – she's just that type of person. She's not bothered by things like age, gender, race or ability.

She'd do anything for her friends and if Julia wanted to be one of them, she would be – no questions asked.

But instead she's chosen to be a bully.

It's sad really – for Julia and her little gang of followers more so than anybody else. They're missing out on knowing the best person I've ever met, and *that* is their loss.

Those girls are part of the reason Violet considers me to be her only 'real' friend and they're also to blame for Violet thinking that people are out to embarrass her.

Mum strides back into the room, phone still in her hand and a pissed-off expression still firmly on her face. "We'll discuss this on Monday, Trevor, I'll see you at nine A.M."

Oh heck, she's moved onto first name basis now, which means she's *really* angry.

I bet Mr. Filby will be regretting the moment he decided to rat me out to my mum.

She hangs up the phone and I watch her take three deep breaths.

"Right, what are you waiting for, let's go," she announces finally.

"Are we going to throw eggs at Julia's house?" I answer hopefully as I jump out of my seat.

"Nope." She reaches into the cupboard and pulls out a bottle of red wine. "We're going over to the Miller's."

"Can I ask you again about the eggs after you've had a couple glasses of that?" I reply optimistically.

"You could try."

I grin. "Should I bring the toilet paper? We could TP her house?"

Mum laughs then, and some of the tension in her shoulders disappears.

She slings her arm around me and kisses the top of my head. "I'm sorry I doubted you. You're a good friend. Violet is lucky to have you."

My heart warms at her words, but I know I'm not the only lucky one; Vi would do anything for me too.

"You're just happy I didn't punch Julia, right?"

She mumbles something under her breath that sounds suspiciously like 'she would have deserved it', before ushering me out of the house.

"C'mon let's go visit our friends and see if we can't get me drunk enough to throw some eggs."

God, I really do love my mother.

Chapter Twenty-Five

There's one birthday in particular over the years that stands out to me more than any other. I was ten years old and I was finally allowed to have a party with the kids from my school.

Every birthday I've ever had has been celebrated fiercely by my family – I know it's because no one's ever been sure if I was going to get another one the following year, and I'm grateful for the attention, cake and ridiculous amount of gifts I received.

But if there was one thing I missed it was handing out invitations in class like all the other kids.

When I was younger I remember thinking that Mum and Dad were just being mean by not letting me have a big party every year like my classmates did, but now I realise it's because they didn't want me to be the kid that had no one turn up.

I missed a lot of school back then. Every time my class was hit with a bout of germs or bugs; it took me twice as long to get over it – sometimes when something was doing the rounds, Mum would pull me out and keep me at home as a precaution so there was no extra risk to my heart.

As a result of missing so much school, I didn't make that many close friends. I had Lucy, of course, and she had friends who were nice to me, but I always felt like they were always Lucy's friends, not mine.

Sometimes when I think back I wonder if I made it out to be something more than it was. Deciding that people don't want to know me before they've been given a chance is something I've been doing my whole life.

I guess I'll never know which of the two it was, but either way, it doesn't matter anymore. I've never been the popular kid and now I'm past the point of caring about having a lot of friends – I'd rather have one good one than ten mediocre ones.

But this one particular year however, I must have been feeling brave, because I invited every single person in my class.

I doubt any of them can recall even one thing about my party, but I sure can... and maybe being brave is what I need to do more of, because, despite my worry, they *all* came. I laughed, had fun and felt normal... and back then, it was probably one of the best days of my life.

I smile at the memory as I sit here, in my hospital room on the day that I turn yet another year older, surrounded by the people I love the most in the world and I think about being brave like I was eleven years ago and vow that tomorrow I'll try to be more courageous.

I stare at the flames and smile before blowing out the candles.

I might not have that much to be happy about this year – spending your twenty-second birthday in a hospital room isn't exactly my idea of a good time. Spending Christmas wasn't any better, but at least today I get to make a wish.

I don't have to think long or hard about what to wish for this year.

I know exactly what I want and although it's not a new heart I'm wishing for, at the same time I sort of am.

I'm being sneaky and trying to kill two birds with one stone.

I wish that I'll get to meet the man with the blue eyes, and given that I'm not in the best of shape, I figure I'm going to have to get my new heart first... in fact, I'm counting on it.

I can't see that fate would be cruel enough to save me then, only to take me now, but with every day that passes, I can feel my hopes slipping, and the slope feels far too steep for them to climb back up again.

***

There's a light knock at my door and I look up from my book in surprise. Everyone has been gone a while now and I wasn't expecting any more visitors.

Dr. White appears in the doorway looking fresh and bright eyed. She must be starting her nightshift.

"Come in." I smile at her.

She's not my regular cardiologist, but ever since she saved my life she's sort of taken over the duties. I like her better than the grumpy old guy I got assigned after I switched from child to adult care, so I'm certainly not complaining, and it gives Dr. Ellis some breathing room from my mum – so I figure it's a win for everyone involved.

"I bought you a present."

I frown at her because frankly, I'm confused – she's not holding anything and it's certainly not normal for a doctor to be buying gifts for their patients.

"You can't open it, but I think you'll like it all the same." She smiles as she walks towards me.

"Okay..."

I'm not sure where this conversation is heading, but I can't help thinking back with hope to the wish I made only a few hours ago.

"You're next on the list, Violet, if there's a heart available within a four-hour window that's compatible with you, it's yours."

I don't want to cry, but I can feel it's going to happen anyway.

This is a big development for me. I'm *next*. I've been waiting what feels like forever for this news.

I don't know what to say. I'm at a total loss for words.

I hope to God that any people ahead of me have received hearts and not passed away instead. I consider asking her but think better of it. I won't sleep well tonight as it is. I don't need to be brewing up new worries to concern myself with at two in the morning.

"It's my turn?" I croak. My voice has momentarily got caught in my throat.

"That's right."

I know I've got a real chance now. The possibility that I'll get to live outside of this hospital room and be free of all these wires and tubes is suddenly so much more real.

I know there's still a lot of factors that have to fall into place, and a ton of criteria that needs to be met in order for me to actually get a heart, but it's one step closer and that's the best I can hope for right now.

Just one step at a time...

I'm well aware that I've probably been bumped up a few places on the list. My condition is deteriorating and we all know it – It's no secret that I can't stay on this machine forever... and my time is running out.

"You know, Violet." She sits down on the end of my bed as she speaks. "I've seen a lot of patients in my eight years here, but I've never met one with quite as much spirit as you've got. I've got a good feeling about you – I know better than to make promises, but I really do think we'll find you the heart you need."

I know she doesn't say this to all her patients, so I'm grateful she's here saying it to me. She's a lovely woman and I know I'm lucky to have her on my side.

"It's the universal recipient blood type that's got you so convinced, isn't it?" I tease, referring to the conversation we had all those years ago. I doubt she'll remember, but she smiles at me and winks like it's our own little private joke.

She stands up and heads for the door. "The blood type certainly won't hurt, but it's more than that... you're destined for great things, Violet. We can all see it."

She leaves me alone in the room contemplating her words. She's not as black and white in her thinking as the other doctors. She allows a bit more of her personality to shine through – and she's optimistic, which is something I think others in her field are afraid to be.

She's exactly what I need to keep my spirits up.

There's so much I want to do with my life. I've tried not to dwell on it too much during this hospital stay because I'm not sure if I'll ever actually make it out of here alive, but I know I need to stop thinking like that. I'll never make it through if I have nothing to strive for.

I'm filled with hopes, dreams and aspirations for myself and it's time I allowed myself to believe I have the potential to achieve every single one of them.

There's only one thing I can think of doing now that will soothe my soul, and that's painting.

I've never loved my brother as much as I did when I saw him coming through my door carrying some of my art supplies.

I wasn't even a little bit mad at him for getting into my studio, I was just grateful.

Grateful that he cared enough to do this for me, and in awe that he knows me well enough to see I was struggling big time without my outlet.

I buzz for the nurse and have her set me up with a fresh sheet of paper, and sit all of my paints close enough for me to reach.

I should probably be sleeping seeing as I'm going onto the external VAD tomorrow, and I don't know how that's going to feel, but I'm strangely keyed up.

I've got all sorts of feelings bustling through my mind and body, and the only way I know how to deal with that is to put a brush to paper.

So that's what I do.

I pour my heart and soul into my work – the same way I always have. It's the only way I know to rid my mind and body of thoughts and feelings.

Some people talk, others write... and me... I paint.

Hours later, when I finally set down the brush in my hand and it's well and truly dark outside, I decide that this one I'll call 'opportunity'.

Chapter Twenty-Six

There's a certain vibe in the ward today that I can't seem to put my finger on. It's a bit like hope laced with an air of despair.

I don't know what to make of it, or what it means, but I feel it.

It's got me so on edge I can't do anything even remotely constructive.

I can't focus on my book, I can't sleep, and the TV show that's been on for the past half hour may as well be in Japanese for all I've understood of it.

There's a saying, where if someone is talking about you, your ears burn...

Well, that's how *this* feels.

My ears are figuratively burning hot right now.

I just *know* I'm being talked about.

Nurses and doctors I've never seen before have been popping into my room, checking my chart, and asking me somewhat strange questions.

No one has brought me any food this morning, and even though I'm not eating much at the moment, I'm still curious as to why.

The only thing keeping me from losing my shit entirely is the fact Mum will be here in a few minutes, like she is every other morning, and I know she'll straighten this out for me.

There's probably nothing at all going on, I've probably dreamed the whole thing up – I've always assumed people were talking about me and judging me, but lately it's been worse than ever. I swear it's being in this place for so long that has made me so paranoid.

I lean to the side, trying to watch what's happening outside my window. I'm not sure why I'm bothering, I don't know what I expect to see. They're hardly going to be putting up a big neon sign that flashes the word 'dying' outside of my door.

I'm not even being dramatic this time. I know things are getting bad for me, I look like absolute crap and my oxygen saturation levels are dropping lower and lower by the day. I'm tired *all* the time, yet I never seem to be able to get any restful sleep.

Maybe that's what this is – maybe I'm really going to die soon.

Rationally, I know that they're not just going to leave me here to die – we had a plan… if a heart didn't come in time, I'd have to get the long-term VAD. The only thing I can think of is that they've left it too long – that perhaps I'm not strong enough for plan B anymore. Maybe that ship has sailed.

I can see one of the regular nurses, Jackie, out at the nurse's station, she's got her back to me, but when she turns, it's plain as day that she's been crying.

It's not just a stray tear or two either, it's big, fat, ugly ones and her eyes are so red and puffy I'm not sure she'll even be able to see the computer screen in front of her.

I'm still staring at the upset woman when my mum breezes into the room, but I don't so much as glance at her. I can't pull my eyes from the tear-stained cheeks of the middle-aged nurse who has been so kind to me these past months.

I assume it's me she's crying over – that I'm dying, and she's upset.

This is what I've always been afraid of – the amount of people I'll take down with me when I go... it's the ticking time bomb feeling all over again.

Mum is rambling about something so unimportant that I can't even make sense of it.

"Violet!" she calls loudly.

I snap out of my trance and turn so I'm looking directly at her.

She glances between my face and the window I was looking out of. "What on earth is going on?"

"I'm dying, Mum, that's what's going on."

***

I can hear Mum. She's not yelling, but her voice is right on the cusp of it. She's talking loudly, and her tone has that slight element of terror that gives the distinct impression that she's anything but pleased.

"My daughter is in there, worried that she's about to *die*, for crying out loud. Why is everybody bawling out here?"

I can't hear the reply of the man she's talking to – he's one of the nurses who has been into my room this morning that I don't recognise.

It's unnerving to say the least.

A whole bunch of random medical professionals coming in and out of my room can't mean anything good.

I don't know what he's said to my mum, but she's talking again, only this time she's deadly quiet.

That's when I know for sure.

My time's up.

I thought it'd feel different, I thought I'd know that the end was near, but I don't... I feel no different today than I did yesterday, or the day before that, for that matter.

I've been in here so long; one day is just blending into the next.

I can see the distinct difference between the day I was brought in, and now. But I was expecting something more sudden. Cardiac arrest felt a hell of a lot more like dying than this does.

I pick up my phone, about to text Lucy to let her know she needs to get in here as soon as she can, when I catch sight of my mum walking back through the door.

She's got tears in her eyes and I feel my heart sink further.

It's not until I see the smile on her lips that I release the breath I didn't realise I'd been holding.

Chapter Twenty-Seven

They've found her a heart.

I've still got no idea what half the nurses were crying about out there, but I don't care anymore – they've found my baby a heart and it's the best news I've ever heard.

I know that a transplant isn't a foolproof solution, and that there's a huge risk to any surgery, let alone open heart, but this is the best option we have left. She's made it through so many of these types of operations, I *know* she can do it again.

Violet is deteriorating before my very eyes and there's only so long she can hold on for. It's been hard to watch her like this, but now I think I finally understand her decision – I can see why she wanted to take a chance.

This will completely change her life.

She needs this heart more than anyone else in the whole country and she's *finally* going to get it.

I know I shouldn't feel so entirely elated – someone, somewhere, is probably having the worst day of their life right now. They'll be preparing to say goodbye to a loved one.

I know it probably makes me a selfish, horrible person, but I'm so grateful that it's not me who is having to say goodbye.

I hope that family out there can find some type of comfort in knowing that the person they cared about is going to save others – I hope the knowledge of this gift can bring them a little bit of peace.

I'm so grateful that this person, whoever they are, decided to be a donor. There's a lot of people out there who aren't and that's something I'll never understand.

I've always been a firm believer in the idea that when you're dead – you're dead.

Yes, I believe there's something *more* out there... some type of afterlife, but you don't need your body for that. You don't need to take a perfectly good heart or set of lungs deep down in the earth in order to move on from this life.

There's thousands and thousands of people on waiting lists for organs in this country and only so few people willing to donate something they no longer have use for. The concept truly blows my mind.

I understand it's probably the first-hand experience we've had with recipients that's made me see this in such a black and white fashion – but I can't imagine ever denying someone the chance to live after I was already gone.

"Mum?"

Violet is looking at me in bewilderment and it's then I realise that although my mind is going a mile a minute, I still haven't said a word out loud.

"They're coming in to see you now."

She's about to demand answers from me, I can see it in her eyes, but she's going to have to wait, because they're already here – time is of the essence now, when that heart gets here, they have to be ready for it.

Dr. Ellis, two nurses and a cardiologist whose name I can't recall stand before us.

"What's going on?" Violet whispers.

She's terrified; I can smell her fear from here, but *finally* this time it's good news.

Dr. Ellis gives her a smile and just nods her head.

"Are you... are you saying?" Violet stutters, disbelief thick in her voice.

"I am," she confirms. "We found you a heart."

Chapter Twenty-Eight

I don't know what everyone else is worried about at twenty-two years old… if I were to guess I'd say partying, drinking… sex perhaps.

For most people my age, I'd be willing to bet it *isn't* the fear of having their heart taken out of their body and replaced with someone else's.

But that's what I worry about most in this very moment as the doctors, nurses, anaesthesiologists and surgeons all rush around me like headless chickens, prepping my body and talking to me about what's going to happen next.

I don't hear a single one of their words.

I don't *need* or *want* an explanation.

I already know what happens now.

They'll take out my old, broken and battered heart and give me a new one.

Somebody else's old one.

I try not to think too hard about the fact that in order for me to live, someone else had to die.

I've officially been waiting months for a heart. Unofficially it's been looming for my whole life… and now that one is finally here, I'm scared.

I wish I could talk to Lucy.

I wish that I could be like my best friend – that my biggest concern was whether or not the guy I've been dating is going to message me today or not, or whether the selfie I took a few days ago is going to get as many likes on Instagram as the last one did.

If she knew this was happening right now, which she will soon enough, all of that crap would be quickly forgotten, but for now, I wish I was like her... young, healthy and carefree.

I've had those superficial moments, they've been fleeting, but they're there, and it's not until now, in this very instant, that I realise how perfect it was to fall out with my best friend over something trivial, only to make up again two hours later, or how amazing it was for a boy that I liked to decide that he liked someone else, or how I'd give anything to be absolutely devastated because the top I wanted didn't come in my size.

I'd give just about *anything* for those little moments to be my biggest concern right now.

All other people's insignificant, little nothings are every one of my most treasured somethings, and in this moment, as I'm wheeled out of my room and off to the operating theatre, I hold them close.

Chapter Twenty-Nine

Violet

I open my eyes and blink drowsily as I take in the small, dimly lit room of the intensive care unit.

I glance to the left and smile as I recognise my mother's sleeping form, her neck propped up awkwardly in the armchair.

She's going to have the worst stiff neck, but I wouldn't have expected to find her anywhere other than right here next to me.

She *never* leaves me when I need her. She's still wearing the same clothes as she was when they wheeled me into the operating theatre.

I don't even know what day it is, or how long I've been out – I know I've been awake, but I can't really recall what happened – it's like the memory is covered in a thick haze.

It's dark outside and I feel like I've been hit by a bus. The pain thrumming through my body is too much and I know I need to ask for more pain relief.

I'm opening my mouth to let the nurse in the corner know that I'm awake when I catch a movement out of the corner of my eye and my gaze meets *his*.

He's standing on the other side of the glass window, watching me intensely.

I've never met this man, but I know him right down to my bones. And as I stare into the blue depths of his soul, my new heart skips a beat for the very first time.

after

This is about what my heart wants, not what it needs for once, and all that my heart wants in this moment, is him.

Chapter Thirty

I don't know what I'm doing back at this window; this is the third time I've stood in this spot in the last hour alone.

I know I should do something, *anything* other than just linger here... but I don't know how to break away.

There's *something* keeping me here right now, and in a world where nothing seems to make sense anymore, I *need* this feeling, if only to get through the next few minutes.

I glance back at the girl in the bed.

If I had to guess, I'd say she was about nineteen years old – far too young to look the way she does.

She's pale and gaunt and if I hadn't had to witness first-hand my sister's life in this world coming to an end, I would have sworn that nobody had ever looked as close to death as the girl behind this small glass window.

She's motionless. So, *so* still and I worry for a moment that she's dead too.

The only thing reassuring me she's still alive, even though it's really no business of mine, is the continuous beep from the monitor next to her, making it clear that her heart is, in fact, still beating – that it's doing the very thing that my sister's isn't.

A loud sob rips through my body at the thought.

Doctors and nurses move around the hall but none of them bother me; most of them avoid eye contact entirely.

They know why I'm still aimlessly wandering the halls of the intensive care unit.

My sister may have had no brain function for a couple of days, but now she's officially gone. The machines aren't breathing for her anymore – there's nothing left keeping her alive.

I don't know what to do, I've never felt this alone or unsure in my entire life.

I know I need to leave; I need to be anywhere that's not inside these hospital walls, but I can't seem to make that happen.

I know I can't stay here forever, but I'm terrified that walking out the door will make everything even more real than it already is.

I'm not sure who I'm trying to fool with my logic – this couldn't possibly be any more real, and deep down I know that it's not going to make a difference if I stay or go.

She's gone.

I take one more look at the girl and promise myself that this will be the last time I'll ever see her.

I allow my eyes to linger on her motionless form, and as I finally find the will to turn around, her arm moves, and my breath catches in my throat.

I watch her as though she's some type of miracle, and maybe she is, as she slowly wakes and eventually glances over at the sleeping figure in the chair next to her.

I see the side of her face curve and I know she's smiling.

Her head rolls slightly in my direction and the wave of pain that crosses her features is so sudden and intense that I rush forward a step.

She catches my movement out of the corner of her eye, and I stop dead in my tracks.

The nurse from the corner is rushing towards her, but she doesn't look away from me.

All I really see are her eyes – surrounded by dark circles, they are the most beautiful crystal blue eyes I've ever seen. Even filled with pain, and dulled with obvious sickness, I've never seen anything like them.

She stares at me – a total stranger, and I stare back at her, with one lone tear rolling down my cheek.

Three years later

Chapter Thirty-One

Violet

"What if this guy's a sociopath, huh? What happens then?" I demand.

"Calm down, I've heard he's *really* nice."

"Oh 'you've heard' have you? He could be a killer just waiting for the right opportunity for all you know."

Lucy pauses from applying the makeup to my face and rolls her eyes.

"You watch way too much C.S.I."

I huff out a breath. "You're not wrong, but that's not the point... what if he's a murder rapist, hmmm? You want that on your conscience?"

"Stop being such a drama queen and show me what you think you're going to wear."

"What do you mean, what I *think* I'm going to wear? I'm perfectly capable of putting clothes on my body, thank you very much."

I know as well as she does that she's just successfully distracted me from my irrational fears, but for now at least, I've got bigger fish to fry.

"Baggy t-shirts and jeans don't count as clothes, Letty."

"I wasn't going to wear a t-shirt," I grumble as I slide off the chair.

I pull out a long-sleeve blouse and a pair of black pants from my closet and wave them at her.

She screws up her nose in a look of distaste. "It's a date, not a funeral."

She might only be joking, but I've worn that exact outfit to a funeral before, so she actually has a point.

I shoot her daggers anyway as I rummage through the closet again, this time emerging with a denim skirt and a green knit, high-neck jumper.

"Oh, good God no... *not* the snot colour jersey."

I throw the clothes onto the chair in the corner and groan in frustration. "You find me something then."

We both know she's going to get her way in the long run anyway – she always does.

"I'll do you one better." She grins wickedly, and I seriously fear for myself in this moment.

I may have survived more operations and treatments than I can count, but Lucy's hare-brained schemes still scare the life out of me like nothing else.

Her and her ideas are the reason I'm preparing for a blind date right now.

Her husband, Emmett, is no better than she is. The guy I've been forced into meeting tonight is someone he knows from work apparently – so he's as much to blame for this mess as she is.

"You know, I would have thought that being seven months pregnant would have slowed you down, even just a little bit."

She turns and sticks her tongue out at me over her shoulder. "Not a chance."

She pulls out a shopping bag, and I'm instantly nervous at the sight of it.

Lucy is always pointing items out on clothing racks at stores and telling me how good things would look on me.

She's sweet, and if it wasn't for the big scar that runs down the centre of my chest, she'd be absolutely right.

If it wasn't for the marks on my skin, I probably would have tried on the plunging-neckline dress she'd pointed out to me two weeks ago.

But that's not me. I'm scarred, I'm flawed. And I'm okay with keeping those parts of myself hidden. Lucy, however, doesn't seem to see my scars when she looks at me, and while that's a blessing in itself, right now, it has the potential to be a curse.

She waddles over with the bag and holds it out to me.

I reach for it as though it's a bomb that could go off at any minute, because, quite frankly, it is.

"It won't bite." She laughs as she shoves it into my waiting hands. "Oh, ye of little faith."

"Does it have sequins?" I wince.

"Nope."

"Glitter?"

"Nope again."

She sits herself down in the chair I sat in while she painted my face on.

"Plunging neckline?"

I brace myself for the answer.

"Just open the bag, Violet."

I peek inside and am greeted by the sight of deep blue, soft fabric – so far so good.

I hold my breath and pull the garment out.

It's a dress, with long sleeves and a full coverage front, a tie at the waist and by the looks of it, the length will fall around my knees.

It's perfect.

"It's gorgeous," I breathe.

"You don't have to sound so shocked."

"I *am* shocked. I was seriously expecting at least a leg split or some awful attempt at getting my tits out or something."

She laughs long and loud, clutching her swollen belly as she does.

Pregnancy *becomes* Lucy, she's the most radiant and gorgeous pregnant woman I've ever seen.

"Don't worry, I'm not blind. I see your face every time I point out those types of outfits – I know they're not your thing."

"Then why do you keep suggesting them to me?" I cry in outrage.

"Because they'd look beautiful on you, Letty. Just because you don't see it, doesn't mean I can't."

I feel the blush heating my cheeks – I'm not good with any form of compliment, I never have been.

"And besides..." she winks at me, "you haven't seen the back yet."

I spin the dress around and grin. Now *this* type of plunging I can deal with.

The back drops down low and drapes at what I assume will be near the top of my bum.

I have no scars and nothing to hide back there and it's almost as though this dress was made just for me.

"It's amazing, thank you."

She waves her hand in front of her to indicate that it's no big deal at all, but I'm not having it. She's thought a lot about this outfit. I know she so desperately wants tonight to go well for me.

I don't date. Like, ever.

I'm not even entirely sure how I ended up agreeing to being set up on a blind date in the first place, my sly best friend and her equally as cunning husband must have caught me in a moment of weakness, but I'm here now, and looking far more respectable than I usually do – so I figure I may as well go and make the best of it.

"Seriously, Luce, it's beautiful. Thank you."

"You're welcome. Now put it on," she demands, glancing at her watch as she speaks, giving me a clear indication that I need to hurry up.

"Brown ankle boots," she hollers after me as I rush into my walk-in closet.

I emerge wearing the correct items of clothing and Lucy sighs in satisfaction.

"Perfect."

***

"Promise you'll be right next door?" I plead with Lucy and Emmett as we pull up outside the restaurant.

"I swear on my life," Lucy replies. "Now get out of the car and stop being such a chicken shit."

I've insisted they wait until either one of two things happen – one; I bail and need them to get me the hell out of there, or two; I hit it off with this guy and find my own way home.

I don't even feel bad about hijacking their evening for my own benefit – the two of them got me into this mess, it's the least they can do as far as I'm concerned.

"He's a good guy, Vi," Emmett reassures me in a manner far nicer than his hormonal wife.

"Okay, I can do this," I reply in a less than convincing tone.

"C'mon, woman, you've literally survived dying, and yet you're scared of a date?"

Lucy's right.

I *know* she's right, but that doesn't stop the heart that still feels foreign to me from beating erratically in my chest at the very thought of getting out of this car and walking inside.

"I can do this." I'm slightly steadier sounding this time so I open the door and step out while I'm still able to find the courage to go through with it.

Chapter Thirty-Two

Rylan

I know that running late for a date isn't going to be the best first impression I've ever made, but I've got a pretty good excuse, and if the woman I'm meeting tonight doesn't understand that, then it was never going to work out anyway.

My job can be demanding, and I'm well aware that it's probably what's kept me from having any type of meaningful relationships with women thus far. That, and the lingering feeling something's missing whenever I'm in the presence of other people.

Ever since my sister passed away, I'm left constantly feeling like a piece of me is incomplete.

I've met nice women, but nothing ever feels as right as I know it should – so for years I never felt compelled to invite anybody new into my life.

I'm not expecting to walk into this restaurant tonight and find the solution to that problem, but a guy can dream.

I hear the tone indicating I have a text message as I throw myself into the driver's seat of my car. I stop at a red light and pull out my cell. I shake my head at the picture message I've just received from Emmett.

Emmett and I work together at the hospital, and with a bit of luck I'll be delivering his baby within the next two months.

He and his wife Lucy – they're the ones responsible for this set up tonight.

Emmett's sent me a picture of a woman I assume is Violet – my company for the evening. I can't see her face, and if I had to guess I'd say he took the picture of her as she walked towards the date I'm currently running late for.

The light turns green and I speed up a little; the thought of her sitting alone at a table is making me feel guilty.

After what feels like an eternity, I pull up outside and I must have some type of luck after all because there's a park right outside.

I take a deep breath before pushing the door open and jogging to the front of the restaurant.

Thanks to Emmett I know I'm looking for a woman with long dark hair, and a blue dress.

I'm glancing around as I give my name to the woman behind the desk and she points Violet out at the same moment that my eyes find her.

She doesn't look around as I approach from behind, and I still can't see her face.

I clear my throat in an attempt not to startle her, but still she jumps a fraction in her seat.

She turns slowly to face me and it's all I can do not to gasp as I see her face for the first time.

She's *so* beautiful, but not only that, she's oddly familiar.

I'm certain we've never met, but I feel drawn to her, like souls rekindling.

"Violet?" I question her, my voice sounding not at all like my own.

She looks at me as though she's seeing a ghost and her face pales visibly.

The doctor in me takes over.

"Are you okay?" I reach for her elbow on instinct; I'm worried that she's going to pass out, but for now at least she seems to be holding steady.

She's just staring at me in obvious shock.

She's caught up inside her own head right now, and I know that I won't reach her, no matter what I say. So I don't say anything, instead I crouch down next to her and wait.

It takes a full minute until she blinks once, twice, three times, before giving her head a little shake to clear it.

"Violet?" I repeat.

She reaches for her glass and takes a quick sip.

"I'm so sorry," she breathes as she sets it back down. "You gave me a fright. Rylan?" she questions me back, her eyes lingering on my face for a moment before trailing down my shoulder and arm to where my hand is still touching her.

I let her go hurriedly, as though I'm a teenager being caught doing the wrong thing.

"That's me," I tell her with a smile.

Her eyes are on my face again, as mine are on hers, and I watch in silent appreciation as her lips curve up to mirror mine.

An overwhelming sense of calm that I haven't felt in years settles over me, and I decide that now would be a good time for me to sit down.

Chapter Thirty-Three

Violet

I would have known those eyes *anywhere* – I've dreamed about them nearly every night since I was twenty-one years old.

Three years ago, when I looked into them for the very first time in real life, it had shocked me beyond belief.

Much like right now.

He's saying my name and it's *just* like in my vision.

I can't breathe.

I don't know who this man is, but I know he means *something* to me.

He's literally the man of my dreams and that scares me half to death.

I know nothing about him, but he's here, saying my name and touching my arm and I still can't breathe.

"Are you okay?" he asks me, and I can hear the obvious concern in his voice.

'No, I'm not okay at all' I want to scream, but when I open my mouth, nothing comes out.

I can feel the anxiety clawing its way out of me and I know I only have seconds to get it under control.

I think of the technique one of my doctors taught me when I was younger.

Five, four, three, two, one...

I need to concentrate on five things I can see, four things I can touch, three things I can hear, two things I can smell and one thing I can taste.

Five... I can see *him,* the table, the waiter taking orders, cars on the street, my bag on the seat.

Four... I can touch *him,* the seat, the floor and the table-cloth.

Three... I can hear *him* saying my name, the people at the next table talking and the hum of energy from the kitchen.

Two... I can smell *him*, and garlic bread, and honestly, I'm not sure which smells better.

I can feel my breathing settling now as my body becomes more grounded and calm.

One... I can taste... my eyes immediately dart to his lips, but I grab my glass of orange juice before I do something stupid.

"I'm so sorry," I finally say as I put my glass back on the table. "You gave me a fright."

I look up and he's still watching me carefully.

"Rylan?" I ask, even though it's obviously him.

"That's me," he replies, his face lighting up with a smile so beautiful it actually pains me to look at it.

I find myself smiling back at him; like I don't even have a choice in the matter.

It's not lost on me that all five of my senses were drawn to *him* first and foremost, and considering I don't know him in the slightest, that's an unexpected revelation.

He sits opposite me and I'm overcome with a feeling that maybe my life is only just beginning right in this very moment.

***

"And that's why I was late," he replies with a shrug, only now getting around to explaining why he'd kept me waiting.

"You're an obstetrician?" I ask, surprise clearly colouring my voice.

We've been talking for over half an hour, and so far, I've managed to keep myself from asking him how or why it is that he frequents my dreams at night.

I've also managed not to freak out and panic again, but the more he talks the more I get a feeling of déjà vu that I can't explain.

He nods and smiles, acknowledging that it's somewhat of an unexpected field of medicine for him to be in.

He looks like a real man's man – not someone that looks at women's private parts all day, while periodically delivering little bundles of joy.

His shoulders are broad and strong, his golden skin is freckled from time spent in the sun and his hair is as dark as the night sky.

If I didn't already know he worked in the hospital, and someone had told me to guess, I would have gone with something like a builder or a farmer – something that required him to have strong, rugged hands.

He's tall and lean – he's very obviously physically fit, and I know I *really* need to stop looking at him.

"You got it, I'm an obstetrician," he confirms with a shrug.

"And you were delivering a baby..." I repeat his words back to him, still not quite believing.

He chuckles and the sound is warm and comforting.

I smile at him while I watch the curve of his mouth as the laughter falls from his lips.

"She came early. We weren't expecting her until next week, but really, at this point I should know better than to expect a baby to come on its due date."

"Did you know Emmett and Lucy are having a baby?"

He points to himself. "Who do you think is delivering it?"

I gape at him. "Seriously?"

He nods his head proudly.

"Wow... you *must* be good. You should have seen how long it took her to decide on a car seat. I can't even imagine the process she went through to pick a doctor... did she bring you in for a formal sit-down interview?"

He grins, and once again the breath is stolen from my lungs.

"I know you're joking, but you're actually not far off."

A realisation I'd previously missed appears front and centre in my mind.

"Hold the phone, so *she* knows you? That sneaky little she-devil gave me the distinct impression she *didn't* know you."

My eyes are narrowed now, and my finger is pointed at him in an incredibly accusing manner.

"Hey, don't shoot the messenger." He holds his hands up in surrender.

I make a pretend shooting motion with my finger, and he laughs – really laughs for the first time tonight.

It's a perfect sound and I'm already wishing I was funnier so I could say something that would let me hear it again.

"I can't believe she played me like that." I scowl half-heartedly.

He looks right into my eyes. His stare is strong and un-wavering, and I almost shudder under the weight of it.

"Did she choose wrong?" he asks seriously.

I hold his gaze and shake my head, one small little move-ment that he doesn't miss.

She chose good – *really* good.

He's interesting, kind, funny, and somehow, manages to pull off this intense thing he has going, all the while looking like an absolute dream.

But the thing is, I'm not sure that Lucy and Emmett chose him at all.

I'm forced to think, that after nearly four years of dream-ing of the deep blue eyes that are now focused on my face, watching me carefully, that perhaps this meeting was just meant to be.

I've never been a big believer in fate, because then I'd have to accept the fact that someone, somewhere deemed it my fate to suffer when others don't, but after spending tonight in his magnetising presence, I might have to rethink my views on the world.

"Well... good then," he replies, reminding me where I am and who I'm with, even though my eyes haven't left his for a moment.

The sight of him in my mind has become a sense of calm for me, a comfort even... and I hope to God that I'm re-flecting my behaviour in a way that is appropriate for two strangers meeting, rather than someone greeting a familiar memory.

"Tell me something about you."

I refrain from groaning in response to his request.

I absolutely hate talking about myself. I despised the first day of school every year; the one where you had to stand up in class and tell the group a fun fact about yourself.

I would literally rather stick pins in my eyes than tell another 'fun fact'.

There's very little to tell about me that isn't going to get me *that* look. The look of sympathy.

I loathe the look of sympathy.

I don't want people to feel sorry for me, I want them to accept me for who I am and not what I've been through. I don't want to become my condition, but sometimes I fear I've done exactly that.

"What do you do for work?" he prompts when I don't reply.

I smile at the question because *that* is one I can answer – even if it's not with total honesty. Technically, I don't work – I volunteer, but he doesn't need to know that just yet.

"I work at an animal shelter."

His eyebrows raise in surprise. "That might be as rewarding as delivering babies."

"I actually helped deliver a whole litter just last week," I brag.

"Well then, here's to new life." He picks up his glass and holds it up to me.

I reach for my glass and clink it gently against his, repeating his sentiment back to him.

I spend the entire time it takes for our mains to arrive talking about the shelter and the quirky animals that come through, and he's either an excellent actor, or he's genuinely interested because he asks me questions the entire time.

I get to hear him laugh again and my insides feel all fuzzy and warm.

We eat in a comfortable silence and I'm aware that he's watching me as closely as I'm watching him.

I've already learned that he's the kind of person that eats each element on his plate separately, not starting the next type of food until the last one is finished. He's methodical even in his eating habits.

I, on the other hand, am quite the opposite, I eat a little piece of this, then that, then this again. It's the unrestrained artist coming out in me I think.

"I paint," I blurt the words out before I even consider the implication of them.

I only paint for me, and the reason I don't tell people about it is because the first thing they ask is if they can see my work.

He's watching me again – honestly, I'm not sure he ever stopped, and I can almost feel him rummaging around in my thoughts – like he somehow understands that even though I brought the topic up, I'm not entirely sure I actually want to talk about it.

"What do you paint?" he asks cautiously after a moment of silence.

I fiddle nervously with the gold ring that I wear on a chain around my neck.

"My feelings, my thoughts…" I shrug. "Whatever comes to me."

He nods for more than a few seconds, like he's processing the information.

"I bet they're incredible."

I wait for it – the 'I'd really like to see them sometime', but it doesn't come; he simply picks up his glass and takes another sip.

"That's a beautiful ring." He tilts his head in the direction of the ring I'm still playing with and I'm taken by surprise – he's as observant as he is intense.

I bring it up to my face so I can study it, as though maybe I've forgotten what it looks like all of a sudden.

"It was my aunt's. She gave it to me before she passed away."

And there I go again… speaking before I think, but much like before, he doesn't ask me questions that I don't want to answer.

"It matches your eyes beautifully," he simply replies.

I can feel myself blushing again. Even though he didn't technically give me a compliment, it still feels like one.

It does match my eyes – that's why she gave it to me. My Aunt Rita was more like a grandmother to me growing up, she was fifteen years older than my mother, and their parents – my grandparents, were both gone by the time I was born.

She was an absolute loon and I loved her dearly.

She lived long enough to see me get my new heart, and then she was gone, leaving behind a longing ache in my chest, the most wonderful memories, and a trail of wealth that gave my entire family more than we ever thought we'd have.

"You loved her." He's not asking a question, but merely reading my expression and stating a fact – it seems to be a skill of his.

We might not eat the same way, but we both appear to share the talent of reading people.

"I loved her very much. She was kind, kooky and very generous."

When she passed away, she left me the home I now live in along with a small fortune that will ensure I never want for a single thing. Auggie and Charlie have one each too.

She's the reason I can spend my time painting and volunteering without having to worry about how I'm going to pay the bills.

None of us had any idea that Rita was so well off, or that when she died, she'd leave everything to the five of us. She never had any children of her own, so my parents, my siblings and I, we were it for her.

"She gave me a house." The words come out without thought yet again.

I don't know what it is about him, but my walls keep slipping and I find myself telling him things I'd never normally consider telling a someone I just met.

Maybe it's because he doesn't feel like a stranger to me at all.

His eyes widen in surprise, and just when I expect him to question me further, he brings out the line I was expecting earlier, when I told him that I paint.

"I'd really like to see it sometime."

My heart is beating overtime at the very thought of having this beautiful man in my home, I'm scared, *so* scared to let people into my life.

This all feels like I've been thrown into a pressure cooker. The force is already building up, and I don't want it to explode, or the lid to lift and the air to escape. I just want to stay right here with him and let this pressure build.

I've never felt this comfortable and yet off kilter at the same time, but I think I like it – it feels like living.

"I think that might be okay," I tell him coyly.

He dips his head and grins, like that was exactly the answer he was hoping for, and for the first time in a long time, I think that maybe everything might be okay after all.

Chapter Thirty-Four

Rylan

"This is a beautiful house."

It's an understatement – the huge Victorian home in front of me is as stunning as it is grand, but I've quickly come to learn that Violet isn't one for making a fuss, so I don't say anything more about it.

"I love it." She smiles as she glances up.

We're walking up the path to her front door, and there's nothing out here but us, the silence and the moonlight.

This whole evening has felt this way – like it's just been her and I, talking like neither of us had anywhere else in the world to be.

I glance at her again and shake my head in disbelief that *I'm* the guy that gets to bring her home tonight.

She *really* is a beautiful woman; I'd have to be blind not to see the obvious beauty in front of me, but it's not just about her pretty face, she radiates goodness and warmth too.

She's cautious – I can see that, but she's got a sense of freedom about her that I'm not sure even she knows what to do with.

We're strolling *so* slowly, dawdling even, and I get the impression that she doesn't want this night to end any more than I do.

I can't quite comprehend the feeling I have inside me when she's around. I feel... at peace. It's something I haven't experienced in a very long while, and I'm not ready to let it go just yet.

I glance down and brush the back of my hand against the back of hers. I feel like a teenager all over again, and it's a sentiment I welcome.

It feels like a stage of my life that I can manage right now – it's innocent and pure and there's no expectation on either of us to do anything more than just be here. I'm not walking her to her door with the hope that she'll invite me in and we'll have wild sex all night long.

It's not that I don't want to do that, because as much of a gentleman as I am, I'm exactly that, a *man* – but just not tonight.

Even if that was on her agenda, which I'm confident it's not, Violet deserves more than that, and so do I.

I take her hand in mine when we reach the steps – under the pretence that I'm helping her up them, and don't get me wrong, I *am* happy to help, but this contact is as much for my benefit as it is for hers. I've been dying to feel her skin against mine again ever since I touched her arm. The satisfied smile on her face makes me think that maybe she feels the same way I do.

Her hand is small and delicate in my much bigger one, and I like it. It feels *right*.

I don't let go when we reach her door, and neither does she.

We turn to face one another, and I'm struck again with just how pretty her eyes are.

They sparkle like cut crystal does in the sunlight. Even out here in the dark they shine, and when I look into them I get an inexplicable feeling that I'm not only looking at an important part of my future, but also somehow at my past.

It shocks me to my core that I feel this way about her after only a few short hours, but if there's one thing I've learnt from delivering babies into their parents' waiting arms, it's that a person's whole life can change in a mere fraction of a second.

"I'd really like to see you again."

Yet another understatement.

"Well… you've got my number." She shrugs.

She's nervous – she's not sure if I'm going to kiss her or not.

I step towards her and reach my free hand out slowly towards her face.

There's a strand of hair that seems to find its way across her forehead often, and I sweep it away and tuck it behind her ear.

I lower my lips to her forehead and place a soft kiss there.

She visibly shudders at the action and it makes me want to do it again.

I pull back, one of my hands resting on her jaw, the other still intertwined with her hand. She looks up at me. Her eyes are cautious but curious. She wants to be kissed.

She tilts her face up towards mine, and I slowly lower my lips to hers, pressing them together ever so gently.

Her free hand reaches for my neck and lightly tugs down, inviting me even closer. I go, willing and eager for more of her.

Her lips are so soft and smooth, and I can taste the mint she took from her handbag earlier.

I want more. God, do I want more, but instead I pull away, knowing that I haven't earnt more, not yet anyway.

"Thank you for dinner," she whispers into the small space between us.

"You're welcome." My reply comes out just as quietly.

I lean in and press my lips to hers once more, just quickly before I lose myself in her all over again.

"I'll call you," I promise as I take a step back.

I'm still holding her hand in mine, and as much as I don't want to let it go, I know it's time. I bring her fingers to my lips and kiss her skin one last time before I let go and reluctantly leave.

I watch her from my car. She unlocks her door and waves to me before going inside.

I look back up at the house as the lights come on and allow myself to acknowledge that my long lost feeling of contentment can be found inside those very walls.

***

I see Emmett coming from a mile away, and my feeble attempt to bury my face in my notes goes as expected – totally unsuccessfully.

"Dr. Wilder..." He says my name in the kind of way a voice-over might announce a character in a cheesy movie. "How was the date?"

He's raising his brows suggestively at me. I'm not sure why he doesn't just tell me how my date went, because I have a pretty strong hunch that Violet would have been straight on the phone to Lucy the moment I dropped her home.

I consider blowing him off, but I can't do it. The guy is just too likeable – he and Lucy both are, and right now his obvious excitement is infectious.

"It was good," I reply as a grin breaks out on my face, and I find that, surprisingly, I actually *want* to talk about my evening.

I don't know Emmett all that well, or him I, but he seems to know me well enough to realise that this revelation is a win, albeit a small one.

"She's pretty incredible once you get past her defences, huh?"

He may not know *me* all that well, but it seems he does know Violet, and cares a lot about her too. It's sweet, and I'm happy to know she has such good friends. There's something about her that makes me think she deserves them.

She's a guarded woman, but when her mask slips and you see the real her, it's a beautiful thing to witness.

She's a bit like me in a lot of ways; we're both what I would consider to be old souls. I don't know her story yet, but I get the feeling that she's lived through a lot more life in her twenty-five years than most people have.

"I had a really good time with her."

"You seeing her again?"

One thing I've learnt about Emmett is that he's as straight up and to the point as they come. He doesn't beat around the bush and I like that about him. I prefer to know where I stand with people.

I haven't had much in the way of friends in the past few years and there's something about the big man in front of me that makes me think that maybe I've found one.

"I hope so," I tell him, because honestly, I want nothing more than to see her again. The idea of peeling back another layer of Violet intrigues me in a way that nothing else does.

I'm looking forward to being back in her company already, and that's a *big* deal for me – I haven't looked forward to something that isn't work in a very long time.

"I plan to call her today."

"That's good..."

"I hope it will be."

He seems like he has more he wants to say, so I wait for him to get it off his chest.

"She's been through a lot, doc, so if you're going to see her again, don't expect it to be all smooth sailing." He's still wearing a smile, but I can tell this is a serious statement.

I nod as he walks away, his warning heeded.

This conversation has only enforced the feeling that there's something special about Violet – something that I know nothing about.

I stroll around aimlessly for a while after that; I'm not even rostered on, and I'm ninety percent confident I won't be having any unexpected deliveries today, but I still seem to find myself here anyway.

Wandering the halls has become therapeutic for me. It's bizarre really. Most people, after a trauma, will avoid places and things that remind them of that event, but apparently, I'm not wired right, because I don't operate that way.

I work in the same hospital that my sister passed away in. I still walk the same halls I walked as I tried to accept that she was really gone, and I still linger outside the window of the girl whom I never got to meet.

The girl with the crystal blue eyes...

A visual of Violet smiling and giggling softly last night, the deep dimples visible in her cheeks, hits me like a wrecking ball and I nearly drop to my knees.

She's looking down at the table, but when she glances up to meet my gaze, the same eyes from my memory are looking back at me.

***

It's funny how when you're doing something you shouldn't be, you feel like everyone is looking at you.

They aren't really, but the feeling of eyes on you is suddenly very real.

I know this is a total breach of her privacy, and that I could be fired for doing this, but there's just something about Violet that I need to know, and the more I think about her and her familiar eyes, the more concerned I become.

I've never been a person that's able to let things like this go – so here I am, risking my career, because there's something in a woman's eyes that makes me feel like I've found my way back home.

I type her name into the search bar and peer out my door once more before hitting 'enter'.

I'm pretty sure I mutter a curse word as her file appears on my computer screen.

It's a *mile* long; in fact, I'm not sure I've ever seen a medical history quite this large in all the years I've been practising. Violet Miller has had more hospital stays than I've had hot dinners and that can't mean anything good.

I don't want to violate her privacy any more than I've accepted I need to, but I can't help looking at the first entry ever made – the one from the day she was born.

My hands shake as I read the doctor's notes.

It's her heart.

I know without looking what the rest of this will say... open heart surgery, probably infections, more open heart surgery, medication... and eventually maybe a transplant.

She's twenty-five now, and I hope to God that she's already got the heart she needs. Considering her colouring and the spring in her step, I'm almost certain she has, and I breathe a deep sigh of relief because of it.

I find what I'm looking for in a matter of minutes – the reason I feel like I've seen her and those eyes of hers before is because I *have*.

The month and year leap out at me and slap me clean across the face.

She was here while my sister was dying.

She was here on the same date that brings me to the brink of insanity annually.

She was here when I began wandering the hallways not knowing where to turn.

She was here when I first watched the girl with the crystal blue eyes who looked like she was on the verge of death – she *was* that girl... she *is* that girl.

I don't even read the notes that accompany that particular hospital stay – it doesn't matter what they say, what matters is that it *was* her.

I close the file down as fast as I can and rest my head in my hands.

This only confirms what I already knew.

Violet is the girl with the beautiful eyes. The girl who gave me hope in the darkest of all my hours, and I don't know if I'm more shocked with the revelation, or the fact that I didn't put it together sooner.

Chapter Thirty-Five

Violet

"Has he called you yet?"

I roll my eyes at my best friend's ridiculous persistence.

"It's not even midday; give the guy a chance, would you?"

"He had a great time. It sounds like you two really hit it off."

I groan. "How on earth do you know he had a good time?"

"Emmett saw him at work, so he quizzed him, then he called me. Duh."

Of course he did. I don't know why I would have expected anything less – frankly I should probably just be grateful that Lucy didn't go ahead and call him herself.

"You two have been watching too many of those love match shows. You're both totally out of control, you know that, right?"

She laughs, and the sound is soft and tinkling.

She doesn't say anything more and we both know it's only a matter of time before I crack.

"Fine." I let out a resigned sigh. "Are you going to tell me what he said or not?"

Lucy doesn't require any further encouragement before she eagerly launches into a total re-enactment of the encounter.

I know her and Emmett well enough to know that the details of this story will be strongly inflated and possibly entirely inaccurate, but still, I listen with bated breath and all the excitement of a teenager talking about her first boyfriend. Because frankly, he might not be my boyfriend just yet, but he *is* near the top of a very short list of dates that I've had in my twenty-five years.

"Did you tell him about... you know, your heart and stuff?" Lucy asks me quietly and I feel a pang of guilt in my gut.

It's not that I think I owe him the story – not yet anyway, if I see more of him, then yeah... I'll need to explain to him the reality of my life.

But not having told him yet *isn't* why I feel guilty.

I feel guilty because of the reason I didn't tell him.

I didn't tell him because he's the man from my dream... my premonition, my life flashing before my eyes... whatever you want to call it... *he's* the one.

He's the one whose eyes stayed with me as I found my way back to life instead of disappearing into death.

He's the one who I've dreamed of nearly every night since.

I don't know what I would have said. I have no idea what I could possibly say to him that wouldn't send him running for the hills – so instead I said nothing.

There's also guilt because I've never told Lucy all of this.

She's my best friend, has been since we were babies, and this is the one and only thing I've never shared with her.

I don't even know why. Maybe one day I will bring her in on my secret, but for now at least, I know I'm not ready.

The only person I've talked about those moments with is Auggie, and suddenly I'm filled with an overwhelming desire to talk to my big sister.

"I didn't tell him," I respond quietly. "I will… if it goes anywhere, I'll tell him."

"I know you will, Letty."

"I still can't believe you forgot to mention that you actually know him," I grumble, hoping that I'll succeed in changing the subject.

"Well, technically, he knows my lady bits better than he knows me, so I didn't think I needed to mention it."

I groan again. "I really did not need a visual of the man I was kissing last night, looking at your lady bits."

"Um… back the truck up. *Kissing*? Now who's holding out on information, huh? You conveniently forgot to mention that you were locking lips with the hot doctor now, did you?"

I intentionally left that part out when I was texting Lucy last night. She'd barely managed to refrain from asking me five thousand questions when I let her and Emmett know they were relieved of their chaperone duties, and the minute I got home she jumped right back into it.

Lucy is *all* about the questions.

I laugh into the phone. "Cut the fake outrage, I'm telling you now."

"Oh, you bet your ass you are. I want all the details, right now."

I smile and revel in the feeling of being normal, even just for a few moments.

***

"Hey, stranger." I lean in and whisper hoarsely in August's ear as I approach from behind her.

She startles so easily, and I just can't help myself.

"I told you to stop doing that to me!" she cries once she realises it's me and not some creep trying to hit on her.

"And I keep telling you that I've lived this long for a reason, and if driving my sister crazy isn't one of them, then I just don't know what it is I'm meant to do with my life."

"You *really* need a boyfriend," she tells me as I sit down opposite her.

I smirk. "Well if I *did* have a boyfriend it would have made my date last night pretty awkward now, wouldn't it?"

Her jaw drops. "Did I just hear the word *date* come out of your mouth?"

"You did."

"Oh my God, who? Where? How did this happen? Who is he? When can I meet him?"

I take a sip of her coffee. "Calm down."

"But I have *so* many questions."

I laugh. She wouldn't be August if she didn't. Between my best friend and my sister, I could spend the rest of my life answering questions.

"It was a blind date, courtesy of Lucy and Emmett."

"How the hell did they get you to agree to that? I've been trying for years." She pouts at me.

"Does it really matter?"

"I tried to get you to go out with that guy I met in class and you wouldn't do it."

I roll my eyes. "Focus, Auggie."

She's not really listening to me, she's picking the information she wants out of my words, while ignoring everything she deems irrelevant.

"Who was the guy?"

She scowls at me when she reaches for her coffee and it's not there.

I hand the cup back and grab one of the little packets of sugar from the jar in the centre of the table.

I'm nervous, and when I'm nervous I fiddle with things... anything to keep my hands busy.

"That's actually what I wanted to talk to you about..."

She must notice that I'm uneasy about it because she puts down her cup and gives me her full attention.

"What did he do?" she demands.

August may be a lot of things, but deep down I know she'd go to the ends of the earth to hunt someone down if they hurt me. Thankfully her services won't be required today.

"It's nothing like that."

"Why don't you tell me how it is then?" She narrows her eyes at me.

I go back to picking at the label on the sugar packet. "Do you remember back before my transplant when my heart stopped?"

"I think I'm familiar," she answers, her lips tight.

No one in my family likes talking about that time in my life.

It took me a long time to comprehend just how close they'd come to losing me.

Hearing that my whole family had sat in a waiting room for hours with no clue if I was alive or dead was absolutely heart breaking.

"Do you remember me telling you about what happened... what I saw?"

We haven't talked about this for four years, so I'm half expecting her to have no recollection of it at all; she is Auggie after all.

"You seriously think I'd forget my little sister's vision of her future?"

I shrug.

"I remember, Vi. The baby, the guy with the blue eyes..."

"You called him the man of my dreams," I prompt her.

She looks proud of herself. "I did."

"I never told you this, but I saw him... in person, he was outside in the hallway when I woke up from my transplant."

Her eyes widen, and I can tell she's about to bombard me with questions.

"I didn't tell you because I knew you'd freak out, and to be honest, I wasn't entirely sure I didn't dream the whole thing up," I explain before she has the chance to speak.

"Why are you telling me this now?"

I don't answer her right away.

She reaches across the table and pulls the now shredded packet from my hands.

"Spill it, Vi."

"It was *him*…my date was with him," I whisper.

I hear her gasp.

"You've got to be shitting me?" She gapes at me in disbelief.

I huff out a little laugh and shake my head. "I shit you not."

"How? What? I don't get it…. what? But how? I can't deal, I just can't…"

She's rambling now, and I almost suggest my five, four, three, two, one method to her, but think better of it.

Auggie needs information and she needs it right now.

"He's a doctor. He works at Royal West with Emmett; so that could explain why he was there in the hallway after my transplant," I offer.

"Hold the phone. He's a *doctor*?" she asks quickly, and I laugh. Just like that, August's back.

"*Yes*, he's a doctor, and yes he's handsome, tall *and* he's a gentleman, before you ask."

"Holy crap, did you marry him?"

I know she's joking, but just those words put me right back in the pressure cooker.

I can't explain why, but all I know is that this is so important, *all* of it – I can feel it in my bones.

"You're sure it's him?"

"I've got no doubt. I'd know those eyes anywhere."

"Well… heck…"

It's not often in my life that I've seen August lost for words, but right now is one of those moments.

"Maybe he was one of your doctors; you said it yourself that he works there... you could have woken up for a while and seen him before they got you back under. That can happen, right?"

It's not a bad theory, and it's one I have considered over the past few years, but I've always known it's not what happened.

"He's an obstetrician, so that'd be a little weird."

She nods in agreement.

"Okay, so did you tell him?"

She says it as though it'd be as casual as mentioning the weather.

"Of course I didn't tell him! He'd probably submit me for a psych evaluation."

"He might be a spiritual guy..." She shrugs.

He'd have to be a little more than spiritual to think this was normal.

"I haven't told him anything about *anything* yet. It was just one date, Auggie."

"Has he called you today?"

I groan. "You sound just like Lucy. *No.* He hasn't called yet. Maybe he never will. I probably wouldn't. I've got more baggage than a freaking airplane's cargo hold."

She raises her brows at me. "You done with your pity party?"

"I'm not sure." I pout back at her.

For someone who basically lives in a constant state of self-involvement, August has always been the first to tell me to snap out of it when I'm feeling down on myself.

Whether that's because she doesn't like me feeling that way, or because she'd rather I was focusing on her instead of me, I'm not sure, but either way, it's hard to feel too down in the dumps when she's around.

"Don't be such a sad sack. Besides, think of it this way, if he doesn't call you, you can't even blame it on your heart, because you didn't tell him about it."

"Thanks for that. So if he doesn't call it's just due to the fact that I'm terrible company then?"

She winks at me. "*Exactly*."

"That makes me feel *so* much better," I deadpan.

She smirks at me. "Don't say I never do anything for you."

We sit in silence for a moment as the drink I ordered is brought over to our table.

"So, what are you going to do, Vi?"

I don't have an answer for that. I can't possibly. I don't even know if Rylan wants to see me again, and until I do, it's all a moot point.

It sure seemed like he was interested, but considering I don't know a single thing about romance with boys, let alone men, I really can't be sure.

I don't particularly want to agonise over a decision that may never be required from me at all.

"I think I'm just going to wait and see what happens."

She nods in acceptance and sips from her cup again.

"I still can't believe it's him." She breathes out a breath of disbelief, and I know exactly how she feels.

I'd felt the same way when I looked into his eyes last night.

"I know you don't really believe in fate and things that are 'meant to be', but it might be time you started to think again." She says the words quietly, and that's how I know she means them.

And to be honest, she's not wrong about it either.

One short evening with Rylan Wilder has made me re-think everything I thought I was sure about.

Chapter Thirty-Six

Rylan

I don't know how I'm supposed to feel after what I've just seen.

I know damn well that most men would run a mile when faced with a woman that lives with the things Violet does every single day.

But then I've never really been like 'most men'.

I'm shaken by what I saw, undoubtedly, but what's really rattled me most is the fact that Violet is *the girl*. She's the one I watched all those years ago, and I don't know how to process that, or what to make of it.

Strange coincidences happen in the world, and I get that, but this doesn't feel like one of those times.

I've experienced instances in my life where everything has just felt like it's falling into place – like I'm exactly where I'm supposed to be.

I felt that way when I stood outside her room all those years ago, after my sister died.

It scared me then, and the thought of it still confuses me now.

I felt it again last night, when I held Violet's hand and kissed her under the moonlight. Only this time, I didn't feel fear – I felt relief.

I've got so much to learn about her, and her, I, but hell, I want to know it *all*.

She's probably been put in the too hard basket by people her entire life, and I don't want to be the guy that does that to her too.

Hell, I'm not even sure if it actually bothers me.

I'd be lying if I said I hadn't thought about her situation at all. I don't have any real idea what her condition is like, or how her heart is responding to whatever treatment she's received over the years.

There's no quick fix. There are procedures, surgeries and medication – but the battle she's facing is a lifelong one. Even a new heart can't last her forever, if she's got one, that is.

I desperately want to open her file again and find out her entire medical history, but I can't.

I like Violet. I respect her, and I've already violated her privacy far more than I ever should have.

I vow to myself that I'll never go behind her back for anything like this ever again. If she wants me to know something – she'll tell me herself.

I know it's the right decision, but it's one that doesn't help ease my apprehension in the slightest.

I'm scared for her. I don't know how I couldn't be.

I felt something for that woman last night, something *real,* and if I can feel like that after only a few short hours, I can't even imagine what a whole day with her could do to my head.

I want to find out everything there is to know. I want to spend many more days talking and laughing, but the harsh reality is, I don't know how many days she's got. I doubt anyone does.

The doctor in me tries to analyse the situation with rational thought and logic, but already I'm past the point of rational when it comes to Violet.

I know there's no real choice for me.

I *have* to see her again.

She evoked emotion in me that I'd long thought was dead and buried, and I need to feel that way again.

I *need* to see her and her beautiful eyes... and above all else I need to figure out exactly why she already feels so vitally intertwined with my life.

Chapter Thirty-Seven

Violet

"Hello?"

My voice comes out breathless and rushed as I answer my phone.

I know it's him on the other end of the line, and that knowledge makes my heart beat frantically against my rib cage, like it's trying to make its escape.

"Hey, Violet, it's Rylan..."

"You called," I reply stupidly, because frankly, I'd convinced myself that he wasn't going to.

"Did you really think I wouldn't?"

I shrug before realising he can't actually see the action.

I really am terrible at this dating thing.

"I wasn't sure, but I hoped you would..." More truths – they seem to just fall from my lips where he's concerned.

"I like that." I can hear the smile in his voice.

I'm lying on my back across my bed, my legs dangling off the side, and I feel the way I imagine the teenage girl in movies does when she's talking to the captain of the football team.

My heart is racing and there's butterflies going crazy in my stomach.

"Well I like that you called," I reply lamely.

He laughs lightly down the phone.

Neither of us seems to know what to say, and this is beyond awkward, but there's still nowhere I'd rather be than here, with him on the other end of the phone.

"I had a really good time last night."

"I heard." I giggle.

Lucy and Emmett are an unstoppable force of nature. There was never any way that Rylan was going to be able to escape unscathed.

He laughs again, louder this time and it makes my smile grow wider. "Emmett isn't really one for personal boundaries, is he?"

"Pffft." I snigger. "You think *he's* bad, you should hear what I've been dealing with since I walked in the door last night. Lucy's been asking every five minutes if you've called me yet."

"You'll have to tell her I'm sorry for keeping her waiting, I ended up at work all day."

"I'll be sure to pass that on." I laugh. "So did you have any deliveries today?"

"Not today... actually I didn't really *need* to be at work, but you'll probably learn that taking time away from the hospital isn't something I'm very good at."

I bite down on my lip, my smile so wide I'm a little afraid my face might split in half.

He's just implied that I will get to know him better, and whether or not he intended for it to come across that way or not, it's how I've taken it.

"You think I'll get to learn about you?"

"I hope so, Violet. I plan on learning a lot about you." His voice sounds hoarse, and there's a sincerity there that I can't possibly deny.

I can understand in this moment why people are so eager to date and to fall in love. This feeling of excitement and euphoria is like nothing I've ever experienced.

For the first time in a long time, I welcome it; I think that maybe I might finally feel ready to put myself out there.

Rylan is like no one I've ever met before, and he's a far cry from the guys I've been turned down by in the past.

He's mature, kind and gentle. He's not some silly little boy, he's a man.

"What are you doing right now?"

I glance at the clock next to my bed. It's seven on Saturday evening, and my plans consist of nothing at all, as do most of my Saturday nights.

"I'm lying on my bed, with not a thing on the agenda."

There's silence for a moment, and when he speaks I can hear the smile in his voice.

"Do you want to go for a walk with me?"

I don't even have to think about it, I've never heard a better idea in my life.

***

"This is my favourite spot. I've seen a lot of places, but nothing comes close to this."

He's right, this *is* a beautiful sight.

We're up on a clifftop along the coast, and considering it was only a half-hour walk up here, I don't know how I've never done it before.

I'm a little short of breath, and while it's frustrating, it's nothing out of the ordinary for me.

The sun is beginning to lower in the sky; soon it'll set. The ocean is calm and glistening, and the clean waves are crashing against the sandy shore.

The smell of the sea air is so relaxing; I close my eyes for a moment and just breathe it in.

That's one positive about coming so close to death – you learn to appreciate the little things.

I'm not sure I would have ever stopped to smell the flowers, or lie in the long grass, or chat with strangers if not for the condition I've lived with for twenty-five years.

I don't take a single moment for granted anymore, and I certainly wouldn't dream of taking this particular tick of the clock for anything other than the miracle it is.

I breathe deeply and take a second to acknowledge just how lucky I am to be here, alive and well, and when I open my eyes, Rylan's looking at me with a stare that asks so many questions, but at the same time, understands so much.

"It's sort of sobering up here, isn't it?"

I nod my head and look out at the horizon. "I've never felt so small or insignificant."

Out here in the cool evening air, with no one else around, is so refreshing. It makes me realise what a little part of the universe I really am.

In my world, everything is always about me and my health, my good days and my bad ones; it's all about my heart.

But not out here... out here I'm just a woman looking at the sea.

Most people wouldn't like the idea of being a no one, but for the most part I'd be happy to be of little significance.

All my life I've felt like some type of experiment. No one ever knew what to expect from one day to the next and it was always a case of trying something out and then waiting to see what happened.

It's been one big high-risk game of trial and error, where the ideal outcome is that I live, and in the worst case – I die.

"There's some serious thinking going on in that head of yours."

He startles me; for a moment I forgot he was right here next to me.

I can feel the weight of his stare on me again and I can't help but marvel at the fact that when faced with such an in-credible view, he's still choosing to look at me instead.

"I've got a lot to think about," I say as I turn to face him.

"Anything I can help you with?"

His smile is so sweet and genuine I seriously consider taking him up on his offer.

I *could* tell him. I could open my mouth and let the words all fall out. It's not that I don't trust him with the in-formation, but I can't bring myself to taint this picture-per-fect moment.

The golden sun is sinking out of view behind him and I don't want to ruin this small lapse in time.

"I think one day you might be able to."

He smiles at me and looks down at his shoes before meeting my eyes again.

I'm learning this is how he reacts when I give him an answer that he likes – one that really speaks to his soul.

"Violet?" he says quietly as he looks out at the ocean.

"Yeah?"

"You could *never* be insignificant."

He reaches for me and as the sun disappears from sight, I'm left standing in the dim light with my hand held in his.

Chapter Thirty-Eight

Rylan

I can't even remember the last time I had what I would call a *good* dream.

It's not that my nights are filled with nightmares or the stuff from horror films, but I haven't had that feeling where you wake up smiling in a really long time.

But I'm smiling now, and I know Violet is the reason for that.

Last night was even better than the first we spent together.

I can't recall a time where I've felt so content in someone's presence.

She's not like others. She's got more depth than half the people I've met thus far in life put together, and when I talk, she listens, *really* listens to the words I'm saying... but more than that, I think she understands my reasons for saying them too.

She's funny, considerate and so, *so* beautiful.

I can't stop myself from looking at her. I know she notices it; the stain of blush on her cheeks assures me she's aware, but she's not once complained.

I smile again as I picture her hand in mine. My skin still tingles in the spot where it met hers. It's unbelievable really;

I never thought a walk and a scoop of ice cream could bring me so much happiness.

Happiness... it's something I wasn't sure I'd truly experience again. My sister dying sort of sucked all the joy from my life, but ever since I met Violet, I feel it again.

It's there.

And when I kissed her goodbye, under the stars and the moon once again, I'd felt the last of my reservations slip away.

She is the girl with the blue eyes – the girl who gave me hope.

I've got no choice but to see where this goes, and even if I did have the ability to choose, I know that she's what I'd decide on.

This is one of those situations in life where it seems as though it's less about me making a choice, than it is about a choice making me.

I've had moments since I made this realisation where I don't understand why I couldn't have met her *then*, why we couldn't have had the past three years to get to know each other instead of just the past few days.

The past three days have been better than I thought was possible, whereas I've *endured* these past three years.

There's no other way to describe it. I get by okay now, but when I'm with Violet, it doesn't feel like just 'getting by', it feels like living.

I realise in an instant that it doesn't matter why or how this has all come to be, all that matters is that she's here – that she's in my life *now*.

Maybe it is fate – Daisy was always a big believer in fate.

Maybe this is our time.

Maybe I wasn't meant to meet her three years ago... neither of us were in a place where we could have been ready for another person in our lives... but I think we're both there now.

I think I'm ready for not only someone, but for *her*... I hope to God that she's ready for me too.

She's on my mind so constantly, there's no space for darkness anymore.

Once again, *she* is my light.

Chapter Thirty-Nine

I scrawl the word 'happiness' on the back of the canvas and collapse into my chair with a thud.

I'm so totally exhausted, but at the same time, I've never felt so alive.

My eyes can barely stay open, and I know I'll be paying for pulling this all-nighter for days to come, but as I turn the canvas around and look at it one more time, I know it was all worth it.

It's everything he's making me feel, exposed and raw on the surface in front of me.

I've felt a lot of things in my life, but never anything that's come close to this.

I can't tell if this is what it always feels like when you meet someone you like, or if this is something more than that... I'm too inexperienced to know.

My gut tells me it's more – that this is *so* much more than some crush, but I'm scared to say it out loud, I'm scared to do anything that might jinx it. The last thing I want is to tar this with my usual bad luck brush.

I want this to be real.

I remember the way Lucy was when she met Emmett, I'd never seen her so smitten. She fell in love with that man the moment she met him, and she still loves him just as fiercely now.

I've never given much thought to the concept of soul mates before, but when I look at the two of them, it's a hard notion to deny.

I've wondered for a long time if I'd ever find love. I know it's worried my mum a lot too.

I guess as a parent, you sort of just assume that one day your children will find someone to cherish them. Most parents probably just hope that when their future son or daughter-in-law is chosen, that they're a good person.

My mum's worries run a little deeper... as do mine.

There are all the normal considerations, like personality, looks and chemistry, but I've got the added pressure of finding someone who is equally as considerate as they are good looking, and as accepting as they are funny.

Not everyone out there has it in them to love those of us who aren't quite 'normal', and finding someone who loves me, despite the state of my heart, was never going to be a simple task.

I think of myself as a bit of a hazard.

Loving me carries so much risk. I read a book when I was younger, and the main girl talks about herself and her illness as being like a grenade – that one day she'll blow up and that everyone in her life will be casualties.

I feel that on a deep level. That's the reality of my life a lot of the time. I can't fathom that the value of knowing me is worth the risk of the fallout from losing me.

Mum, Dad, Charlie and Auggie, they don't really have an option... you can't choose your family, and they're stuck with me whether they like it or not.

Lucy though... she's here by choice. Nobody tells Lucy what to do – and believe me, I've tried. She's as stubborn as an old goat and there's no way she's going anywhere.

She really is the best friend a girl could ask for.

And then there's Rylan... I know we've only been on two dates, but it feels like so much more than that.

We share a connection.

I know I'm going to have to tell him soon... and when I do, he'll probably flee. Any sane person probably would.

I hope for his sake that he does.

I can already tell he's an incredible man. He's got so much going for him, and his future shines so bright it's like looking directly into the sun.

He deserves someone who can give him so much more than I can.

A family, good health, time...

None of those things are promised to me.

Not one doctor has been able to tell me what *my* future holds.

There's statistics and averages, possibilities and chances, but none of those things are guaranteed and they're certainly not certain.

All I can do is hope for the best.

I guess I'm one of the lucky ones when I think about it.

I lasted twenty-one years before my heart really tried to kick the bucket, and it took less than a year to find a new heart for me – which, in the scheme of things, isn't all that long.

I've made it three years past transplant now, and the chances of my body rejecting the organ are significantly reduced.

There's a long list of risks and problems that can arise from having a heart transplant, but so far, I've got by okay – a couple of infections my body had trouble fighting off, a little bit of emotional trauma, and one significant hospital stay... but all in all, it's been pretty uneventful in comparison to the year that preceded my transplant.

I don't know how long this heart will last me, or whether it might just give up on me one day... I don't know if I'll need another transplant or if medical science will evolve to the point where there's another option.

It's all the unknown. My whole life is one big unknown.

Rylan has everything going for him. He's smart, attractive, kind and funny – he's a doctor for crying out loud.

He could have any woman he wanted.

I know that worrying about this is probably totally unnecessary, but I can't seem to help it – maybe I did inherit some personality traits from my mother after all.

I know that Rylan might decide to wake up tomorrow and never contact me again. Rationally, I understand that, but I've got my hopes up and for someone who has spent her whole life *not* getting her hopes up, this is a big deal for me.

It's clear there's only one thing for it.

I have to tell him.

I need to make sure he's fully informed about me and my life before I let myself or him get anymore invested.

Sometimes the only way to move forward is by going back.

***

"I'm going to tell him."

Lucy looks up from her lunch in surprise. "What? Already?"

I stare at her in confusion. I could have sworn this was the same Lucy that was telling me I shouldn't keep it a secret any longer.

"I thought you wanted me to tell him?"

"I *do*," she blurts out quickly. "I *totally* think you should tell him. I'm just surprised that you're agreeing to it so early in the piece... that's all."

"I mean... I dunno... I think he needs to know." I shrug.

She narrows her eyes at me as she sets her knife down, and now I know I'm in for it. Lucy – especially a pregnant Lucy, doesn't let *anything* come between her and her food. I watched Emmett attempt to take a French fry off her plate the other day and he was lucky to make it out of there without her fork stabbed into his arm.

"What do you mean by that?"

I avoid her stare and push my own food around my plate.

"*Violet...*" she warns me when I don't answer.

"I just think he should know what he's getting himself into, okay? I'm damaged goods, and I'd hate for him to start to like me and then change his mind once he found out. I'd rather it happen before then."

I'm looking right at her now so I don't miss the softening of her eyes.

"Oh, Letty… that's not going to happen…"

"You don't know that."

She goes to repeat her statement of denial again but stops herself. "You know what, you're right. I *don't* know, but I do know that he's a good man, a really good man… *and* a doctor – a little bit of a heart defect shouldn't be able to scare him off."

I can't help but laugh at Lucy's downplaying of my condition. I know she's not being serious and I also know she's achieved exactly what she set out to do – she's made me smile.

"Please don't write him off just yet, let *him* be the one who decides to stay or go – don't make that choice for him."

She's right. I'm doing what has become habit for me – I'm expecting the worst.

Maybe just this once I should try hoping for the best instead and see what comes of it.

I'm staring at my plate, quietly contemplating what to do when she speaks again.

"You really like him then?"

Once again, she's hit the nail on the head.

Telling him is as much about me as it is about him.

Yes, I want him to know the whole truth, so he can make his own choices, but I also want him to know so that I can limit the damage to my own heart if he walks away. I'm aware that I'm getting invested in him already, and I don't want to catch any more feelings if he's just going to leave me.

"I've never felt this way, Luce. I'm really scared."

She reaches for my hand and gives it a squeeze. "It's good to be scared sometimes... it means you're alive."

I like that she doesn't try to dig for more information, I know that she will, but for now she knows I need the support of my best friend, not the full Spanish Inquisition.

"I've got a good feeling about him, Violet."

I've got lots of feelings about him too – but that doesn't help my nerves in the slightest, in fact if anything, I think it makes it worse.

Chapter Forty

Rylan

To: Rylan
From: Violet
Okay, there's something I have to ask...

I'm smiling at my phone like some kind of crazy person. Thankfully I'm in the privacy of my exam room, so no one can see me anyway, but honestly, I'm not sure anything could wipe the smile off my face right now – not even my colleagues thinking I'd lost my mind entirely.

This light-hearted banter has been going on for the past hour or so, and it's lucky really that I'm here in my spare time again and not on shift, because I'm not sure I'd be able to focus on anything other than Violet and her messages.

My phone beeps indicating another text has arrived, and I smile even bigger as I anticipate her question.

To: Rylan
From: Violet

So you look at... you know... *lady parts* all day... I mean wouldn't you get sick of seeing that... like in your personal life?

I laugh out loud at that one.

I can almost see her blushing from here. She's adorable really.

To: Violet

From: Rylan

You know what; it *is* just vagina all day around here... it's really a wonder I haven't turned gay over it.

I wait for her reply almost anxiously. I'm not sure how she'll respond to my teasing.

To: Rylan

From: Violet

You just made me spit a mouthful of water across the room, so touché... I'll give you ten points for that one. I'll also take that as a no to my question.

I'm thinking about how incredible she is when another text comes through before I have a chance to reply.

To: Rylan
From: Violet
P.s. While I have no issue with gay men, I'm really glad you aren't one.

She's funny too.

No one has made me smile like this in years, and here she is, making me laugh without even trying.

I'm dying to see her again; she's like an addiction I can't satisfy.

To: Violet
From: Rylan
I like you, Violet Miller.

Her reply is instantaneous.

To: Rylan
From: Violet
I like you too, Rylan Wilder.

***

"What are you doing tomorrow?"

Her eyes are bright and excited and it's infectious. When she smiles, I smile.

I've got a strong suspicion that whatever Violet was feeling, I'd feel it too. It's like there's a direct link between her emotions and mine.

It might be invisible to the eye, but I *feel* it... it's there, and while it terrifies me, it also excites me like nothing else.

"I've got the day off tomorrow actually."

I don't know why she's asking, but it doesn't matter, if there's anything on offer, I'll take it.

I had to work the last two days, and they were the longest days of my life. Knowing I had a date with Violet waiting for me tonight made the hours seem to drag on forever. I can't recall a time when I was actually more eager for something outside of the hospital, rather than something within it.

"Perfect." She grins at me as I open the door into the bowling alley – our destination for the evening. "I've got somewhere I want to take you."

She's so pretty when she smiles. It lights up her whole face and causes those deep dimples in her cheeks that I'm beginning to crave.

"I'm intrigued."

"I'll pick you up, okay?"

"Tour guide *and* chauffer, huh?"

"At your service." She winks.

She strolls off ahead of me and I find myself following along behind her like a little puppy dog.

"Are you not going to tell me where we're going?"

She turns back to face me, her eyes sparkling with mischief.

"I bet you're one of those people that hate surprises, am I right?"

She's *exactly* right. I thoroughly dislike them, but I'm not about to tell her that.

I like to have a plan. I get enough of the unknown and unexpected with my job, so I tend to avoid it in my personal life – when I actually bother to have a personal life that is, but I already know I'll make some type of exception for her.

"Me?" I make a show of balking at her statement. "I *love* surprises."

She giggles, and I'm filled with warmth. "You're a terrible liar."

She's right about that too. I always have been... my sister always said I couldn't lie to save my life.

It bothered me as a child, but now I like to think of it as one of my better qualities.

I give the young girl behind the counter the name on the bowling lane I've pre-paid for. Violet has been making a good show of insisting that she was going to be treating *me* to this date but there was no way I was going to let her hand over a cent.

It's not that I'm stuck in the dark ages, but in my mind, when a man is courting a woman, *he* should pay for the privilege.

That's how my grandfather courted my grandmother and how my father courted my mother.

It's the way I want to do it too.

Violet pouts at me when she realises what I've done. "Rylan! I told you *I* was paying today."

"You're going to have to be faster than that then." I wink at her and she scrunches up her nose in frustration.

She hurriedly hands her credit card to the girl. "I'm paying for the snacks then."

The girl, 'Kate' according to her name badge, grimaces. "Ummm... he's kind of already ordered *and* paid for all of that too..."

I watch Violet's jaw drop as she turns back to me. "You're impossible... we had a deal."

I shrug and grin. "You might have *thought* we had a deal... I never agreed to let you pay, Violet. Call me old fashioned, but I want to take you out – so I pay, okay?"

"Girl, you should just let him... I mean hell, I wouldn't say no if some cute guy wanted to spoil me."

I shoot Violet a 'see' look.

Violet blushes as she looks between me and Kate, who is now setting our bowling shoes down on the counter.

"Well I can see I'm outnumbered." She sighs. "Fine, thank you, it's very sweet – albeit totally unnecessary," she adds in a grumble.

There's a small smile playing on the corner of her lips and I know she can't hold this grudge for long.

"C'mon..." I grab both pairs of shoes before slinging my arm around her. "I've got a real deal for you."

"And what would that be?"

We approach our lane and I look at her, unable to keep the huge smile off my face. "If I win, you have to tell me where we're going tomorrow."

She laughs. "And if *I* win?"

I think about it for a moment. "If you win... I'll let you pay for our next date."

She blushes again, and her lips turn up in a coy smile – I know she's thinking about the fact that I've just committed to another date, and while she seems pretty damn happy about it, this deal is still very clearly stacked in my favour.

She holds out her hand for me to shake. "Alright then, deal."

***

"You could have told me you were a pro," I grumble. "I got hustled."

She giggles gleefully – I think she's still pretty pleased with herself about her win.

Actually, *win* doesn't quite cut it, she whipped my butt good and proper.

"A deal's a deal, Dr. Wilder. I get to pay for the next date."

It's me who's pouting now.

That'll teach me for underestimating her – I'd been so sure I was going to win the game *and* our little bet.

She's walking backwards so that she's facing me, as we stroll through the park.

I want so badly to find out about her heart; she's so radiant and filled with life, I almost wonder if I looked at the wrong patient's file. If it weren't for the fact that I've seen her, frail and extremely unwell with my very own eyes, I'd probably have decided by now that I *had* made a mistake.

I won't ask her though. I can't. Not without revealing I violated hospital policy or that I somehow know her from a hospital corridor years ago.

Neither of those things are something I want to share at the moment, or perhaps ever, so I just have to wait... wait and hope that she'll trust me enough to tell me when she's ready. There's so much more to her than just her heart, and I can't blame her for wanting to share who she really is as a person before she's forced to confess the thing that's probably defined her for her whole life.

Maybe it's better this way – that I'll learn about her first and her heart later.

I want to know everything about her – the *real* her... and this is probably the best chance I'm going to get.

"Hey... do you want to come and have dinner with me?" she asks unexpectedly, breaking me from my thoughts.

"You mean at your house?"

I'm yet to set foot inside Violet's house, but I want to so badly I have to stop myself from yelling the word 'yes' at her.

"Yeah... I've got a heap of food; it's kinda hard to cook the right amount for just me... I mean if you're not busy..."

She's rambling, and as soon as I recognise it's because she's nervous I'll say no, I almost *do* yell the word at her.

"That sounds perfect, Violet," I interrupt her chatter.

"Yeah?" She looks up at me, her crystal blue eyes filled with hope.

"Yeah."

Chapter Forty-One

I might be a person who tries my hardest not to lie, but I sure was talking complete and utter bullshit when I told him I had 'heaps of food' at home. My cupboards have never looked so bare.

Inviting him over for dinner was not the best plan I've ever had. I just wasn't ready for our time together to end, so I panicked and threw out the first idea I thought of.

Rylan's sitting in my living room, and he's undoubtedly the best-looking thing that's ever walked through my front door – so even though I have nothing but baked beans to feed him, I still have to admit it was definitely worth the little white lie.

He's made himself at home in here. His shoes are off and his jacket is draped over the back of my couch.

I like it – I like it so much I'm actually having trouble focusing on the problem at hand... the fact that it'll be time to start dinner within an hour, and I have next to nothing here to cook for him.

"What are you planning to have for dinner?" he calls out to me, like he can somehow sense my distress from across the room.

I grimace and glance around, hoping for some type of suggestion to jump out at me.

"Well I know how much you like surprises," I reply coyly as I stall for time.

He laughs and the knot in my stomach eases.

"Do you want some help, Vi?"

He's never called me 'Vi' before, and even though most of the people in my inner circle call me either 'Vi' or 'Letty', it's different when it's coming from him.

It feels like a sign of us growing closer – growing together.

It's enough of a sign for me to take a deep breath and let go of some of my nerves.

This isn't a big deal.

He won't care that I have nothing to feed him – I'm yet to meet a male that has an objection to eating takeout and I doubt he'll be any different.

I just need to relax, stop stressing about things that don't matter and enjoy having him here with me while it lasts.

I'm about to admit my predicament and suggest we order Chinese food when I hear my front door open.

"Knock, knock!" calls the familiar voice from *inside* my house. "We're early."

I bring my hand up to my forehead in disbelief. I can't *believe* I forgot what day of the week it is.

It's pizza night tonight.

Lucy and Emmett, along with my *entire* family come over here for pizza every Sunday night.

"Oh *crap*," I mutter under my breath.

I'm not sure if I'm ready for Rylan to meet my family, or more to the point, for my family to subject him to the rounds of interrogation that they're bound to, but at the same time, I can think of nothing worse than him walking back out of my door so soon after arriving.

Rylan obviously hears the unexpected visitor too because he appears in front of me in the kitchen.

He must see the expression on my face because he chuckles. "You forget you were expecting company?"

I groan. "I'm so sorry. It's Lucy and Emmett... we have dinner every Sunday with my *whole* family... I guess it slipped my mind."

He smiles and steps forward to take my hands in his. He intertwines his fingers with mine and looks down at me with the sweetest expression on his face.

"It's okay... we can do this another night. It's no big deal."

All I can think about is stretching up to kiss him – so I do.

My lips meet his in the way I've been craving all day long. He sighs in satisfaction against my mouth and my legs turn to jelly.

"Ooh la la... hello there, good doctor." Lucy's voice comes from behind me, and the intrusion is enough to break our lips apart, but not our eyes.

The brief yet passionate contact tells me everything I need to know – he's right where he should be and there's no way I'm letting him leave now.

"*Stay*," I whisper to him.

***

I can't recall what I was worried about.

It's almost as though he's been part of Sunday night dinner forever. He fits in so effortlessly that I'm waiting for the moment where the penny drops and it all goes wrong.

Sadly, that's what the circumstance surrounding my life has taught me to expect. But for now, at least, everything seems to be going better than I could have hoped for.

My mum *loves* him. Even if she hadn't cornered me in the kitchen earlier to tell me exactly that, I would have known anyway – it's obvious to see that she's absolutely smitten with him.

Charlie's looking at him with total admiration – like he wants to be him when he grows up. Even Auggie is a fan. She told me, and I quote, that 'he really *is* cute... *and* a doctor too', so as far as August goes, that's praise of the highest kind.

My dad hasn't threatened to shoot him if he hurts me like he did to August's first boyfriend, so that too is a win in my book.

Lucy is sitting in her usual spot, watching the whole thing play out like she's some type of cupid genius. She might be awfully smug that things are working out well so far, but I can also see how genuinely thrilled she is that there's finally a man in my life. I know she's been worried; we probably all have – that I'd never find someone to share myself with.

Sure, it's early days yet, and he might run a mile when I tell him the truth, but this is still so much more promising than any other relationship I've had. It's *progress*. And regardless of the result, it's going to be a good learning curve for me.

There's a chance that meeting my family could even work in my favour – maybe it'll help him to separate me from my condition.

Even Lucy's mum is a little bit in love with him.

I should have realised that they would know each other – Linda has been a nurse in the paediatric ward at Royal West since before I was born.

She, Emmett and Rylan all work in the same place so it's like a little hospital reunion in here.

Linda doesn't join us every Sunday, but I can tell she's awfully chuffed that she decided to attend tonight.

I can't even blame her really, Rylan is more than worth looking at, and when he opens his mouth, he only gets more attractive. He's smart and funny and I can't speak for everyone in the room, but I can't help but be drawn into his presence.

Much to my relief, no one has mentioned my heart – not that they often do on these nights, but still, the worry was there.

Considering this evening was entirely forgotten by me, I couldn't have planned it better if I'd tried.

Lucy's mum and my parents have just left, and my brother and sister are about to follow suit.

Everyone seems a little more reluctant than usual to go and I'm under no illusion that there's a reason other than Rylan that's responsible for their hesitation. He's been a hot commodity at this little get together – he's captured the attention of all of us.

Charlie is chewing his ear off about some surf spot down the coast, and to be honest I don't even know if the man

I'm dating knows how to surf or not, but if he doesn't, he's making a really good show of seeming interested in what my younger brother is telling him.

It warms my heart to watch.

August has been quiet tonight, and considering she usually talks more than anybody I've ever met, I'm slightly concerned that she's unwell.

"Auggie."

She's watching our brother and Rylan talking with an inquisitive expression on her face – she doesn't appear to be aware that I've even spoken.

"Auggie."

I break her focus and she looks around, almost as though she's forgotten where she is.

"Huh?"

"Are you alright? You've barely said a word all night."

She shrugs and her gaze flickers back over to Rylan and Charlie before meeting mine. "I'm fine. I guess I'm just curious."

"About Rylan?"

She nods. "He's the man who saved your life..."

Technically it was Dr. White and her team who saved my life that day, but I know what she means – if it weren't for his voice and his eyes, I'm not sure I would have had the strength to hold on and stay.

I hope I get the chance to tell him about it someday – to make him see all that he's done for me before we ever even met.

I hope I get to make sense of it at some point too.

There's no logical explanation as to why it was him I saw, but maybe one day it'll all click into place.

I don't know how it could, but since he came into my life for real, I feel like I don't know anything for certain anymore, other than the fact that *he's* here... and because of him, so am I.

Chapter Forty-Two

Rylan

"*Stay*," she whispers for the second time this evening.

Blush stains her cheeks as she asks her unspoken question.

"I mean it seems silly... I'm picking you up tomorrow anyway..."

I sweep a strand of hair off her forehead.

I've found myself at her front door once again, the two of us alone under the stars.

Her arms are wrapped around my waist, tugging me tight against her, while one of my hands is resting on the back of her neck, the other cupping her jaw.

I'm not sure I'll ever tire of the feel of her mouth on mine. Even now, we've been apart only thirty seconds or so, and I'm already yearning for more.

"It *does* seem silly," I murmur before brushing my lips ever so softly against hers again.

She sighs, a soft, breathy sound that I'm beginning to really love.

I want to stay, God do I want to stay here with her all night, but I won't – that much I already know.

Not yet.

"Oh wow, I've just realised what I've implied..." Her face somehow manages to go a deeper shade of red. "I'm not talking about sex… I just thought we could sleep next to one another…"

I'm biting back a smile as she stumbles over her words, her nerves blindingly obvious.

"I'm digging myself a hole here; can you say something *please*?"

"Breathe, Violet."

She nibbles on the corner of her lip and forces her eyes to meet mine.

She's so beautiful it pains me – she appeals to me in a way no woman ever has.

I can't put my finger on exactly what it is about her that I find so intriguing, it's not just her eyes, but the stories that they tell and the secrets they keep, it's not just her lips, but the way they move and the seduction they exude. Every feature on her face is not only pretty, but filled with depth, knowledge and power too.

To top it all off, she's got absolutely no comprehension of how stunning she is and that only adds to the appeal of her.

"I know you didn't mean sex." I grin at her, both because I'm amused and because I want her to relax.

I never considered for a second that she would be inviting me up to spend the night with her in that way – things might be moving fast, and I might already like her more than any woman I've ever dated, but neither of us is ready for that yet.

When that time does finally come, I'm going to make sure I do it the right way. I've got a pretty strong hunch that Violet isn't equipped with a whole lot of knowledge on this particular topic, so I want to take things slow.

"And even though I can think of nothing more satisfying than having you fall asleep next to me, I think we should take a rain check, okay?"

"You're such a gentleman," she teases.

I might not have been this way my whole life, but she brings the chivalrous side out in me... she makes me want to say and do things that will sweep her off her feet.

"Can I make a confession?" I ask her.

She nods at me and smiles. Those gorgeous little dimples appear in her cheeks and for a second I can't remember what it was I was planning to confess.

She raises her brows in question.

"These past few days, every moment I'm not with you... I'm wishing I was."

She doesn't say anything, but the huge smile on her face is enough of a reply for me.

She's happy, really happy, and that's when it hits me – If I never achieve another thing in this lifetime, then I would still die a satisfied man.

***

Leaving her just now was the hardest thing I've done in a long time.

Especially after meeting her family – they're what a family should be... loving, warm and welcoming.

I've not been part of a family like that in a long time, but I truly felt as though I was tonight. They welcomed me with open arms and made me feel like I belonged there.

I hope I do belong there – right there with her.

Hanging out with her, Emmett and Lucy had been as easy as breathing. I can picture us as two couples, off in the distant future. We're friends – we're in each other's lives constantly. The minute the image hits my mind I realise just how badly I want exactly that.

I want it all. Her family, her friends, but most importantly, I want *her*.

It would have been so easy to stay... to fall asleep with her in my arms, but I *had* to leave.

I know she's beginning to trust me, I can see it in her eyes. Just the fact that she invited me into her home, let alone her bed tells me that.

But she hasn't found the time to tell me about her heart yet – which means she doesn't trust me entirely.

I'm more than aware it's up to me to earn that trust from her.

Nothing comes free in this world and having faith in a person is probably the biggest testament to that.

She needs to understand I'm in this for a long time, not just a good time, and until she does, I'll be kissing her goodnight at her front door and not between her sheets.

The fact that I was able to do it – that I found it within me to walk away from her when I so effortlessly could have stayed, has given me the strength to do something that I haven't done in a long time.

I know it's kind of creepy to visit a cemetery so late at night, but it's been far too long since I was here, and I have a feeling I won't be able to sleep a wink until I've done this.

I need to talk to my sister, and even though I live in the house she once called home, this is the only place that I seem to be able to feel close to her anymore.

It probably makes me appear crazy – coming to a ghost for advice, but I don't have anywhere else to go.

My father's been gone a long, long time. My mother doesn't even recognise me anymore, and I don't have a lot of friends left.

You spend three years drowning in grief, throwing yourself into your work and pushing people away, and eventually they stay there.

I learnt that the hard way.

There's only so much you can do for someone that doesn't want to help themselves, and while, on the outside, I might have appeared to be together and whole – I've actually been anything but.

Daisy was my rock, my sounding board and my best friend. Losing her destroyed me.

And she might be gone, but I still need her now.

I'd give anything to hear her voice again, even just one more time. I know that I won't get to – that miracles like that don't happen in real life, but it doesn't stop me from wishing for it.

I want to tell her about Violet so badly it hurts.

I know she would have loved her. I don't see how anybody couldn't... she's so pure, and sweet and *good*.

She's so damn easy to love.

The realisation that I'm falling for her doesn't scare me the way that I expected it would. My cold, black heart somehow still beats in rhythm and now it's as though it's beating just for her. Ever since she fell into my orbit I've felt a sense of purpose again.

I smile.

I laugh.

I'm enjoying my life – I'm actually living it.

No longer am I just floating through my days. I'm grounded and I'm *feeling*... I'm feeling things I've never felt before.

I approach the spot where my sister was laid to her final rest and I whisper into the darkness.

"I found her, Daisy... I think I've found the one."

Chapter Forty-Three

Violet

"The movies?" He guesses his approximately one hundredth wrong guess.

"Nope." I shake my head. "You really are terrible at this, you know that, right?"

"You mean the aim of the game *isn't* for me to get it repeatedly wrong?"

I haven't told him that I'm only a volunteer at the animal shelter – not a paid employee, so I would imagine that's why he hasn't guessed it's where we're headed.

I'm really nervous about this entire day.

I've decided that today is the day I'm going to tell him about my heart.

I have to – it's time.

I'm starting to feel things for him – *real* things that seem to be boarding the train headed for love.

I don't know how he's feeling about me, but if he's even looking in the same direction as I am, then I need to tell him now before he gets in too deep.

It's not fair to keep him in the dark. Even though life has dealt me a whole series of unfair cards, I still try my hardest to play that hand with respect and dignity – especially where people I care about are concerned, and he's quickly become one of the people on that list.

"Well," he announces. "I'm out of ideas."

I giggle at his perplexed expression. My eyes trace over the curve of his lips as his face breaks into a cheeky grin.

I linger on his blue eyes, the same ones I still picture in my sleep most nights.

My dreams have shifted slightly, where before it was only his eyes and his voice that stayed with me; they've now evolved to include the smile that lights up those eyes, and the warmth of his hand in mine.

The man of my dreams has turned out to be exactly that, and I hope more than anything that he'll still be that man after he learns the truth about me.

"We're here." I grin. "Do you think you might be able to figure it out now?"

He glances around out the window before spotting the sign and laughing – presumably at his own foolishness.

"You're right. I really do suck at this game."

I eye him carefully. "If you'd rather do something else, we can—"

"I can't think of anything else I'd rather do," he cuts me off.

I beam at him. I'm glad he feels that way, because there's nothing I'd rather be doing either.

***

"And this is Smokey, Fluffy and Socks." I point into the enclosure housing three cats, one grey, one ginger and fluffy, and one black with white feet.

He raises his brow at me and smirks. "Original."

I grin. He's not wrong.

"Where did they all come from?" He glances around the large room where we keep all the cats.

I shrug. "Most of them get dumped, some are brought in hurt or unwell, some get taken from their owners... we do our best to fix them up, get them fed and healthy and then find them homes."

He sticks his fingers through one of the gaps and Fluffy rubs up against him.

I can't stop myself from smiling as I watch him scratching under the cat's chin.

There's just something incredibly attractive about a man who's kind to animals.

"Don't you just want to take them all away with you?"

"I have to talk myself out of it every time I leave," I confess.

We stroll past a few more enclosures, heading out towards where they keep the dogs.

There's someone special I want him to meet out there.

"Have you ever given in and taken one home?" He takes my hand in his and swings them between us as he asks.

"Once. I've got a cat, but he hates everyone." I giggle.

He frowns at me. "Why'd you take him then?"

"I dunno. He's just a real grumpy old thing. He hisses if you go near him... he would have been in here forever, and that just made me sad. All he does is sleep all the time, and he eats more than he should, but at least he has a home."

I catch his eye and he's looking at me like I'm something amazing.

I can feel the blush creeping onto my cheeks – it never fails to make an appearance whenever he's around.

I glance over his shoulder and see Avery approaching, and even though I know she's bound to say something that will embarrass me further, I'm so happy that she's here today and she'll get to meet Rylan.

"Hey!" she calls out as she rushes over to us.

I get a half wave and Rylan gets an extended hand. "Hi, I'm Avery, you must be Violet's boyfriend."

The blush I had before is nothing compared to the way my face is flaming now.

"This is Rylan. Rylan, this is my friend Avery," I reply quickly. "Avery is one of the full-time vet nurses here."

I'm hoping to save him from the embarrassment of having to clarify that he's not actually my boyfriend by offering him a piece of information to cling onto.

"I'm Rylan," he confirms as he takes her hand in his. "But between you and me, I like the sound of *Violet's boyfriend* better."

He winks at me and I'm at a loss for words.

The buzzer in Avery's pocket lets out a shrill tone and I'm literally saved by the bell from what was bound to be an awkward interrogation for all involved.

"Gotta go, Violet's boyfriend Rylan." She grins at him and much to my surprise, he grins right back. "It was nice to meet you."

"It was nice to meet you too, Violet's friend Avery."

I don't know precisely what just happened here, but it's making my heart race.

"What?" he questions the perplexed expression I have on my face as I watch her jog off to help out with a new arrival.

"Nothing..." I shake my head.

He looks so happy and carefree; it's a real transformation from the man I met such a short time ago. He's relaxed somewhat and he's more comfortable with me now – he's still got the potential to be intense and smouldering at the drop of a hat, but I like that about him. I actually like it a lot. Being the sole focus of that intensity makes me feel interesting and attractive, and I welcome that feeling.

"She seems nice."

His obvious cheerfulness makes me feel even guiltier for the secrets I'm keeping from him.

I want to be able to call him my boyfriend so badly it almost hurts, but I'm not willing to discuss that label again until he knows what he's getting himself into.

"She is," I agree. "Now come on." I tug on his hand before he can say anything more. "Come say hi to Bear."

Bear is my favourite animal in the whole shelter, and as much as I want him to find a home with people that will love him, I can't imagine this place without him.

"Let me guess, he's big and cuddly?" Rylan drawls.

I don't need to answer, because the dog in question spots me then and comes bounding toward us, all one hundred kilograms of him.

"Bear!" I call to him.

He's so excited to see me, his tail is wagging like crazy as I crouch down to pat and cuddle him.

"When I said big and fluffy, I wasn't imagining it quite to this extreme."

I laugh as Rylan squats down next to me and gets a lick on the face from my best canine friend.

"I think he likes you."

"I like you too, bud, but preferably without your tongue down my throat, huh?" he teases as he scratches the huge St. Bernard on his belly.

"What do you do with him?"

"I normally take him for a walk down to the river..."

I'm not sure how much of his day Rylan was planning to spend in this place with me, but as I watch him with Bear, he certainly doesn't seem in a hurry to get out of here.

"You walk him, or he walks you?" He raises one of his brows at me.

I laugh again, because it's true. I weigh about half of what this big boy does, and if it weren't for the fact that he's decided he's happy to listen to what I say, there's no way I'd be able to make him do anything he didn't want to do.

"It's a bit of both." I giggle.

"How about you pick on someone your own size." He grins at the big dog like they're already best friends.

If I wasn't already falling for this man, I know I would be now.

"Let's go then. Where's his lead, gorgeous?" he asks me over his shoulder.

I don't know if I'm more thrilled that he wants to come with us, or that he called me gorgeous, but either way, I don't speak, I just smile and point.

***

"Urgh, *Bear*!" I cry as he shakes the water out of his long coat right in front of where Rylan and I are seated as we throw sticks into the river for him to fetch.

"Get it, boy." Rylan sends another stick flying into the cool river and Bear bounds off after it.

I smile as I watch him leap in with a splash.

"I've gotta ask... why don't you adopt him? It's obvious you love him."

I've been waiting for this question from him ever since I introduced him to Bear.

There are a few reasons, but I still haven't found the nerve to tell him about my heart, so for now I decide to start with the easiest excuse to explain.

"My place isn't fenced, it'd be no good for him."

I realise just how lame it sounds the moment I say it out loud.

"So build a fence?"

"I'm not exactly known for my construction skills."

He raises a brow at me as though he knows I'm full of crap.

He's right too. If that was all there was to it I would have had the section fenced the moment Bear got brought in to us.

I'd love a dog to keep me company in the big house I call home, but I know I can't take care of him the way he deserves. He'd need walking every day, and if it's too cold for me to go out, or too wet, then Bear would be stuck at home with me instead of getting the exercise he needs.

Then there's my life expectancy, I'm more confident these days, but I've lived with fear in the back of my mind for the past three years that my body would reject my new heart and I'd drop dead.

Bear is only two years old, he's still got a lot of life ahead of him and it wouldn't be fair of me to take him on when I'm not sure I could outlive him.

I try to live my life to the fullest and make the most of the second chance I've been given, and a huge part of me wants to take him home for that very reason alone, but it wouldn't be fair of me – and I can't imagine making such a selfish choice.

I don't realise that I've fallen silent as I watch Bear swimming out towards the stick.

When I look up, Rylan's eyes are watching me intensely, seeing things I'm not sure how to find the courage to explain.

"What's the real problem, Violet?" He asks the question in a soft voice, but there's a hoarse edge to his tone, like he's sensed that bad news is coming his way.

This is it. This is my make or break moment.

I know what I need to do, this is as good of a time as any and I *have* to do this now. I've just got to, as Lucy so diplomatically puts it, 'find my lady balls'.

"There's something I haven't told you." I whisper the words, but he hears me, I know he does.

His eyes never leave mine as he gives me a look that indicates I should carry on.

"I know I should have told you sooner, but I didn't know what *this* was..." I indicate between the two of us. "I promise

I was never trying to deceive you." My voice is louder now, but I'm almost shaking with nerves.

"Violet," he murmurs as he takes my hand in his. "Just take a deep breath and say what you need to say."

"It's a long story," I warn.

"I've got nowhere else to be."

I search his eyes for a hint that he'll run – that what I'm about to tell him might scare him off, but I find nothing to confirm my fears, all I see looking back at me is a tender gaze.

"Tell me," he whispers, his voice sounding like gravel.

So I do.

I tell him about the condition I was born with. I tell him about the surgeries and all the hospital stays. I tell him about my heart transplant and the medication that I take each morning. I tell him why I can't take Bear home with me and what I live with every single day.

I tell him everything except for the part where I nearly didn't make it – I don't tell him about seeing his eyes or hearing his voice. I'm not ready to share that with him yet. If he sticks around after this, which I can't possibly imagine he will, then maybe one day I'll find the courage to confide in him about that too.

When I finally finish spewing out my life story, I'm out of breath. I don't know how long I've been talking for, but Bear is out of the river now and has lay down in the sun to dry... and Rylan, he's still staring at me with the same tender expression he was when I started speaking.

There's no pity in his eyes, there's no anger, resentment or disappointment there either. In fact, if anything, he looks relieved, and I have to wonder if he's known all along that there's something I've been keeping from him.

He's an incredibly insightful man, and it's a possibility I can't discount.

"I'm sorry I didn't tell you sooner, but I just wanted to feel... *normal*, I guess... I wanted to be the woman falling in love with the man for just a little while longer before my heart got in the way."

He's doesn't say a word, just reaches out with his free hand and tentatively places his palm against the spot where my heart beats.

I thought he'd have questions, accusations perhaps... but he's silent. I don't know what this means, but I allow myself to enjoy the moment of what feels a lot like wordless acceptance.

"I can feel it beating."

I don't recall closing my eyes, but upon hearing his whispered voice, my lids flutter open again.

I don't reply, I'm waiting for something, *anything* more from him.

I need him to respond – to tell me that I shouldn't have kept this from him... to tell me that he doesn't want to be with the girl with the broken heart.

He slowly pulls away his hand, and I watch the movement with a fierce intensity.

He's bound to talk now, he *has* to. There's got to be something he wants to say to me.

I'm waiting for it, so when he does finally speak I don't anticipate being taken by surprise by the words he chooses.

"You're falling for me?"

It's the last thing I expect him to say. In fact, it's not until he asks the question that I realise I said those words aloud to him. I was so caught up in my story, in my heart... that I didn't even acknowledge what I was admitting.

I consider denying it, but I don't know what the point would be in that. I've laid out almost all my cards and there's no reason I can think of that I should hide the truth from him.

I can only control *me*, and right now, I want him to know exactly how I feel about him.

"I am... I'm falling in love with you."

His answering smile is so blinding I literally have to look away.

He's ecstatic, and I'm confused.

He reaches for my jaw and runs his thumb gently down the skin on my cheek as he tilts my gaze back up to meet his.

His stare is so intense; I feel it all the way down to my toes.

He leans in so our faces are only an inch apart. "I'm right here falling with you," he whispers before pressing his lips against mine.

Chapter Forty-Four

Rylan

It's so much worse than I imagined, but at the same time, it's better too.

Violet has been to hell and back, *repeatedly*, but she's still here... living and breathing... she's *alive*.

She's a fighter and I believe she's already made it through the worst of what life will throw at her.

Looking at her, such a bright, beautiful woman, you'd never guess the horrors she's endured – the opponents she's taken on and won.

There are already so many things I can think of that I want to ask her in regards to what she's been through, but I don't.

There will be plenty of time for that later. I'm not going anywhere and if I have my way, neither will she.

I'm in this for the long haul, and if she thinks that her heart is going to make a difference to the way I feel about her, then she's going to have to think again.

The only thing I need to know about her heart right now is that I hold a piece of it.

I can tell she's worried, and I've got a feeling she's expecting me to walk away. I don't blame her for her insecurity surrounding what she's just shared with me. I can't even begin to imagine everything she's been through. It literally brings a tear to my eye to imagine that she must feel that way for a reason – that people must have steered clear of her in the past due to something she has not an ounce of control over.

I've had people avoid me too – leave me all alone, so I sort of understand what it's like... but I also know that's on me – I didn't give anyone a reason to stay. Violet gives people all the reasons in the world.

I may not have known her for a huge amount of time, but it didn't take long to figure out what kind of a person she is.

She's open, kind, strong, warm and loving... I know I'm not the first person to feel this kind of love from Violet, but I think that maybe I might be the only man whom she's not related to that's ever been allowed to get this close, and that's not an honour I'll take lightly.

Her lips are still on mine and she's kissing me back with the fervour of someone who might never get another chance.

That's when it hits me that it's probably *exactly* the way she feels.

She's just laid everything out bare for me – literally put her heart on the line and I haven't said a word about it.

I undoubtedly know it changes nothing about the way I feel for her, but *she* doesn't know that yet.

I pull back, breaking our kiss but she's not done, she has the front of my shirt fisted in her hand and it pains me to think she's holding on for dear life.

"Violet," I murmur against her lips as she kisses me again.

Her breath is heavy as she releases me before resting her forehead against mine.

Her eyelids are flickering open and shut and it takes me a moment to recognise that she's crying.

"I'm here," I whisper. I wrap my arms around her and pull her onto my lap.

I wrap my arms around her like a vice as she clings onto my neck and shoulders.

Her small frame is wracked with sob after sob, and I just hold her as tight as I can.

As much as it pains me to see her upset, I don't bother telling her not to cry. There would be no point... she needs this release and after all I've just heard, she deserves a good cry.

She deserves a lot of things, and I'm going to do everything in my power to give her all I have to offer.

Bear wanders over and nudges Violet with his head. It's a small gesture, but it warms my insides.

She's like a magnet; it's not only me she's pulled in, but this big dog too.

She reaches out and strokes his head and reassures him that she's okay, that she *will* be okay.

He curls up at our feet and I smile.

Violet's sobs have subsided, and she turns in my arms so she can look up at me.

"I'm sorry."

"You don't have to apologise for being human."

"I got your shirt all wet."

"I think I can live with that."

She's looking up at me with her big crystal blue eyes, and even though they're brimmed with tears, I've never seen her look so beautiful.

She's staring at me, searching for answers that it doesn't appear she's finding.

"Why aren't you running?" she finally whispers.

I reach my hand forward and wipe away a stray tear from her cheek.

"I'm not going anywhere."

"But aren't you worried... don't you have questions?"

I nod. "I have questions, but they can wait... I'm not going anywhere, and no answer you could give would change how I feel about you anyway."

She opens her mouth to speak but no words come out, so I continue.

"And as for being worried... truthfully, I *am*."

She sighs in defeat, like maybe this is the 'but' moment she's been dreading.

"I'm worried that I'll lose you, and I don't mean because of your heart... I mean because of your head. I'm worried you'll convince yourself this isn't a good idea and you'll leave me."

Her chin lifts slowly until she's looking into my eyes and I see the deep-seated fear she usually keeps hidden there.

She's scared, and rightfully so, but she doesn't have to be scared on her own anymore.

Sure, she's got her family and friends, but until now she's never had me, and I'm willing to do whatever it takes to make her happy. I know I can't make the things she fears disappear, but I can share the load with her – I can lighten the weight on her shoulders, if nothing else.

"I worry about letting people in... it hurts me to think what will happen to those closest to me if I die."

She may have just told me all of the facts about her heart, and shared with me some of her most tightly kept secrets, but this right here is possibly the truest thing of all to fall from her lips.

Her biggest fear of death isn't for herself, but for those she'll leave behind.

That one sentence sums up exactly what type of person she is, and I fall a little bit further down the rabbit hole of love because of it.

She's got to be the most selfless person I've ever met.

I make a vow to myself that I'll never be someone she can push away, that I'll never let her see herself as a burden to me, because she isn't.

I know her fears are justified, and there's no point in telling her otherwise, because she's right – loving her carries the risk of losing her, but there's one thing I know for absolute certain in all this, and it's that this is a risk I'm willing to take.

Bear might not have a choice about whether or not he goes home with Violet, but I sure as hell do, and I'm not going to let her go without a fight – and if I'm honest, probably not even then.

Chapter Forty-Five

Violet

"So you really like this boy, then?"

The unexpected voice sends me jumping in the air.

"Jesus, Mum, you scared me... what are you doing in here? Is everything okay?"

She's sitting in my living room, making herself at home on one of my couches.

It's not that she's not welcome, but she's never done this before – I've never come home to her alone in here like some type of creeper.

"Everything's fine. I was just waiting for you to get back from your date."

"*Why?* Why didn't you call? How long have you been here for?"

I strip off my jacket and toss it over the back of the seat before joining her on the couch.

"I haven't been here long, and I'm sorry, I shouldn't have just let myself in like that."

I've never been particularly concerned about boundaries with my mum before this point in time, other than with my paintings that is, but now that I have a real life boyfriend and I'm not a child anymore, I'm suddenly hit with the desire for privacy.

My phone chimes in my pocket with an incoming message and I can't pull it out fast enough. I already know it's Rylan. He's like a drug to me, and even though I don't need him like I need my anti-rejection pills and my other daily dose of medication, I can feel myself beginning to rely on him like he's keeping me alive the very same way.

To: Violet

From: Rylan

Ever since you left I've been trying to convince myself I don't miss you already.

It's not working.

I can't help the smile that spreads wide across my face as I read his words. I've momentarily forgotten all about my mum sitting only an arm's length away, but she hasn't forgotten about me it would seem.

"Well that answers my question about you and that boy then, doesn't it?"

As I sit the phone down I can feel myself blushing. "I'm not sure he should be classed as a boy, Mum. A *man* might be more appropriate."

She raises her brows at me and I realise that I've just insinuated that I'm familiar with his manhood.

I cover my eyes as I feel my face flaming even deeper red.

Mum laughs at my predicament.

"Not like that! You know what I mean... he's not a kid, oh God, this is so embarrassing."

"So... he seems very nice," she prompts me for more information, clearly not yet having got what she's after from this little talk.

"He is, and *yes*, I do like him... I like him a lot actually."

I don't know where she's planning to go with this conversation, but just in case she's about to give me the birds and bees talk, I decide to get in first.

"I know I've never had a real boyfriend, but I'm not fifteen anymore, okay? I'm a grown woman and I can take care of myself."

She nods her head in acceptance, but I can't help but feel a little guilty that she's missed out on that particular milestone with me.

It's a mother's rite of passage to stress about their daughter getting drunk and winding up pregnant, but that was never going to be an issue for me. She more than got her money's worth with Auggie however, so I guess it all evened out in the end.

"I just worry about you."

She's always worried about me and she probably always will, but at some point she's going to have to let go and let me live the life she's fought so hard for me to have.

"I know you do, but I'm fine, really I am. He's a good man."

"Does he know about your heart?"

I nod, and it feels so incredible to be able to answer that question with an honest yes.

"I told him today... it was like I'd confessed something as trivial as the colour of my eyes." I huff out a laugh of disbelief. "Must be the doctor in him."

Mum smiles at me in a knowing way and I instantly feel like a little girl who still has so much to learn.

"I've seen the way he looks at you, Vi, and it's got nothing to do with the fact that he's a doctor." She shrugs. "He's in love with you."

The way she says it, like it's totally straightforward and uncomplicated makes the heart in my chest gallop like a race horse.

I might be too old for the safe sex lecture, but I'm not too old to talk to my mum about the new man in my life, so I do.

I tell her everything about him and by the end of it, I'm well aware that I'm in love with him too.

***

He might not have asked me anything much when I first told him about my heart, but he's certainly making up for it now.

He wants to know *everything*.

Only, the questions he's firing at me aren't the ones I expected to hear.

He doesn't seem to want to know about my illness so much as he does my life – he wants to know what I've done with my new heart these past three years.

So I tell him.

"Before my transplant I was studying business."

He raises his brows at me in surprise.

"Mmm hmm." I nod. "I don't know what I was thinking... I dropped it as soon as I was well enough to convince Mum I'd thought it through."

"What did you change to?"

"I didn't..." I shake my head. "I decided that I wanted to explore my real passion."

"Painting." He nods in understanding.

It probably should surprise me that he got the answer correct in one, but it doesn't. He sees *me*, and even though he hasn't seen any of my work – he already seems to know it's important to me.

"I signed up to some local art classes and some short courses. I've done painting, photography, drawing, sculpture, design... you name it, I've probably taken a class."

I taught a few painting classes too, but I decide to leave that part out. This conversation is teetering on the edge of dangerous territory as it is, the last thing I want to do is encourage him to ask to see my work for himself – because I'm not sure I'd have it in me to say no.

"I could have studied art and gotten myself a degree, but what would be the point? I don't need a degree to paint."

He's smiling at me like he agrees with my logic.

"So when you're not working at the shelter, you're painting?"

I crinkle my nose sheepishly. "So, I don't actually work there... I'm a volunteer."

"Huh... that's cool. Do you volunteer anywhere else?"

"Sometimes I hang out with the Heart Kids group I used to be a part of, but that's about it. I'd love to spend some time in the children's ward at the hospital, because I spent so much time in there when I was little, but I can't. My immune system isn't what it should be. Animals have a lot less I can catch."

I don't go into details about the medication I take and how it suppresses my immune system in order to reduce the risk of my body rejecting my new heart – he's a doctor and he probably understands my condition better than I ever could anyway.

That's when the thought occurs to me. He delivers babies, and the defect I have – I was born with. Someone like him probably brought me into the world.

"Have you ever delivered a baby with a heart condition like mine?"

He looks at me with a pained glance and my stomach flips.

"You have, haven't you?"

"I have."

"The baby didn't survive, did it?"

He shakes his head. "The parents decided against medical intervention."

Tears spring to my eyes and I blink them back fiercely.

That could have been me.

If my parents weren't as strong as they are – not that I think those other parents necessarily made a weak choice – they did what was right for them, but in my mind, the strength is in the fight.

I'm so thankful that my parents chose to fight.

"So, you sell your art?" he questions, no doubt in an attempt to distract me from the current topic of conversation.

I laugh nervously. "*God* no."

That would require people to actually see my paintings.

His expression is confused. "Sorry for the intrusion, but how exactly do you pay the bills?"

He sits down his chocolate milkshake on the table, picks up my strawberry one and brings it up to his lips to suck it through the straw.

This conversation was bound to come up at some point; I knew it would, and it's not that I don't want to tell him, but discussing my financial situation always fills me with a feeling of guilt.

"You remember I told you about my Aunt?"

He nods. "Rita, right? She gave you the ring and the house."

I like that he hasn't forgotten what I told him about the ring around my neck, and I appreciate that he recognises it's just as important to me as the big, beautiful house is.

"That's the one... She also left me money – a lot of it. It's invested well and turns over a pretty solid income, so given my medical situation and the fact that I don't really know what I want to do for a job, I've just been volunteering my time and living off the money she left me, even though I don't feel like I deserve that luxury most of the time."

If it was anyone other than him I'd be expecting a question about just how much money I inherited, but I know he won't ask – he's not that type of guy.

"She must have loved you very much. Why wouldn't you deserve it? She obviously wanted you to have it."

I think about the truth in his words for a minute.

She did love me; she loved me like I was her own daughter. She'd been a big part of my life since the day I was born, and I know all she ever wanted was for me to have a real life. It's a hard pill to swallow that I finally got one, and she's not around to see me enjoy it.

She passed so quickly and unexpectedly, none of us saw it coming or had time to process it. She never even told anyone that she was unwell.

"She knew she was dying. She had everything all mapped out, her money, her assets, letters for us all... even her funeral was planned for us. She didn't even look sick." There's tears pooling in the corners of my eyes and I know it won't be long before one escapes down my cheek.

He reaches out and intertwines his fingers with mine across the top of the table.

"You miss her."

I shake my head. "Well I mean, yeah..." I sniff. "I miss her like crazy, but that's not it. It's the guilt that gets me. She left us a couple of months after I got my new heart. All that time she was unwell and the only thing she worried about was *me* and my family. She was there supporting us when it should have been the other way around."

"I'm sure she had her reasons for that."

I don't doubt that she did – Rita had her reasons for everything, but that doesn't make it any easier for me to accept.

"I just *don't* understand. Why did I get to stay when she had to go? Why was my life deemed more important than hers?" I choke the words out.

He squeezes my hand but says nothing – I think he knows I'm not really looking for an answer to my question.

"In a way it feels like I'm responsible for *two* deaths," I whisper.

"You're not responsible for *any* deaths, Violet."

He pulls on my hand so I look at him. His blue eyes are burning into mine with sincerity.

"I know I didn't kill them, but I benefitted from them dying, Rylan. How is that not the same thing?" My voice cracks as I voice my guilt. "A donor – someone I didn't even know – gave me their heart, their actual *heart*. The very thing that keeps us alive was taken from their body and put into mine. I can literally feel another person's heart beating in my chest."

"I'm not going to pretend to understand how it feels to live because somebody else died, because I don't, but I *do* know that none of this is your fault – you didn't ask to be born with this condition, Violet. This isn't on you."

He makes a valid point, but it's still something I have a hard time getting my head around.

"I know they were going to die anyway, and that I need-ed this organ to live, but it's just so conflicting to think about."

He gives me a sad smile.

"And Rita, she gave me *so* much – she's not just given me money and a roof over my head, she's given me freedom. She gave me the means to do everything I ever wanted... she's the reason I got to travel the world."

"You travelled?"

I nod and smile. "I saw *everything* I've ever wanted to see." I rest my hand over the spot where my heart it. "When I was stuck in the hospital, I promised myself if I ever got a second chance to live, that I'd tick off all of the boxes on my list, so when I got my new heart, that's what I did."

I'm not sure if he's grateful for the change of subject, or if the sights of the world is something that gets him excited, but his face breaks into a smile and his eyes light up.

"Tell me."

"Lucy, Emmett and I went for six months; and Charlie joined us for a month over his summer break."

I sigh as I think about all the incredible places I went and all the amazing things I saw.

"I saw the Louvre and the Mona Lisa in Paris, the Sistine Chapel in the Vatican City, Michelangelo's David in Florence, Banksy in London, The Colosseum in Rome... we went to Vienna, Venice, New York, Barcelona, Mexico, Istanbul, Athens... if it had art, I saw it."

"I think she would have been happy to give you that, Vi. She didn't leave you all of that because she wanted you to feel guilty, she gave it to you so you could live."

He squeezes my hand and I can't help but smile in agreement.

"I think the only reason you'd have to feel guilty is if you weren't doing exactly that."

Chapter Forty-Six

Rylan

I wince as the giant dog bounds around my small living room, he knocks into a shelf and sends books flying all over the place.

"*Bear!*" I groan.

It wasn't until I got him in here in this confined space that I realised just how big of a dog he really is.

I didn't even bother to ask if he was full grown yet or not – but he damn well better be, or we're going to have some serious problems with this new arrangement.

He leaps up onto the couch and begins to make himself comfortable in my favourite spot.

I swing open the double doors that lead out to the back yard.

The house might be small, but the yard is huge, and I'm hoping he'll decide that his time is better spent running around out there than it is in here.

"Out you go, boy," I call.

He looks up at me and doesn't budge an inch – we're clearly going to have to work on the command training. It seems the only person the big guy is willing to listen to is Violet, and she's not here, nor does she know of my harebrained scheme to surprise her, so I'm going to have to find another way to get him to do what I want.

I grab one of the tennis balls off the table and suddenly I have his attention, I throw it out the door onto the grass and he damn near bowls me over chasing after it.

I shut the door behind him, just in case, but it seems he's been distracted from his reign of terror by the scents around the yard and all the objects that need peeing on.

I'll be the first to admit that I didn't think this through particularly thoroughly, but even though he's turned my house upside down in a matter of minutes, I still can't bring myself to regret my decision.

I couldn't stop thinking about the look on Violet's face when we said goodbye to Bear last week. She was heartbroken. She knew as well as I did that a beautiful dog like that wasn't going to stick around an animal shelter forever.

Losing him would have broken her and I couldn't let that happen. Violet's had more breaks in her heart than anyone I've ever met, and I couldn't allow her to endure yet another crack.

Bear had a rough start to life, but thanks to Violet and the other staff at the shelter, he's been nursed back to health, he's put on some weight and he's ready to enjoy himself.

He and Violet have that in common, they've both been dealt a harsh hand in life, but they've both come out stronger for it.

Maybe that's why Bear chose her.

Maybe that's why I chose her too… maybe I need her passion for life to inspire me to do better – to *be* better. Maybe it's time I came out stronger too.

If Violet can live through everything she has and still come out of it with a smile on her face, then I don't think I have a choice than to believe that anything is possible.

I glance back out the window and see that Bear has moved on from peeing on everything and has now begun the process of digging up every plant in my small garden.

I can't even be mad – that dog makes her happy, and seeing her smile is going to be more than worth the mess.

I glance at the time on my watch.

It's my day off, and Violet is about to start working a shift at the shelter for the next five hours, which means I need to get my ass into gear.

I've got a fence to build.

***

I glance around at the progress we're making. I have to stop working for a moment to stop myself from getting all choked up about the support around me.

I know they're all here for Violet, and not for me, but I guess it's just been so long since I felt like I was truly a part of something bigger.

I haven't felt like I've had people I could call on for a favour, for years, but it seems I do now.

Emmett didn't hesitate to agree to help me out and he didn't miss a beat before asking Charlie and Shaun to chip in too.

Even Leanne turned up to get her hands dirty, although I think she's possibly got an ulterior motive for being here.

She wants to know if I care about her daughter. She needs to know that she can trust me with her.

She hasn't said those words, but I can read the woman like a book. She wears her worries on her sleeve and her concerns might as well be tattooed across her forehead.

I don't blame her. Violet might have got a raw deal in life, but I can't even begin to understand the things that Leanne and Shaun went through as her parents. It seems like an impossible situation to imagine, let alone witness those things happening to your own flesh and blood.

I can understand why she's protective of her daughter, and it's up to me to prove that I'm here to stay and that I'd never intentionally do *anything* to hurt Violet.

It's *my* responsibility to show her that I'm capable of taking on the role of protector – not that Violet seems to need it, but I think that perhaps Leanne does... I think that maybe she might need to know that someone is there for Violet, or maybe it's just a matter of having someone to share the worry with.

Whatever it is, I'm putting my hand up for it – I'm *all* in, and I'm hoping that this plan I've put in motion is the first step to proving exactly that to Violet *and* her family.

Violet and I have spoken every single day since her confession by the river. When we haven't been together in person, we've spent countless hours on the phone and every single minute I've spent with her on the other end of the line has had me falling deeper and deeper.

She's a complex creature with so many layers to unwrap and decipher. She's like a puzzle you think you've got all figured out, but then you realise there's a piece hidden under the rug you're yet to even see.

It's what I've decided I love most about her, because it's more than clear to me now that I do love her.

It's why I'm here – why we're all here. We may all be very different people, but we each have one thing in common – *Violet*.

*****

We've still got a lot of work to do, but it's a start, and hopefully it's enough of a gesture to show Violet that I'm in this with her for good.

I know she'll be due back soon, and she's bound to be upset over Bear being gone.

I feel bad about convincing Avery it was a good idea to lie to her, but I wanted to show Violet this in private.

Bear spots a bird in the far corner and takes off in an attempt to catch it.

He loves it our here in Violet's newly fenced back yard, and much to my disbelief, he's not dug up a single one of her plants or peed on any of her outdoor furniture.

We've still got the entire front yard to fence, but it's something at least, and it'll give Bear somewhere safe to run around for now.

"I can sort that later," I call to Shaun and Charlie as they restack the leftover timber against the side of the house.

They both proceed to ignore me and carry on doing what they're doing. They've done so much for me already and I feel guilty for hijacking their Saturday the way I have.

Even Lucy is here now. She's far too pregnant to do any type of lifting or building, but she's kept the snacks and drinks flowing for us while we work.

I can feel her watching me – she's been doing it for a while now, and I know sooner or later I'm going to have to hear whatever it is she's planning to say to me.

Violet must be due back any minute, so I decide that now is as good of a time as any.

"Just the man I've been waiting for." She confirms my suspicion as I sit down next to her on the garden bench.

"At your service."

She glances around at our day's work, her eyes lingering a little longer on Emmett than anyone else as she takes her slow appraisal.

"This is going to mean a lot to her," she finally says.

"I hope so."

"*You* mean a lot to her."

I know I do. There's no denying the love in Violet's eyes when she looks at me, and I wouldn't dream of disagreeing with what Lucy said, even if I weren't able to see the truth for myself. She knows Violet better than I do.

"She means a lot to me too."

"I can see that."

Her gaze strays from the yard and lands on my face. She smiles at me.

"I guess you're expecting the speech where I threaten to hunt you down and kill you if you hurt her, right?"

The thought had crossed my mind.

"You should know I don't assume anything when it comes to pregnant women." I chuckle.

"You're a wise man, Dr. Wilder." She grins. "I'll admit, I've been thinking about the little talk you and I would have... but after this I'm not sure you need to hear it."

"I won't hurt her, Lucy."

She smiles at me again. "I know you won't. You adopted a giant freaking dog just to make her smile – I think we're good here."

I laugh as the dog in question leaps up at Leanne, slobbering all down the side of her face as she laughs.

I might have got him with Violet in mind, but truthfully, I kind of like having him around too. He's just another thing I have to thank Violet for. Lucy too – it's because of her that this whole thing began.

"I never got a chance to thank you."

She looks at me quizzically. "For what?"

"For forcing me to agree to that blind date... for *Violet*... for all of it."

"That smile on her face is all the thanks I need."

Lucy's looking past me; back up at the house and when I turn, I see the very smile she's referring to.

Violet's hand flies up to her mouth as her eyes land first on Bear, and then on me as she realises what's going on.

"That's your cue to get over there." Lucy shoves my shoulder and I stumble to my feet.

I don't even make it halfway across the lawn before Violet flies down the steps and throws herself into my waiting arms.

Bear chases after her, leaping and barking in excitement as he goes.

"*You* adopted Bear?" She's staring up at me, her blood-shot eyes wide in bewilderment.

"Surprise." I shrug.

"You built me a fence?" Her voice is beginning to crack and I know it won't be long before the tears start to fall.

"I can't take all the credit for that. I had some help."

I glance around and it's only then that I notice we're alone out here.

They've all left us to enjoy our moment in private.

"I can't believe you did all this for me."

I shrug again. "You love him," I reply simply, because it's the only explanation I'll ever need.

She blinks back the moisture pooling in her eyes and smiles the sweetest smile at me.

"I love *you*."

The earth might technically still be spinning, but *my* whole world has just stopped.

I know there will never be another moment quite like this one. I hope to hear those words from her for a very long time yet, but I can't imagine anything possibly comparing to this first time.

Now I'm the one with teary eyes.

"I love you too." I choke out the words as best I can.

She presses up onto the tips of her toes and I meet her for a kiss. It's so much more passionate than any we've shared before.

I may have spent all day building a fence, but now I can physically feel a wall crumbling down between us.

She's giving me another little piece of herself and I lock it away safely in my heart.

"Thank you," she whispers hoarsely against my lips.

I could say so many things to her right now, I could tell her that I'm crazy about her, that I'm *hers*... that I can't manage to picture my life without her in it anymore. I could tell her that I think she's had my heart from the moment I first laid eyes on her, but instead I just hold her tight and soak up some more of her light.

Chapter Forty-Seven

Violet

There's not a lot of things I've allowed myself to have in the past twenty-five years.

There's my passion for painting and there's my friendship with Lucy, but outside of my favourite hobby and my best friend, I've made a real effort not to take anything more from the universe – in a lot of ways I feel like I've already taken enough.

I know I'm not responsible for the loss of a life, but I benefited from one and it often feels like the same thing.

So I try not to take. Instead I do my best to *give*.

But now, here in this moment, as I see the deep, unwavering love in his eyes, I know I have to allow myself this.

I have to allow myself *him*.

I'm entitled to live and love, just like everyone else is, and I have to give this everything I have, even though I know I'm going to receive so much more back in return.

Rylan is here in front of me, figuratively naked, baring his soul to me.

He sees *me*. The *real* me.

My borrowed heart is so tangled up with his, it's like they're one and the same – that it seems like they're beating together.

It's just the two of us and Bear in my big house, but I've never felt less alone. He's everywhere I look. I can feel him all around me and I can smell his scent in the air.

He lets go of me and tugs his t-shirt slowly over his head. The sight is so perfect it seems too good to be true. His golden skin stretches flawlessly over his tight, toned muscles and there's not a mark out of place.

My head is screaming at me that he's too good for me – that I couldn't possibly deserve someone this faultless, but the look in his eyes quietens my silent objection.

He reaches for my hand and ever so slowly lifts it to the spot on his chest where I can feel his heart beating. My hand rests there as he mirrors the action, placing his own hand over my heart.

I can feel the steady thrum of his heart and know that he's experiencing the same.

I fill my lungs deeply and as I release my breath, I let my hand wander over his chest and across the grooves of his abdomen. I feel him shudder under my touch and I revel in the reaction I've evoked.

"*Violet*," he whispers as he dips his head and his mouth briefly comes into contact with mine.

There have been plenty of times when I've felt nervous in my life; I can think of half a dozen that spring to mind in an instant, and they're *all* to do with my heart.

This is too, but not in the same way.

This is something new.

This is about what my heart *wants*, not what it needs for once, and all that my heart wants in this moment, is *him*.

"I've never done this before," I whisper back as he places soft kisses along my collar bone.

He pauses and looks up at me. "Never?"

He doesn't seem shocked – maybe a bit surprised, like perhaps I've just confirmed a lucky guess.

I shake my head no.

No one has ever wanted me the way Rylan does. No man has ever got to know the real me like he has.

"I'm broken goods."

I'm embarrassed that I'm still a virgin at twenty-five years old, but there's also a small part of me that's glad, I may not have known I was saving myself for him, but it sure feels that way now.

I can't think of a better man to share this first with.

"We're all a little bit damaged, Violet." He looks right into my eyes as he speaks.

I like that he doesn't argue with me about it, or try to deny the obvious.

This is one of the things I love the most about him, he doesn't lie to me and he doesn't try to make me feel better by filling me up with untruths. He simply reminds me that I'm not alone – that we all have our flaws, we all have a story... he reminds me to forget the rest.

He kisses me on the skin just below my ear and the sensation is so sharp it feels like broken glass.

I've never been kissed like this before.

He wants *me*, in all the ways a man wants a woman. It's pure desire and primal instincts that are driving him to me.

I want this so badly I can hardly think straight, but I'm still afraid of what he'll think when he sees *every* part of me.

I feel like the shy little girl in the changing rooms at school all over again.

My scars aren't red and angry looking like they once were, they've healed and faded somewhat, but for him – seeing them for the first time, it's bound to be a shock.

He tugs on the hem of my shirt, pulling it from the band of the denim shorts I'm wearing.

"Leave it on." I can't stop myself whispering.

It's my shield – my last line of defence, and if he takes that away, he'll never be able to unsee what's beneath it.

He pauses and lets go of the fabric before tipping my chin up so I'm looking right at him.

"You can't hide from me."

"But—"

He shakes his head. "There is *nothing* you need to hide from me, Violet, I see *you*."

He's right... I *know* he's right. I want this with him and I know I can't stay hidden forever – not if I want this to work, and I do... more than I want anything else.

I nod, just one small movement.

Ever so slowly he reaches for my shirt again and one by one unfastens the buttons until it's hanging open in the front.

His eyes are no longer on my face, but on my body now, and the weight of his stare threatens to make my knees buckle.

His strong hands slide the fabric off my shoulders and I watch as it falls to the floor and lands at my feet.

I've never felt this entirely exposed to a person. I know full well I have been – rooms full of doctors have looked at my body in far less than what I'm wearing now, but this is different.

He's not a professional who is looking at me as a patient.

He's just a man who is looking at me as a woman.

I gasp as his fingers run ever so gently over my scar.

"*This* is what you were worried about?" His voice is raw, it sounds like sandpaper.

I nod – I can't speak. It's taking everything I have just to breathe as he exposes more of my secrets one by one.

"You really think I'd scare that easily?"

He doesn't wait for an answer; instead he leans in and kisses my collar bone again, before moving lower and kissing the very spot where the heart I was born with vacated my body.

"Let me help put you back together, Violet."

They're the exact words I need to hear in this moment.

I almost feel stupid for worrying the way I did. I should have known that he wouldn't run... that he wouldn't care about something as superficial as the marks on my skin.

"Rylan," I whisper.

"I'll *never* leave," he whispers back and I feel his lips move against me. "I might need you to put me back together too."

He hears my unspoken fears and soothes them instantly.

I run my hand down his bare front until I reach the waistband of his jeans.

I'm scared, *so* scared, I think I might be more afraid of doing this than I've ever been of anything that came before it, but I take that leap, because it's not just some guy in front of me.

It's *Rylan*.

I love him, and he loves me back – every last broken bit of me.

Chapter Forty-Eight

Rylan

I can't recall us having the conversation, but it seems something unspoken has passed between us this past month.

I haven't spent more than twelve hours away from Violet since the night she gave me another of her firsts.

We're joined now – bound in a way I can't even begin to understand.

I'm not the same man I was a few months ago. He's still there, deep inside me, but he's evolved somewhat.

I no longer live and breathe my job – I still love what I do, but for the first time ever, I love something else more.

I love *her* more.

I love her more than I love anything else in my life.

She makes my pulse speed up and time slow down.

Our two separate paths have been diverted to flow alongside each other almost effortlessly.

It seems too easy most of the time – we fit together so naturally that it almost seems too good to be true.

We laugh and play, we watch movies and talk about books, we take Bear for walks and lie out under the stars, we discuss everything from politics to fan fiction theories and cook together nearly every day.

I don't have to worry about missing out on time with her because of my job – she's more than comfortable adjusting to the long shifts and erratic callouts. When I work, Violet paints or volunteers and when we sleep we do it together.

Painting, I'm beginning to learn, is Violet's escape from the world.

Sometimes my phone rings in the middle of the night, and when I return to her place, there's a jar of dirty brushes sitting in the sink.

I don't know if she paints to fill the time that I'm gone, or if she paints *because* I'm gone.

She's never offered to show me her work, and I know her well enough to know that it's not a slip of her mind.

She's not ready to show me yet and I can respect that for now.

There's things I'm not ready to share with her yet either – things like my sister.

Every now and then something will happen and the pain of losing her hits me like a slap to the face.

Today was one of those days.

An old friend of Daisy's – a nurse that had worked with her, came back from overseas this week. She didn't do anything wrong, but she obviously didn't get the memo that all my other colleagues did.

She talked about Daisy, she laughed and reminisced about the good times they'd had together.

I know that's how it should be – that years after someone's gone you *should* be able to talk about them, but it doesn't seem to work that way for me.

Where others seem to light up at an old memory, I feel like I'm being filled with lead, and I'm about to be dropped into dark, murky water with no way out.

It's moments like these that I feel most lost and alone. Only I'm *not* alone anymore.

I've got Violet, and right now I need her more than I ever have.

***

I arrive back to a sight that steals all of the breath from my lungs.

Violet is sprawled on her couch, Bear on the floor next to her. She's sketching in a book that I've never been allowed to look in and she's dressed in tracksuit bottoms and a tank top – the type of top that *doesn't* cover the marks on her chest.

I know her scars still bother her, but this small step where she's chosen not to cover up feels like huge progress in my mission to assure her that I don't see her for her struggles.

As much as I want to celebrate this incredible milestone, I'm so emotionally spent that I don't think I can manage anything more than to hold her close.

She'll make everything better just like she always does.

She hears me come in and there's already a smile on her lips before she even raises her gaze to meet mine.

I'm not sure what she sees when she looks at me, but judging by the look on her face, it can't be anything good.

"Rylan." She scrambles up off the couch and the normally treasured sketch pad falls to the ground with a thud.

She doesn't say another word until she's in my arms.

"What is it?"

I want to tell her, I *do*, but I don't know how. I can't figure out how to make my mouth open so the words can come out.

I try, over and over, but nothing happens, so I give up trying.

Instead, I bury my face in her hair and just breathe. Each breath is more calming than the next and I find the tight coil inside my gut loosening with each fill of my lungs.

She's gripping me tight, like she can't get close enough.

I hoist her up and she clamps her legs around my waist, her arms are wrapped firmly around my neck, holding me as close to her as I possibly can be.

When I'm here like this, with her in my arms, the thought of talking about my sister doesn't seem so life shattering anymore – I can't help but consider the possibility that I could do *anything* as long as Violet was right there with me.

"Rylan?" she whispers after what feels like forever.

"I'm okay..."

"Do you want to talk about it?"

As much as I want to tell her yes, I can't right now, I'm dead on my feet and I know I'll need every ounce of strength to share my story with her.

"Could we just go to bed?"

"If that's what you need," she replies softly.

"I just need *you*."

"You've got me, Rylan."

Chapter Forty-Nine

Violet

I clutch my chest and drag in a deep breath.

"You scared me," I tell him as I pull my ear buds out and hit pause on the playlist on my cell phone.

I can't work without music. I prefer it blaring over the sound system in the corner, but when I'm up here in the middle of the night, that's not exactly possible.

His intense blue eyes watch me carefully as a wide smile graces his full lips.

"Sorry, I didn't mean to..." His gaze shifts, and his apology is lost. "Are these yours?"

I feel the blush colour my cheeks – I don't make it a habit of showing people my work and he's still no exception to the rule.

Even Lucy, my best friend since we were in nappies, has never seen the entire collection of my work. I've shown her only two pieces, one of which she begged for until she wore me down and I agreed.

That particular piece sits proudly on the wall in the entry to her and Emmett's house, with a pinky promise from her that she'll never spill the beans on where she got it.

Rylan has never seen anything more from me than a doodle on a napkin and the 'safe' paintings my mum and dad have on their walls.

"Yeah… they're mine. I thought you'd be sleeping… I didn't mean to wake you. Do you want to go back to bed?"

"You didn't wake me," he murmurs as he slowly walks past me, his eyes studying one canvas before moving onto the next, ignoring my question about returning to the safety of my sheets.

I normally don't paint when he's here, but ever since he came home broken, I haven't slept much at all.

It was a rookie error on my behalf – leaving myself exposed this way, and even though I don't want to hide all of this from him forever, I'm not mentally prepared to have him in here right now.

This room is filled with my work and as he slowly takes appraisal of each piece, it's almost as though he's stripping me bare of an item of clothing.

These are my inner most thoughts and feelings – some of the images on these canvases are so raw and real they take me right back to the specific moment in time and the feelings hit me with such force it can literally knock me backwards.

That's why I keep it all up here, in the large attic, with a locked door.

The light provided from the huge skylights makes it the perfect place for me to paint –it's my happy place. But right now it feels more like a prison cell I can't escape.

Rylan's gently flicking through the stack of canvases against the wall now.

I suck in a ragged breath because I know exactly what he's seeing.

I haven't laid eyes on those paintings in close to two years, but each and every one of them is burned into my memory for all eternity.

Those are some of the hardest hitting works of art I've ever created.

I'm paralysed, almost gasping for air as I wait for him to question me on them, for him to ask things I can't answer.

But he doesn't.

When he reaches the last one, he rubs forcefully with the ball of his hand at a spot on his chest and glances around at the collection I have displayed on the far wall.

The relief I feel almost brings me to my knees.

These I can talk about, mainly because they make little to no sense to me.

He turns to face me for the first time in what feels like an eternity. He raises a dark brow at me. "What's with all the flowers?"

I shrug. "I'm not sure to be honest... I just started painting them one day, and I've never stopped."

"I like them," he whispers, his voice thick with an emotion I can't place.

"Thank you."

I don't tell him about the dream or *vision*, if you want to call it that, that I had a few years ago.

I don't tell him about the fields of daisies that everything important to me, including he himself was in.

I don't tell him that as soon as I was allowed home, I was back in front of a canvas, painting daisy after daisy, with no real idea why they were so important.

I can't tell him all of that. If I do, he'll have questions, and I'll end up telling him that he was there in my dreams – that I've been picturing him in my mind for nearly four years.

I'm still not quite ready for that revelation yet.

He strolls back over to me, leaving the other half of the room and the work in it safe from his intense stare.

There's a lot of memories over there too and a pair of blue eyes he was bound to recognise as his own, but I don't feel relief knowing he didn't see that particular painting, instead I still feel stripped bare as though he's already seen everything.

If there's one thing I've learnt about him in these past two months, it's that he misses nothing.

His mind is sharp, his eyes are focused, and his soul is curious.

He sees *everything*, even the things I don't say or show... he sees them too.

"Can we go for a walk?"

I'm surprised by his request, given that it's after midnight, but I'd give just about anything to be out of this room right now, so I nod eagerly, and when he holds out his hand to me, I take it.

Chapter Fifty

Rylan

We've walked for four blocks in total silence.

It's just us and the moonlight – much like it was after our very first date.

It's ironic really, that we've found ourselves out here again, only this time we're so far from strangers it's almost laughable.

She might not know everything there is to know about me yet, but right now, in this moment, I feel like I've seen every part of her soul.

Of course, I knew Violet painted.

I also knew she liked to keep her work to herself.

I've been dying to see even a glimpse of the magic she creates behind that door, but nothing could have possibly prepared me for what I saw tonight.

I'm under no illusion that me viewing her work was anything other than terrifying for her, but I had to do it.

There's this invisible barrier between us that's growing higher with each passing day we don't talk about our secrets.

On her side, it's her heart, her scars, her insecurities, and who knows what else.

On mine, it's the secret I'm keeping from her, it's my grief, my anger and my pain.

But that's about to change. Right now.

"There's something I need to tell you."

Her grip on my hand tightens and I feel terrible for my choice of wording.

I can't even imagine the things that might be going through her head right now, but instead of addressing all the things that I'm not holding back, I'm just going to come out with the thing that I *have* kept from her.

"You know our blind date?" I question her, and I see her nod out of the corner of my eye. "I didn't realise right away... but that wasn't the first time I'd ever seen you."

She stops walking and pulls me to a stop with her.

I'm expecting questions, confusion, and disbelief maybe... what I'm not expecting is for her to whisper the two words she does.

"I know."

She's looking down at her feet and I don't like it. Violet is the embodiment of the saying 'eyes are the windows to the soul'. Her eyes can conceal nothing, and I need to see them right now so I know we're okay.

I reach for her chin and tip it up so she can't hide from me any longer.

"You remember me?" I murmur. "From outside your hospital room?"

She nods, and I see her eyes begin to well up. "I recognised you the minute I saw you."

Suddenly it all makes sense. The panic attack she had on our first date – it was because she recognised me as the man from outside her window.

"Why didn't you say anything?"

She shrugs and the tears start to fall. "Why didn't *you*?"

I know what she means, and she's right – her reasons for not speaking up are probably the same as mine have been.

I don't know how I'm supposed to explain to her that she was a lifeline for me. That seeing her wake up gave me hope that maybe everything in the world wasn't so bad after all.

I've never told her about my sister, but I know I need to tell her now.

I want a life with Violet, and you can't build a life upon a mountain of secrets.

"You looked so lost," she whispers into the darkness.

"I've never been as lost as I was in those hours, Violet, and for some reason, *you* stopped me from falling apart."

"I don't understand..."

"I'm not sure I do either." I shake my head as I try to make sense of something that truly can't be explained.

"I didn't just happen to pass by your room, I'd been watching you for a while."

Confusion is written all over her face, and I don't blame her.

"I was in the ICU for...." My voice cracks, and I suck in a deep breath in an attempt to regain my composure. "For my sister."

She squeezes my hand again and rubs her thumb gently up and down the side of mine.

The small contact and comfort she gives me is enough for me to find the strength to go on.

"Her name was Daisy, and she died... there was a car crash... she fell asleep at the wheel after a twelve-hour shift and ran herself off the road."

Violet gasps and her hand flies up to cover her mouth. "Oh my God. I'm so sorry, Rylan, you never told me…"

"And then I saw you lying there and I couldn't stay away. My sister was dead, and I was drawn to you, I *needed* you to wake up and be okay. I had no idea what was wrong with you, but I could feel your struggle, Violet, and the moment you woke up and looked at me… I guess I felt hope again."

"I've never seen a person look the way you looked." Her voice sounds like sandpaper.

"You were the light for me, I was surrounded by darkness and *you* were what helped me see through it."

It feels like a huge weight has lifted off my shoulders. I've told Violet my truths, my secrets… and she's not mad at me for keeping it from her… she's still here and she loves me.

"I saw it in your eyes tonight – that same look."

I swallow the lump in my throat. "One of the nurses… she talked about Daisy today. It all hit me again… and then I came home to you, and you saved me, just like that first time."

"You saved me too, Rylan…" She goes to say something further, but I see the moment she catches herself. "Seeing you there, it did the same thing for me. You gave me hope too."

There's more – I can tell that she's holding something back from me, what, I have no idea, but I have a feeling that it's vitally important and I'm suddenly desperate to know.

"I need you to talk to me, Violet, please." I grasp her other hand in mine and tug her close. I know I'm begging, but I don't care – this is a pivotal moment for us, I've never felt a sense of urgency like I do here and now.

Her expression flickers between brave and ready, to frightened and wary.

She opens her mouth to speak, *finally,* and I brace myself for whatever it is she's about to tell me, but right at that moment, my cell phone rings in my pocket.

I drop my head forward in defeat, resting my forehead against hers.

It's my emergency ringtone and I know what that means – one of my patients is in labour.

I'm needed there, but I know on a deep level that I'm needed here just as much, if not more.

"You'd better get that."

She's looking down at my pocket as I stand unmoving.

I'm terrified that if I let this moment slip by right now that I'll never get it back.

She must sense my fear because she pulls her head back and looks at me, *really* looks at me.

"We can talk when you get back."

"You promise?" My voice is gruff and unsure, but I know I don't have another option.

I can't leave my patient and we both know it.

She pushes up to her tippy toes and kisses the side of my mouth. "Answer the damn phone, Rylan; you'll wake up all the neighbours."

She looks different; her face is serene – peaceful, as though maybe she's come to accept something in the same way I have.

She's also right; if I leave this phone ringing much longer there's going to be trouble.

I take the call and as I suspected I'm needed in the delivery ward immediately.

There's no time for any more talking, but as I back out of the driveway I see Violet in the window. She blows me a kiss and I fall even deeper in love with her.

I know in that instant that it doesn't matter what she tells me, I know it's only going to make me love her more.

***

I snap my gloves into place as I use my back to push open the door of the delivery suite.

"How are we doing in here, Luce?"

"Oh, thank God you're here," Emmett calls from his spot next to the bed.

Lucy has his hand in a death grip and I almost laugh – almost. If there's one thing I know, it's that women in labour do not tend to take jokes well.

I grab her chart from the maternity nurse and flick through the notes.

"Seriously, man, you gotta give her something, she's gone crazy."

"She's in labour, Emmett," I reply calmly at the same moment that Lucy screams at him.

"I'm in freakin' labour, you big dumb idiot!"

I hear Kristie, the nurse, try to muffle a laugh and I make the mistake of meeting her eyes.

I'm doing my best, I really am, but the look on Emmett's face right now is priceless.

"You had better not be laughing at me, Rylan Wilder, or so help me God… urrrrggggghhhhhhhhh." Another contraction cuts off her threat.

"We're getting close now, Lucy."

I glance at my watch and make note of the time.

"How about I promise no more laughing, Emmett promises no more being a big dumb idiot, and we get that baby out of there, alright?"

She looks up at me for the first time and I see that she's all bark and no bite.

Lucy looks terrified.

"You've got this, I'm right here," I reassure her.

Emmett wipes a cool flannel across her face, and I can see that despite his wife's anger towards him, he is in fact doing a great job.

"I'm scared," she whispers.

"You can do this, baby, I'm right here with you." He kisses her forehead and I smile.

These two really are great together. They're going to make incredible parents.

"I want Violet." Lucy whimpers as another contraction builds. "Oh my God!" she cries as it hits full force. "I want Violet right now!"

Chapter Fifty-One

Violet

I race down the corridor that leads to the maternity wing of the hospital.

The baby that Rylan is delivering right now isn't just *any* baby, it's Lucy and Emmett's baby, and even though I was never planning to be in the delivery room with her – she needs me.

The fact that it was Emmett who called me and not Rylan, makes me think that perhaps I might be too late anyway, but I still run as fast as I can.

Lucy has been there for me through more than any friend should have to over the years. She's seen the absolute worst in me, and this might be the only chance I get to return the favour.

I approach the nurse's station panting for breath. "I'm looking for Lucy Hale," I say, far too loud and much too fast.

She points down the hall. "Room fourteen, Violet."

I yell my thanks over my shoulder as I take off running again. I'm pretty sure that not just anybody is allowed in here, so dating the obstetrician must have its perks.

I reach the numbered door and I can't hear anything, no screaming, no heavy breathing... *nothing...*

"Hello?"

I tap lightly on the door and I hear Lucy's voice call out to me.

"Come on in, Aunt Violet."

I slowly push open the door in wonder.

I know I'm not technically the baby's aunt, and that one day when August stops being so self-involved and settles down, or when Charlie grows up and stops serial dating – I might get some nieces and nephews that *are* related by blood, but the little bundle that I can see wrapped up in my best friend's arms – the sister I chose, will always be my family.

"Oh my God." I breathe the words.

I don't want to make even a sound and risk disrupting this moment of perfection.

Emmett is sitting on the side of the bed, right next to Lucy, and they're the most beautiful little family I've ever seen.

"You're only ten minutes too late."

I don't even have to look up to see who that voice belongs to. I would know it anywhere.

"It looks like you had it covered without me," I reply softly, my eyes still solely focused on the tiny baby in my best friend's arms.

"She's beautiful, huh?" Lucy catches my eye. She looks exhausted, but I've never seen her happier or more content than she looks right now.

"*She*?"

"You bet." Emmett nods. "My little princess." It's clear to see that this little girl already has her daddy securely wrapped around her finger.

"Her name is Harper Violet Hale," Lucy tells me. "We named her after her godmother." And with that statement I feel the tears start to fall.

***

"Did you know I was born in this hospital?"

I haven't turned to check he's there, but I don't need to, I know he followed me out here.

"You were?" he replies after a moment of silence.

I've been here for hours, watching my best friend be a mother, and I've literally never seen a sight more perfect. It fills me with warmth and cuts me deep in the very same breath.

Lucy deserves *every* ounce of happiness that little girl will bring her, but according to fate, I won't be afforded the same sense of joy.

I nod at him.

The silence stretches between us and I know he's waiting for me to speak.

"You were right earlier; there *is* something I need to tell you," I whisper, my voice shaky.

He moves closer to me and I take a minute to marvel at the feel of his warmth against my arm. He's such an amazing man – the fact he just ensured that my goddaughter made it into the world safe and healthy is an absolute testament to that. Knowing how special he really is just makes me all the more afraid I might lose him.

He's shared his most tightly kept secret with me tonight, and I owe him the same in return – it's time he knew everything about me, the same way I know him.

It can't have been easy for him to talk about his sister, but he did it. For me – for *us*.

His life reads like some type of sad story.

I might have experienced a lot, but he's been through his own brand of heartbreak too and I think that maybe he needs me as much as I need him.

I'm scared like I've never been scared before. It seems to be a reoccurring theme where Rylan is concerned. Maybe this is what being in love is like. Maybe I'll always be terrified about what will happen next.

"Tell me."

His hand reaches for mine and I take it gladly.

We're standing side by side, me watching Lucy, Emmett and baby Harper, and him watching me.

I don't know where I should even begin when it comes to telling this tale, but I figure the beginning is as good of a place as any.

"They tell me I died in this hospital too."

I hear his sharp intake of breath as the words hang in the air between us.

Chapter Fifty-Two

Rylan

"Come with me, there's something I need to show you."

She takes my hand and leads me towards the stairs, right up to the room where she paints.

I'm surprised by this, I wasn't expecting to be allowed back in here again anytime soon after my last intrusion, let alone welcomed with a personal escort, but after what she told me at the hospital I should have known that all bets were off.

She pauses outside the door and looks warily back over her shoulder at me.

"It'll be easier to explain if I show you as well as tell you."

I nod, even though I don't really understand where she's going with this. It doesn't matter, because I do know one thing – that wherever she's going, I'm going there too.

She rests her hand on the door handle and takes a deep, steadying breath.

I can feel the fear and insecurity radiating from her, but I don't say a word. I know she needs to work through this – whatever this is – for herself, and for us.

She eventually pushes the door open and I see why she's shaking like a leaf.

The display she's created is so confronting I can barely breathe.

I understand now exactly why she's kept all this hidden. These paintings say so much without actually having to say anything at all.

I'm gasping for air as my eyes start at the beginning, tracing over one work of art before moving onto the next.

She's so incredibly talented – the amount of emotion and passion that has gone into these is rivalled by nothing I've ever seen before.

"This is only a small part of my story. But it's the part that I think you need to hear the most."

My eyes dart around the room until I find her – standing by the very first painting in the big half circle she's made. It's one I've already seen, only a few short hours ago, but seeing it up on display makes it seem new again.

"I was twenty-one when my heart went into cardiac arrest less than a year before I had my transplant; they had to revive me twice. I was technically dead for a while there."

I look at the painting she's standing next to and I feel fear. Deep, irrational fear – I know I don't need to be afraid, because she's right here and she's okay... she's *alive*, but I can't look away and I can't seem to slow my heart rate.

"When I came back, I painted all of these."

She's never told me this part of her story and that scares me – I can't think of a reason she would have decided to keep it a secret.

I'm instantly filled with worry that maybe everything isn't as it seems – that perhaps there's still something threatening her life.

I love her – I love her more than I ever thought I could love another person, and the thought of a world where she doesn't exist just about brings me to my knees.

"Have you ever heard people say that their lives flashed before their eyes when they came close to death?" She's talking about something so life altering, yet her voice is serene, she looks like she's at peace.

I nod in acknowledgement – right now I can't speak.

"I saw it, Rylan, I saw my *whole* life. I saw my parents, my brother and sister, Lucy... they were all there."

She walks slowly past each painting as she speaks, and I feel like I'm right there on the verge of death with her. I feel like I've stepped into the so-called light and now *my* life is flashing before my eyes – because her life is my life now too. I'm not doing it without her.

My eyes follow her every movement, only leaving her face to look at each piece of art.

"But this was different than what they tell you in books or in the movies... I didn't see the life I'd already lived; I saw the life I should have had – the life that was mine if I survived..."

I don't understand what she means by that. I always assumed that before you died, if in fact your life did flash before your eyes, that you saw everything that had meant the most to you in the time you'd had.

"I guess it wasn't my time yet." She smiles, and I let out a breath I didn't realise I'd been holding. "Maybe one day, when it *is* my time, perhaps I'll see the past then..."

I don't even want to imagine the end of her life – I know it's been a very real possibility for her over the years, but I just can't allow my brain to go there.

"I think it was the only way to get me to come back, you know? To show me everything I should have had..."

"What did you see?" The words are out of my mouth without conscious thought, but I'm glad I said them. She's nearing the end of the paintings now, and there's only one left, but there's still so much left to tell – I can sense it.

The final piece is huge – it's covered with a sheet and I have a feeling that everything she's been keeping from me will be revealed once she lifts it.

I can already see so much of what she was looking at in those moments, the images, colours and scenes on the canvases in front of me are expressive and gut wrenching – but they're not why she brought me up here, I'm sure of it.

It's the painting under the sheet that I'm really here for.

She looks at me, her eyes pleading, for what, I'm not sure...

Understanding perhaps... forgiveness?

She tugs on the sheet and it reveals the painting behind it with a whoosh.

At first I don't understand. It's a set of eyes, deep blue eyes, and in the reflection of those eyes are daisies – fields of them, just like I saw earlier in her other paintings.

"You want to know what I saw, Rylan?"

I'm staring at the painting and I still don't understand what I'm looking at, but I think my brain is getting close to figuring it out.

"I saw *you*."

It's not until the word falls from her lips that I make the connection.

Those are my eyes.

My eyes are on a canvas that she painted four years ago – before I'd seen her for the first time, and I don't know what that means.

I can't fathom how any of this possibly makes sense.

"I saw *you*, Rylan... the last thing I saw was your eyes and the only thing I could hear in the darkness was your voice. You saved me."

"Me?" I stutter the word as I take a step closer. "I didn't know you, you didn't know me..."

"Yet you were outside my room all those months later... I don't know how to explain it, we'd *never* met... I don't know how it's possible..."

I tear my eyes away from the image and meet her gaze with what I'm sure is a look of utter confusion and wonder.

"But it *was* you, Rylan, I *do* know that."

***

"This might sound stupid, but it feels like I'm here for *you*," she whispers. "Maybe I survived because I hadn't found you yet... ever since I woke up, it's as though every moment has led me to this one."

I know exactly what she means.

The past three years never felt like they were going anywhere at all, but now that I'm here with her in my arms, it does seem like a journey.

It feels like there's a map imprinted on my heart, and every single road leads to her.

If it weren't for my sister's accident I never would have laid eyes on Violet. I never would have moved into Daisy's house and got a job at the hospital she worked in. I never would have met Emmett or Lucy, and I wouldn't have been set up on that first date with Violet.

I wouldn't be here now.

It devastates me to think that my sister dying had set something like this in motion – that without her leaving me, I never would have found the woman I love with everything I have.

There's a million thoughts flying through my head and I've got so many questions, but one thing seems to stand out among the rest.

Daisy... it was Daisy that brought us together.

I stroke Violet's hair before placing a tender kiss to her forehead.

We're out under the stars – in the place that's become ours.

Bear's here with us, and nothing has ever felt more right.

Even though I'm missing so much, I somehow feel complete.

I have everything I need right here, it's not everything I want from my life, but I know for certain that it *is* all I'll ever need.

I glance down at Violet and she's staring up at the dark vastness with a look of total wonder on her face. They're the very same stars we look at most nights, but each time she searches that sky it's like she's seeing it all for the very first time.

I've often found myself wondering what she sees through those eyes of hers.

She doesn't perceive things like the rest of us do. I know she has fears and worries, I know that she has more insecurities than most, but she has a sense of peace that surrounds her... it *envelops* her.

She sees the good in *everything* and that good is reflected back to her, almost as though she's absorbing it into her soul.

I'd give almost anything to look at the world through her eyes, even just for five minutes. I bet there's no one on earth that sees those stars the way she does.

"Rylan?" she whispers into the cool night air.

"Yeah?"

"What do you think it means?"

She's apprehensive about my answer. I can see her teeth worrying her bottom lip the way she always does when she's nervous.

I'm not sure I have an answer for her. When it comes to things like fate and destiny, I've never been a big believer, but there's no other way to explain this. I brought her back from the brink of death and in turn, she saved me in my darkest hour.

There's credit due to something or someone for that, but I don't have any idea where to begin with my thank yous.

I also don't know how to answer the woman I love.

I turn and push up onto my elbow so I'm leaning over her. "I think it means we're exactly where we're meant to be."

"You and me?" She whispers the words in a voice so uncertain it threatens to break my heart.

"You and me... *Us*... maybe it's as simple as the fact that we we're meant to put each other back together again."

Chapter Fifty-Three

Violet

"That's it... that's the whole story." My voice has wound up being so quiet I'm not sure she will have caught everything I said, but when I look up it's obvious she understands exactly what I've told her.

I didn't come over here with the intention to spill my guts to Lucy like this, but when beautiful little Harper fell asleep in my arms, the story had just flowed from me for some reason.

I'm still not entirely sure why I never told Lucy about what happened to me – and as strange as it was to have a secret from her all these years, in a way I'm glad I did.

Auggie might have known this whole time, but it was all just a dream until Rylan turned up. Now that he's here and we're together, it really has developed into one hell of a story.

"So I can't take credit for you two after all?" She pouts, and I laugh.

Of course *that* would be her first response.

Luce is so proud of herself for setting us up; her and Emmett haven't stopped gloating about it since we became an official couple.

I am incredibly grateful to them both, and I don't want to burst her bubble, but I think she was just a pawn in something much bigger than any of us.

"I hate to break it to you, but I think I saw him first."

I'm surprised she isn't bombarding me with questions and demanding answers, but right now she seems to just be absorbing everything I've told her.

I can't blame her for needing a minute to process, it's taken me a long time to get my head around, and I'm the one who experienced it.

I wouldn't fault Lucy if she didn't believe me at all – it's a pretty surreal and farfetched tale, but she always has been a bit more spiritual than me, so she's likely to deem the whole thing as destiny.

"I think I felt it, you know? The first moment I met him, it was *you* that popped into my head. In my brain at least, the two of you have always been connected."

It makes me happy that she thinks of the two of us like that.

I've thought a lot about it lately – how we're all intertwined with one another's stories. Lucy and I, Lucy and Emmett, Rylan and I, Emmett and Rylan, Emmett and I... all three of these people are responsible in their own way for saving my life – for keeping me alive both emotionally and physically.

I may have been dealt a really shitty health hand over the years, but I've been handed an absolute winning combination when it comes to company, love and relationships, and if I think about it, I'm not sure I'd trade one for the other.

I'd rather experience the struggles I have and be around these incredible people, than have a perfect bill of health with no one of any significance to share it with.

"I'm *so* glad you found him, Letty – even if it wasn't because of my match making skills – you deserve to be happy."

I've got goose bumps on my arms and legs still – it happens every time I think about what I saw in my vision.

"You know, I pictured him in my sleep every night for years... but I don't have to dream anymore, Luce, I can just roll over and he's there. It's surreal – my whole life feels like a dream now."

"That must be the *weirdest* thing."

"I have to keep convincing myself that it *is* real..."

"It's real." She smiles sadly at me and I know it's because she understands why I'm always waiting for it all to go wrong – that's the way it's been my whole life. "He's not going anywhere, I've seen the way he looks at you – he might be willing to fight for you even harder than I have."

I can't imagine anyone other than my mum and dad fighting harder for me than Lucy has, but when I picture Rylan in my mind, I can't help but consider that maybe he might be the strongest fighter of all.

***

Rylan is still out in the garage working with Emmett – he's helping him build a set of shelves for Harper's room and while they're out there throwing around their testosterone and man skills, I'm getting my baby fix.

"She's seriously *so* cute, how do you get anything done? I just want to stare at her all day." I swoon.

"Why do you think my washing pile is so huge?" Lucy grumbles half-heartedly.

She's not joking either – I do at least two loads every time I come over and it barely makes a dent in the huge mountain.

Harper is still sleeping peacefully in my arms and she's just so unbelievably beautiful. It's hard to believe she's real – until she's exercising the strong set of lungs she's got on her anyway.

I run my finger lightly over her cheek and smile at her total perfection.

I hear the click of a camera. I look up and Lucy is smiling at the picture she's just captured of me and her little girl.

I scowl at her, photos have never really been my favourite thing, but I don't bother complaining, it would only fall on deaf ears.

"It suits you, Letty." She looks between her daughter and me.

A lump forms in my throat the instant the words leave her mouth and I have to fight to swallow it down.

I don't know why I'm getting so emotional about it, but all of a sudden, I can feel tears forming in the corner of my eyes.

The fact that I'll never have my own baby isn't a new revelation; in fact, it's something I've thought about a lot over the years. Especially lately, after I've spent time with my goddaughter – it's a topic that's been pretty front and centre in my mind.

It's not that I want a baby right now, because I don't – not yet... but one day I would have loved to be a mother.

I know there are other options like adoption and surrogacy, but I also realise that those are easy things to talk about, but unfortunately not so easy to make happen. They're expensive and time consuming, and even then, there's no guarantee.

"I'm not sure it's on the cards for me."

"You *saw* a baby, Letty."

"That doesn't mean it'll happen."

I'm aware that I saw Rylan, and I got him – but that doesn't mean this will work the same way.

A baby is in no way promised to me because of something I conjured up in my mind in a near-death experience.

I've been given *so* much; I know it's not fair of me to expect anything more. I already owe so much more than I'm owed in return.

"Violet," says the voice I'd recognise even in my sleep.

I had no idea Rylan was listening to us, so when he speaks it startles me.

He steps into the room and the sight of his intense stare on my face takes my breath away.

"If you want a baby, I'll do *anything* I can to make it a reality for us."

He crouches down next to me and wraps his arms around my body. It makes me feel safe and while he's right here, holding me close, I believe what he's telling me.

He rests his forehead against mine and glances down at the precious little girl in my arms.

"I can't promise you a baby, but I can promise you we'll try every option there is, if that's what you want, okay?"

I know he means it – babies and reproductive organs are literally his speciality, but I can't allow myself to get my hopes up where this is concerned.

"And if it doesn't happen?" My voice cracks.

"If it doesn't happen then we'll get through it *together*. I don't know how many times I have to say this before you'll believe me, but *you* are all I need."

I *do* believe him, but that doesn't mean I don't feel guilt or worry over it.

I know I'm enough for him, and he's enough for me too.

I do want a baby one day, I want one *so* badly, but deep down I know that *he's* enough.

We've got each other and that'll always be everything I need, but I can't help but wish that it wasn't another sacrifice he has to make because he's fallen in love with a broken woman.

Chapter Fifty-Four

Rylan

"Tell me about your sister."

Violet's lying on the couch, with her eyes closed and her head in my lap, and I honestly thought she'd nodded off.

I have a feeling she's been up all night painting while I slept because she's been totally exhausted all day.

"What do you want to know?" I ask as I twirl a strand of her hair around my finger.

"Anything," she breathes. "Just tell me *anything*."

I feel guilty for not being more open with her – ever since I told her about losing my sister we have talked about her, but it's been those types of conversations where you do a lot of talking but at the same time, say nothing at all.

Violet knows my sister's name and that she was a doctor... she knows that after she died I moved here and into her house.

I've told her about my dad passing away when I was a teenager and about my now elderly mother who suffered early onset dementia back home.

She doesn't know anything about who Daisy was as a person or the fact that she basically raised me at times. She doesn't know that we shared a mother, but not a father and that we were all each other had for a good portion of my life.

I want to tell her everything, I really do, but every time I try, the words get caught in my throat and pushed back down deep.

I know I should talk about her more – Daisy deserves to be remembered and not forgotten, and I know it's important to Violet too, so I put down the book I was reading, take a deep breath and start talking as best I can.

"I remember when I was eleven, Daisy would have been about twenty-one, it was my birthday, and my parents had promised me a skateboard. It was the only thing I wanted, and I was so excited to finally be getting one. Anyway, the day came, Dad was sick, and Mum was already beginning to forget things, and that's what happened to my skateboard – they forgot to get one for me." I'd put on a brave face and told them it didn't matter, but truthfully, I was devastated.

I know now that it's just a toy, and if I'd known at the time that only a year and a half later my father would be gone, and that my mother's mind would be taken from her not long after that, I doubt I would have cared about doing anything other than spending the day with the both of them.

That's the real kicker about hindsight.

"I'll never forget the look on Daisy's face when she realised what had happened. She disappeared for an hour and when she came back she had with her the same exact skateboard I'd pointed out in the store a few weeks before."

"She sounds like a good big sister," Violet murmurs, her eyes still shut.

"She was the best."

It hurts my heart that I have to say 'was' instead of 'is' – that I have no choice but to talk about her in past tense rather than present.

"It was a beautiful sunny day, and the four of us went down to the park so I could practise using it. Daisy stayed there with me all day, long after Mum and Dad headed back home. She wasn't too cool for her little brother, or too busy either. When she moved away she always made sure to come home for things like birthdays and holidays. She loved me the same way a mother loves her child – *unconditionally*."

"You miss her a lot." It's not a question, but a statement.

"Every single day."

Violet yawns and wiggles around to get more comfortable. "Tell me another story."

So I tell her the very next thing I can think of.

"She's the reason I went to med school."

"Yeah?" she answers sleepily.

"I got really good grades in high school, but I had no idea what I was going to do when it came time to leave. I went to visit Daisy once; she was working as a GP in a small town while she furthered her study. She was running late so I went into the clinic to wait for her.

A lady in the waiting room started talking to me. She went on and on about how much Daisy had helped improve the symptoms of her arthritis, but it wasn't just her Daisy had helped, it seemed that everyone in town had a problem my sister had looked at and done her best to fix. She was *helping* people – giving back to the world, and it just dawned on me that I wanted to do that too.

Daisy's always done that for me – lead by example. She never put any pressure on me to make a decision about my future; she never even suggested medicine as a potential field for me. Instead she just showed me the way.

I enrolled last minute, and I don't know how, but I got accepted, and as they say, *the rest is history*."

I realise I'm smiling as I talk about my sister. This is the first time I've associated her memory with any emotion other than despair and I'm shocked that I've managed it.

I look down at Violet, so I can share my achievement with her, but when my eyes land on her pretty face, it's obvious she's finally let sleep take her.

Her lips are parted, and her breathing is deep and steady.

She might not be able to hear me, but that doesn't mean I can't talk.

I tug the blanket off the back of the couch and drape it gently over her before telling her story after story – filling in her sleeping form about exactly who my sister was.

Chapter Fifty-Five

Violet

There's something I need to do – something I've been putting off for a long while now because it just seems too... *hard*.

I need to make contact with the family of my donor.

It's been four years now since they lost their loved one and I still know nothing about the person who in death, saved my life.

I don't know if it was a man or a woman, or if they were young or old.

I don't know how they died or if their organs were used to save anybody else.

I don't know what they did for a job or how many people they left behind.

I don't know a single thing about them, so I know it's time to reach out now.

The only option I have is a letter. I can give a letter to the hospital's transplant co-ordinator, who will pass it onto the family of my donor. It's up to them if they want to reply, or even read it at all, and even if I never hear back, at least I'll know I tried.

I don't know what I'm supposed to write – I don't know the right way to thank someone for the unbelievable gift I've been given.

I could ask Rylan for help, but he already does so much for me, and this feels like something I need to do on my own.

I started this journey a long time ago, and I need to finish this final chapter. Who knows what might happen after that – maybe sometime soon I'll be ready to close the book entirely.

I think about the selfless gesture that organ donation is.

I think about the people my donor left behind.

I think about the heart beating in my chest and how I owe my life to someone else.

Each thump of the borrowed organ is so important, so *significant* that suddenly I know exactly what I need to say.

I reach for a sheet of paper and a pen and write from deep inside my soul.

To the owner of my heart,

You don't know me, and I know you can't read this, but I still need to write it.

My name is Violet Miller, and four years ago, you saved my life.

If you hadn't have ticked that little box labelled 'donor', it's entirely possible I wouldn't be here right now, so for that I thank you – you chose to be selfless where you could have been selfish instead.

There's no possible way I could ever repay you, so instead I'll spend the rest of my life living, really living each moment as it was intended to be lived. I can't give you much, but I can do that – for both of us.

There's so many things I wish I could say to you, and it hurts me to know that I'll never get the chance.

I want you to know that I'm so, so sorry. I can't even begin to explain the guilt I carry with me every day, knowing that your life was given in exchange for mine.

Why am I here, and you're not?

I know that's a question I'll probably never get an answer to.

There's a lot of things in this world that make sense to me, but why I was spared when others were taken is something I'm not sure I'll ever understand.

I hope that whoever you left behind is managing as best they can. I may not have met you, but I don't need to have known you to understand the hole you left in the lives of those closest to you.

I've thought a lot lately about fate, and what happens when we die... I'm still not sure exactly what I believe, but I do think that there's some place good for those who deserve it, and I know that wherever that is, you're there.

I have so many questions about you, but I know it's not my place to ask. I don't expect your family or friends to give me those answers, they've given me enough already. I just hope they can find some peace knowing that I'm alive because of you.

Thank you for my life, I promise to live it.

Violet – The keeper of your heart.

Chapter Fifty-Six

Rylan

I knock lightly on the door to the small office I haven't set foot in for over four years.

I'm in such a different place now than I was back then, that it really doesn't look like the same room at all as I open the door.

The paintings on the walls are brighter now, the room doesn't feel like it's caving in around me anymore, and I notice the light streaming in through the window, rather than the dark shadows that light creates.

I'm a different person than I was.

I have Violet to thank for that.

The only constant between my life then and my life now, is *her*.

She was the light back then, and she's been that same light every day for the past year I've spent with her.

"Dr. Wilder." The middle-aged woman smiles at me.

She's a work colleague I don't see often – this hospital is a big place, but yet I don't think I'll ever forget her face.

She was my counsellor for a year. I may not have thought that we made one single inch of progress in that time, but given that I'm here now and I'm doing so much better, I have to admit that maybe it did help me in some small way.

"Rylan, please," I tell her as I take the seat she's indicating I should sit in.

This whole set up feels like I've been sent to the principal's office. I don't know why I'm here, but I have a feeling in the pit of my gut that it's serious.

"Rylan." She smiles at me.

I don't smile back; I can't seem to make the muscles in my cheeks work.

"You're probably wondering why I asked you in here."

"I am."

"I was wondering if we could talk about your sister for a minute."

I can't fathom for a second what she would possibly want to talk to me about in regards to my sister.

Daisy has been gone for a long time now.

As much as I'm confused by this topic, I'm also proud of myself for thinking of Daisy without the pain and heartache I've long since grown accustomed to.

I'm making progress – they might only be small steps, like contacting some of the people I let slip away during my grief, but for me, it feels like a huge leap I'm taking in the right direction.

I know I have Violet to thank for that too.

I still don't talk about Daisy a lot, and I haven't managed to put up or even share with Violet all our old photos yet, but it's progress, and my heart doesn't ache the same way when I think of her anymore.

I still miss her like crazy, and I think there will always be a little piece of me that's missing, but this is the most whole I've felt in a very long time.

"Rylan?" she asks, and I realise I never answered her.

"Sorry, sure, go ahead."

"Do you recall, when you began your employment here, that you were asked to fill out a few pages of questions?"

I know exactly what she's talking about.

The questionnaire is designed as a safe guard – a guide for the families and loved ones of the doctors and nurses that work in this hospital should anything ever happen to us.

I've seen what can happen in an emergency situation, a patient is brought in and their family has no idea what they would have wanted in terms of medical intervention.

When I started here, I answered questions about who I wanted notified if anything might happen to me, whether I'd want to be resuscitated or have my life artificially prolonged... if I agreed to have my organs harvested for donation or my body donated to science.

"I remember," I tell her.

"Do you also remember giving authority at the time of Daisy's death to honour all of the decisions she made on *her* form?"

My sister worked here too – she answered the same questions I did.

I nod, my throat feeling suddenly thick with emotion.

I can remember the moment as though it were only yesterday.

I signed that sheet of paper without a second thought – whatever Daisy wanted, that was what she got. She always knew better than me when it came to these kinds of things, but even if she didn't, I would never have gone against the wishes of my sister on the day of her death.

I still don't know what her final requests were, but I agreed to all of them without a moment's hesitation.

"I have a letter here for you... it's from a patient whom Daisy donated an organ to."

I don't even realise that I've been staring at the ground until I hear her words and my head snaps up.

"Daisy was a donor?"

She nods at me. "She donated to five deserving people."

I don't know why the possibility never occurred to me before now, but *of course* Daisy was a donor.

She was one of the most generous people I've ever met.

"No one told me," I whisper.

"Perhaps you didn't want to hear it?" she offers.

When Daisy was brought in, I couldn't bring myself to ask the extent of the damage caused by the crash, let alone if something like organ donation was a viable option, so instead I stuck my head in the sand and questioned nothing at all.

Much like I did my friends, I shut out any and all things Daisy for a long time, so there's a good chance someone did try to tell me, but I just wasn't willing to listen.

I don't know how I feel about the fact that there are five people out there in the world, each carrying around a little part of my sister, but I know that Daisy would have wanted it to be this way.

"You said there was a letter?" My voice is hoarse and scratchy.

She nods and hands it over to me. "I'll give you a minute alone."

I don't look up as she exits the room.

There's a thin envelope in my hands that feels like a heavy brick, and all of a sudden, I *have* to know what it says.

I tear the flap open and pull out the letter from inside.

My hands are shaking so badly it takes me a couple of attempts to read the first few lines, and when I do, the sheet of paper falls to the floor.

To the owner of my heart,

You don't know me, and I know you can't read this, but I still need to write it.

My name is Violet Miller, and four years ago, you saved my life...

Chapter Fifty-Seven

Violet

Even though we've unofficially been living together with Bear for what feels like forever, it's never felt more real than it does today. Rylan's not even here right now, but my home is so filled with him I can barely remember what it was like before he appeared in my life.

There's a whole pile of boxes stacked against the wall, and even though I'm expecting him home any time now to help me, I can't seem to stop myself from taking one down and starting to unpack it.

It's labelled 'photos' and I have to admit that it's got my curiosity piqued.

Rylan talks about his parents often and while I've seen a couple of pictures of his late father and his elderly mother, I'm still yet to see even one of his sister Daisy.

I know it's not for the fact that he doesn't want to show me, but that it just hurts him too much – he never fully dealt with his sister's death, but I think that these past few months he's finally starting to heal.

I glance at the clock again.

There's a sensation lurking around me like I'm doing something wrong, but I shove it aside. Rylan and I are in this life together – I know that nothing that lives in a box could possibly come between us.

I lift the lid and find a few albums, some frames and a couple of stacks of photos.

I shuffle through a few until I spot an envelope.

There's only two photos inside, I recognise one as Rylan's mum and dad when they were younger. I smile at the obvious love between them – his dad is looking at his mum the same way that Rylan looks at me.

This photo deserves to be in a frame, displayed proudly on the wall, so I sit it down on the table to tell Rylan when he gets home that we'll be doing exactly that with it.

I pull the other photo from the envelope at the same time as I hear the front door open.

I clutch my chest in shock, I can't believe what I'm seeing.

The image that has taken my breath away is of Rylan, he's about ten years younger here than he is now and he's *so* handsome, but it's not that – it's the woman next to him, who I now have no doubt is his sister, that's caused me to gasp aloud.

I *know* this woman, and the realisation of exactly who she is steals the last of my reservations about fate.

"Violet." Rylan's voice startles me.

I turn and look at him, and he's there, his eyes filled with what appears to be total disbelief.

We stand unmoving, staring at one another in wonder.

In my hand is the photo that's just completely blown my mind, and in his, he holds a sheet of paper that signifies the final piece of our puzzle clicking into place.

Epilogue

Violet

I hear someone clinking cutlery against glass, indicating that they want to make a speech and I spin around, looking for the speaker.

I recognise his voice a fraction of a second before my eyes land on his face, in all its smiling perfection.

The earth has circled the sun five times since he officially came into my life, yet every time I look into his startling blue eyes; it feels like the very first time.

"I'd like to make a toast." He smiles at me and my belly flips.

I don't know how he does that. He *still* has the power to turn my insides to mush, even after all these years.

"Thank you all for coming... there's two very special women I need to make mention of tonight, the first being my beautiful wife."

He smiles so wide at me that everybody else in the room follows suit, looking at me and smiling along with him.

I know I'm bright red, but I don't care, his words mean more to me than anybody else's and right now, he's *all* I can see.

"The art you're about to witness, she has been working on for literally her entire life. She has laid herself bare on those canvases, and for her to allow the whole world to see them is certainly no small feat."

He looks at me with such tenderness in his eyes I have to fight to hold his gaze rather than shy away from it.

"I can personally vouch for the rollercoaster of emotions that you'll experience when you walk through those doors... because trust me; some of those paintings have the power to bring you to your knees."

The skin on my arms has broken out into goosebumps now; all the individual little hairs are standing up on end. He's the only person close to me to see my collection in its entirety thus far, and I know he means every word he's saying.

Lucy reaches for my hand and grips it tightly in hers.

Her belly is round for the third time and her skin is positively glowing again, only this time it's not her bun she's cooking in her oven, it's *mine*.

I squeeze her hand back appreciatively; I'm so incredibly grateful for the selfless woman I get to call my best friend. She knows me as well as she knows herself, so she of all people understands exactly how nervous I am right now.

"Congratulations, gorgeous, I can't think of a single person who deserves this moment more than you do." Rylan lifts his flute of wine in my direction.

I hold back tears as I walk towards him and he wraps me in his strong, safe arms while everybody around us claps and cheers.

"Thank you," I murmur against his chest.

He kisses the top of my head and when I pull away, he tucks me into his side, his arm wrapping protectively around me, the same way it always has.

"But there's also one other woman I need to thank tonight."

I already know what he's going to say next, and just the mere thought of it has the first of what I'm sure will be many tears slipping down my face.

"My sister."

Everyone is watching him closely, intrigued by his words. He's always been the kind of man that commands the attention of a room, but I think we can all feel that this is something more.

"All of you already know that some years back, Violet's life was saved when she received a heart transplant... but there's one thing that some of you probably don't know, something that neither Violet or I knew when we first met either."

I think back to the moment when I decided that I undoubtedly believed in fate.

"A few years ago, Violet reached out to her donor's family, she wrote a beautiful, heartfelt letter expressing how grateful she was... and not long after, I *received* a letter. It was from a bright, incredible woman who told me that someone in my family had saved her life... it was only then that I realised *my* sister was her donor."

I hear a few gasps from the crowd.

He looks down at me now, his eyes glistening with unshed tears, but his expression bright and happy.

He's finally made peace with the tragedy that took his sister's life and in turn, gave me mine.

"My sister gave life to the woman who would later become the love of mine and I know it was her that brought the two of us together."

He kisses my head again, but I know this time it's for his benefit, not mine. He draws strength from being close to me, and he needs that strength right now as he talks about the possibility of my life coming to an end and as he relives the memory of his sister losing hers.

"Violet's told me about how she technically died once, when she was twenty-one years old... she told me about her heart going into cardiac arrest and about the woman who brought her back from the brink of death. But it wasn't until much later on that I knew without a shadow of a doubt that it was my sister Daisy that brought Violet and I together."

My mum, dad and brother are eyeing me curiously now, but Auggie, she just looks totally serene – like maybe she already knows what's coming.

He turns so he's speaking directly to my family. "My sister was a cardiologist... you knew her actually... she would have introduced herself as Dr. White – she was the woman who saved Violet's life that day."

I can hear my mum sobbing now as the weight of what he's saying presses down on all of us. We chose to save that final piece of information for this exact moment and I'm glad we did. Daisy's memory deserves this honour.

The fact that Dr. White – the woman who brought me back to life and then treated me for the months that followed afterwards – is not only his sister, but also my donor, still blows my mind each and every time I think about it.

"So…" he takes a deep steadying breath, "I just wanted to thank her, because it takes an incredible woman to not only save lives *in* life, but also in death."

He raises his glass to the sky now.

"To Daisy, *thank you*, even though you're gone, you've somehow managed to do what you've always done – you gave me a life worth living."

The group surrounding us erupts into applause and I feel myself being pulled into embrace after embrace.

Tears are flowing freely down my face, along with everyone else in the room.

I glance up at the daisy chain I painted on the welcome banner and smile. They're the same ones from my vision, the ones I never really understood until that final connection between Rylan and I was made.

The daisies are for *Daisy*.

I've dreamt about this moment for so long – the moment where I'm brave enough to share my work with the world, and also where we can pay tribute to the woman who saved my life on more than one occasion, and now it's *finally* here.

I'm eventually released by my friends and family, and right on cue the doors are opened to allow everyone into the gallery to witness my exhibition for the very first time.

I'm terrified of what people will think, but with Rylan looking at me like I'm *everything,* I know that I have what it takes to be exactly that in this world.

I run my fingertip gently over the cover of the booklet in my hand.

The two words looking back at me, much like the beating organ in my chest, are as much hers as they are mine.

It's the introduction to my life's work, to everything I've ever kept hidden, and it's simply titled *'My Heart'*.

The end

"Every new beginning comes from some other beginnings end."
-Seneca

Other Titles

Love like Yours Series
Rushed – Book 1
Pierced – Book 2
Hunted – Book 3
Chased – Book 4

Rock Games Novels
Paper, Scissors, Rock: Vol. 1
Hide and Seek: Vol. 2

My Heart Duet
My Heart Needs
My Heart Wants
Every Last Beat (Box Set)

Calendar Boys Novels
Mr. January
Mr. February
Mr. March
Mr. April
Mr. May
Mr. June

Mr. July
Mr. August

Acknowledgements

There are a lot of people to thank when it comes to this particular project.

I couldn't have even begun to write this book without the help of Kate, the mother of the little girl whom inspired this duet.

Kate, thank you so much for being so open and helpful and for answering my many, many, strange questions without complaint.

I've learnt so much while writing this book – most of which is knowledge I've gained from you.

To Angela, for being so friendly and accommodating with answering questions and sharing a bit of your daughter's precious life with me – I really appreciate you taking the time.

I'd like to take a minute to acknowledge all of the children, adults and families living with congenital heart defects. I've read so many stories about those of you whose lives conditions like this effect, and I'm in total awe of the things you've overcome.

Stacey, my editor, thanks for working so fast and doing such a great job, I really appreciate not only your work, but your support.

To my readers, thank you, I hope you enjoyed reading Violet and Rylan's story as much as I enjoyed writing it.

Thank you all for the support!

About the Author

NICOLE S. GOODIN is a romance author and mother of two from Taranaki in the North Island of New Zealand.

In mid-2015, she started to write about a group of characters who wouldn't get out of her head. Her first book, Rushed, was published in mid-2016.

Nicole enjoys long walks on the beach, pillow fights and braiding her friends' hair. She dislikes clichés, talking about herself in the third person, and people who don't understand her sense of humour.

Please feel free to contact her either via her website, email, Instagram, Twitter or on her Facebook page, she would love to hear your feedback. If you're feeling really game, you can even sign up for her newsletter.

Visit www.nicolegoodinauthor.com for more information.

Upcoming Titles

Calendar Boys Novels

Mr. September
Mr. October
Mr. November
Mr. December

www.ingramcontent.com/pod-product-compliance
Lightning Source LLC
Chambersburg PA
CBHW021716110726
47902CB00005B/1223